This is a work of fiction. Names, characters, businesses, places, events and incidents are either the products of the author's imagination or used in a fictitious manner. Any resemblance to actual persons, living or dead, or actual events is purely coincidental.

Cover: 2001 a space odyssey

© 2017 Michael Marcovici

Via creativespace

First Edition August 2017

ISBN-13: 978-1548608590

ISBN-10: 1548608599

3

for Nadine

CHAPTER 1

Suddenly I was in the middle of a sea of enormous white steel pistons, every one as tall as a building. The solid steel pistons are moving up and down, each one in its own rhythm, powerful and dynamic. As far as the eye can see, there's nothing but a field of white elongated pistons moving up and down. Between them, black struts made of heavy steel beams suggest that I must be inside of an enormous structure.

Each of the pistons is fastened to a brightly polished steel chain, and every link in the chain is the size of a soccer ball. The rattling of thousands of chains produces a loud but calming sound that gives me the impression of meaningful activity and productivity. The loose ends of the chains hang over the pistons and knock against them now and then. It seems some of the pistons are being moved in between the other pistons via rail across the field. Some of them quite quickly, but without touching the other pistons. Every so often I'm also moved through the pistons, seemingly a distance of several kilometers in a short time. And yet everything looks as it did before. The field of pistons stretches on without end before my eyes, but it's constantly rearranged as if by magic.

There is another level beneath the pistons, a black mass. I can hear a loud rumble like a landslide or an earthquake, but clearer and more homogeneous. The black mass also appears to be homogeneous. When I approach, I can see that the black mass consists of black steel spheres, each one far larger than a person. They're covered by scratches and welts from constantly rubbing against each other, but are still deep black. Their movements are like a crowd of clumsy people pushing ahead in all directions and only moving forward by pushing others to the side. The spheres are forced sometimes upward, sometimes downward, but then they sink down again or reappear. The lower ground, if there is one, appears to be not completely level, but it's not discernible from my position.

The view of the space between the spheres and the pistons takes my breath away. An endless landscape of pistons and spheres lies before me, everything is in motion, an incomprehensible amount of energy is being used here to keep everything in motion.

The rumbling of the spheres slowly overshadows the clattering of the chains, and I can sense heat caused by the friction. Suddenly I'm forced in among the spheres and I lose my bearings.

I'm being pressed under by the spheres when there's a painfully bright flash in the otherwise black surroundings; only a little light comes from above. With all my strength I force my way down and try to keep myself under. Underneath the spheres, there's a sea made of diamonds permeated by flashes of lightning, different kinds of lightning, very brief flashes that are probably caused by static electricity. I feel them in part as painful and in part as pleasurable. But there are also other flashes. These other flashes appear to be from machines, from vehicles that swim about in this sea of diamonds. I dive deeper into the diamonds, and the continual lightning flashes help me to perceive the space I'm in and to regain my bearings. The diamond sea is now closing gradually above me and the roaring of the steel spheres gets weaker. One hears instead the diamonds, bright and clear scratching sounds as they rub against each other.

Now I recognize the source of the other flashes a few meters in front of me; it's from machines, robots with a ring flash mounted on one end and whose remaining body consists of a type of screw by which they move through the diamond sea. Again and again I see robots whose drills are already severely damaged, worn out. Further movement is no longer possible.

I realize that I too need to hurry and find my direction. Downward. Farther below it gets darker and darker, fewer and fewer flashes permeate the diamonds here, and that makes the terrain more easily surveyed. But finally it's pitch black around me. Only my own ring flash still gives me light. Farther below, the diamond sea is polluted by abraded refuse from the drills. The dark mass becomes increasingly viscous until any thought of going forward becomes impossible. I turn around and use my own drill in order to move deeper downward. I drill into the mass of steel and diamonds, my body becomes burning hot, but I know that if I stop drilling now I'll get stuck and die here. I don't know how long I bore through the mass that's constantly getting harder. I'm at the end of my strength as I break through; I throw off the drill and slip into the hole.

I'm standing upright on a flat plane. The surface is made of concrete. In the distance, a few black spider-like beings can be seen. They have black, cylindrical, smoothly polished bodies. Six legs. I run in their direction. Several gatherings of these creatures can be seen. In the middle is something like a carousel. At the end of the many metal struts on the roof of the carousel are spotlights, cameras, and gripping arms. Colorful lights and figures of various people are mounted along the struts. Between clowns and pin-up girls, I recognize Napoleon, Hitler, Goethe, Mao Tse Tung, Barack Obama, Elias Canetti, Jörg Haider, Karl Marx, Tony Blair, Rudi Carrell, Yasser Arafat, and Alfred Hitchcock. Rabbis, soldiers, whores, and elderly people I don't recognize. Over and over, a gripping arm lifts one of the spider creatures upwards and hurls it far away with the aid of centrifugal force. Each time one of the creatures is hurled away, several of the creatures laugh, others whisper with each other or call out "uh oh," "jeepers," or "oh dear."

I'm fascinated by the spectacle and try to move as close as possible to the middle where I can better hear and see the figures, but the crowd is dense. Just as I see Tony Blair above me, a gripping arm grabs me. The feeling is familiar: panic, failure, humiliation. I'm discovered, caught, selected for oblivion. Being lifted up is the easy part. Being hurled away will get painful. I land on my feet, disappointed, but the next spectacle is already right next to me, the next carousel. Again and again I try to push forward into the inside of the carousel, but finally I get tired, crawl out of my spider armor and join the throng of people in hats and overcoats who walk along the street. Crowded tightly, my briefcase in hand and with a fast step. A babble of voices can be heard although no one is talking. My gaze is fixed on the ground, but I still feel like I'm being watched. The mass of people creeps with quick pace along the house walls, crosses streets, goes around the corner. In front of us, stairs lead into a subway station.

The mass of people suddenly presses me downwards, there's no chance of turning around anymore, the pressure, the crush of the other people is too strong. I can tell that there's froth down there, a filthy scum, it smells like a mixture of sharp, cheap bath foam from the supermarket and old, putrid laundry. I scream, try to convince the others to turn around. But the mass of people with me presses forward with steady pace into the froth. Suffocating panic seizes me, I'm sure that no one can see anything down there, no one can breathe.

"David," I hear someone calling. "David, I'm sorry." I know this voice, it's familiar.

"David, I'm sorry to have to wake you, but it's already 11:30 AM, June 26, 2049. You wanted to go eat with Nadine in an hour. Nadine is already awake and would like to get going."

"Oh, man."

"I know you were dreaming. I recorded the dream, but you have to get going now."

"Yeah, okay."

"It's 23 degrees Celsius and sunny. I suggested to Nadine to eat at Thephasadin Plaza."

"Okay, fine. Very good. What else is going on?"

"You have a message from your daughter. You should get in touch with her. Ccoin is trading at 0.392 Monero with a volume of 117 billion coins. The level of ethanol metabolites in your blood is elevated, so your health insurance might go up soon. Drink plenty of water today."

"Good, thanks."

"You might be interested in these news stories: Medvedev was presumably murdered using a nanodrone and several areas of New Zealand are joining the South Pacific Law Society. The last train leaves from the Vienna's central station today. In the Atlantic—"

"Okay, thanks, I'll take a look at everything when I get a moment."

"Do you need anything else?"

"Nothing."

That's enough of Watson, my life companion from IBM. Last night when I was partying in my suite, he kept trying to convince me to drink water instead of mango schnapps. It's my own fault. I'm the one who set his morality level so high.

At my age, waking up after drinking alcohol is almost like rising from the dead. Although I've had a nice long sleep, it takes almost twenty minutes until I'm in the bathroom. I've got something like the opposite of senile insomnia. In the shower there's a thing that sprays ice-cold air mixed with water and pure oxygen at the push of a button. I push it until my whole head is ice cold and I finally feel awake. From the shower there's an amazing view of Bangkok. My room's in the 128th story of the Hyatt Elite after all, and not many buildings on the Bangkok skyline are as tall as this one.

I have to leave now. The SDU[1] here comes directly to the room. You learn to value that at my age, and I don't want to make Nadine wait.

I'm driven to Thephasadin, where there are almost 200 stands selling food on the plaza, which is round, as large as a stadium, and spread over several levels. There are small pools with fish swimming in them, a salt water pool with waves where oysters and muscles are growing, tables and chairs, and between them one booth after another with food, drink, shans,[2] and merchants. Surrounding the plaza is the agricultural sector. Hundreds of varieties of fruit and vegetables, artificial meat and fish grow in the ring-shaped building under artificial light. Beer, wine, and insects are produced, and real fish and muscles are cultivated. In several places you can view the fully automated process. As far as I know, most booths buy their ingredients from the Ring. It's by no means an accident that there's so much street food in Bangkok again. After the radical prohibition of 2019,

---

[1] Self Driving Unit, self-driving cars and other forms of transportation.

[2] A shan is a device for smoking. It contains up to 100 different oils and other substances. Among other things it offers marijuana, cocain, and heroin as well as healthy essential oils and salt water vapor from Normandy.

street food became de facto extinct in Bangkok. The booths only came back in 2037, a while after the city was privatized. Most of them came from distant parts of Thailand where there was still street food. Now street food is booming here again and more and more plazas like this one are being built.

There's the traditional dishes like Tom Yum Goong, Pad Thai, and Pad Kra Pao, but also new creations with artificial meats and insects. Super oils and modern plants, above all the patuga—it looks like a big bean and is sort of like rice, but it actually has DNA from muscles and tastes like delicate fish.

I order a patuga dish and a veggie shake with detovil, an ingredient that helps my system get rid of the alcohol that I consumed last night in copious amounts, and take a seat.

A bot comes to my table at once: "Hello Mr. Wenkart, how is your day, would you like a shan?"

"No, thank you. Maybe later."

My assistant Nadine is already here. I'd get no work done at all without her. Nadine's young, glorious body motivates me. I can't stop thinking about what it would be like to sleep with her, and the very fact that this will probably never happen keeps me trotting along. Nadine is twenty-five and comes from Berlin. I met her in Vienna, where she worked at the Wiegand Gallery on Schleifmühlgasse. I think I was looking at works by Mario Nubauer there, who I've known for 50 years, when I struck up a conversation with her.

A few days later I saw her at the Gutruf Bar, and she told me that the gallery paid her badly and belatedly. I suggested that she should assist me with writing. It took months until I actually relocated to Venice to write, because it wasn't really working in Vienna and I had to leave the city anyway. After I assumed all her expenses and the gallery job was over, she was ready to come with me, at least for a month.

She arrived two days ago, but I only saw her briefly, even though we're staying in the same hotel.

Nadine is studying a combination of history and content under Master Altman, who is named for the famous director. These days you don't study at a local university anymore. Instead you have a master, an artificial intelligence that accompanies you for your whole life. Altman teaches her what they used to call directing, dramaturgy, or theater studies. Before that she studied economics with Mises2[3], which is definitely helpful for my book.

"Hello, David. How are you? Maybe I shouldn't ask."

"It's better if you don't. I need to forget last night. Do you want to get something to eat? Or to smoke?"

"To smoke. Does the bot handle that?"

The bot comes back. He reacts to being seen, just like that look in a bar when you find someone attractive. I look over and it's already coming to the table. Nadine decides on a combination of Canadian pine forest, sea salt from Japan, and Bolivian cocaine. The bot lays the shan on the table, which consists of a base and a sort of electronic cigarette, both made of glass. Inside the base you can see the mixture as it vaporizes. Nadine takes a pull from the shan. It smells exquisite.

"What were you up to yesterday?"

"I was only in the hotel. Uberparty."[4]

"Ah, that makes sense now. How many people were there?"

"Eight people, five of them women."

"That's what I thought. Hopefully everyone had fun."

"It was actually pretty interesting. There was an entrepreneur from Azerbaijan. She's here for a DNA hackathon. And a young Thai woman who curates digital paintings for virtual worlds. It's a really impressive line of work, although the field was declared dead a long time ago."

"So it was a cultural conference."

"Can we move on?"

---

[3] Mises2 is an artificial intelligence named for the intellectual and economist Ludwig van Mises. It serves as the master for students who are studying economics.
[4] Ueberparty is a term for ready made parties. Uberparty handles the organization of between one and a hundred people, taking into account language, theme, drinks, drugs, and sexual preferences. As a rule you can get a smaller party together in an hour with five to ten people you've never met before.

13

"Moving on is good. Or getting started, as I'd put it. Should we do it interview style like we discussed? And at the end we'll rewrite it, or maybe we won't. We'll see."

"That's fine. When were you born? What a boring first question."

"I was actually born in 1975. And you?"

"Actually? I was definitely born in 2024. It's probably best to begin with your earliest childhood memories."

My first memories are of my family in Israel in the late 70s up through the early 80s. I was part of a large family. My father had five brothers and two sisters, and I had at least thirty cousins. We all saw each other every summer. Those were good times. Parts of the family lived in the USA and Canada, and we lived in Austria. But in the summers we were all in Netanya, at the time a rather bleak small town north of Tel Aviv. My relatives had a construction firm and a small hotel there. The family fell apart in the end, but I'll get to that later.

Otherwise I remember school and the synagogue I attended with my father. The tram in Vienna that I had to ride to school every day. That awful school where I wasted so much time—it's hard to believe, but you used to have to spend eight hours a day in a room at school. I've never seen most of my school friends since.

I always used to think that my parents and grandparents had seen so much, but actually it's almost impossible to comprehend how much life has changed since I've been alive.

When I was a child, there was only a landline connection at home. For a phone that you could call one person with. The telephone on the other side was inside the house of the person who you were calling.

Mobile phones, smart phones, iPhones, retinal projection, VR,[5] AR,[6] SDUs and all that, we didn't have that yet. But precisely because of that, everything was different. When we went out, we arranged to met at the Schottentor station by the televisions. Those were monitors where you

---

[5] Virtual Reality.
[6] Augmented Reality.

could watch the two state television channels, as there weren't any others yet. Whoever was at the meeting place on time was along for the evening. There was no way to get in touch with someone or to ask how the party was somewhere else. Everything was a bit different.

In order to stay informed, you bought a printed newspaper, and if you wanted to get to know someone, the only way was just to talk to them, on the street, in a bar, or somewhere else. The most successful people weren't the ones who looked the best or had the best DNA, but the people who had the most self-confidence. Which were maybe the same people.

Okay, let's get to the point.

My memories really begin after my father's death in 1987, when I was twelve. My family—that was my mother, my father, my sister, and me—lived in the seventeenth district, a middle-upper-class neighborhood on the outskirts of Vienna, in a nice villa. In 1986, my father was diagnosed with cancer, and the few memories I have of him are unfortunately almost all from this time. My mother was a housewife with a deep passion for literature, my father was a businessman with a deep passion for poker. My sister Anna was six years older than me.

After my father's death, our extended family fell apart. My aunt Rifka, my father's sister, stole a million shillings—a lot of money back then—from him while he was seriously ill. She claimed she was buying a parcel of land in Miami, but she was really financing my uncle's campaign for state surgeon general of Pennsylvania.

But the biggest thief was Abraham, my father's brother. A good-looking, ever-friendly, back-slapping smooth talker. I'm fundamentally suspicious of people like that. Around a week before my father died, he came from Netanya to Vienna in order to be with my father and help my mother. At the time, all the wealthy Jews in Vienna kept their money in Switzerland. After the war, Jews were skeptical of the new Austrian state, and probably of every other country as well. Three days before my father died, Abraham urged my mother to fly to Switzerland to make sure that the money there was set up as it should be before my father died. My mother didn't see the point of the trip and didn't want to go so she could stay with my father instead, but Abraham kept pushing the matter. So they flew to Zurich in February 1987. My mother had to go to UBS on Bahnhof Street. From the airport, they took a taxi into the city. Just before they got to UBS, my father's bank on Bahnhof Street, Abraham said he had to take care of something and would follow along to UBS in a moment.

The UBS account advisor explained to my mother that there was nothing to do at the moment. As expected, there was no point in my mother's trip. The account was registered in both their names so everything was fine. But the trip definitely had a point for Abraham, because he got out of the taxi on the corner in front of Hoffmann Bank. My uncle, who closely resembled my father, had brought my father's passport, withdraw the money from his account, and brought it next door to Credit Suisse. It took a while before my mother found out, but my father's missing passport gave my uncle away. The money, several million shillings, was gone. Almost all our assets at the time.

In the mean time, a family feud in the literal sense was going on. My uncles were actual criminals. They tried to murder each other, and Molotov cocktails were thrown into my cousins' homes. One uncle had his ear pierced by the bullet of a hired killer. Offices were destroyed, and threats, blackmail, and criminal complaints from the tax offices of various countries were part of the daily agenda. Things only calmed down after Abraham and my uncle Emmanuel in Vancouver were six feet under. The family never met again after that.

"That's an incredible story. I don't know what I should ask now. It sounds so trivial after that...but why was the money in Switzerland?"

"My father intensely distrusted governmental institutions. My mother, too: "Don't even brush up against it" was her motto whenever coming into contact with government offices was under discussion. As a Holocaust survivor, she knew only too well what it meant to have problems with the authorities. And my father survived Auschwitz. Romania didn't protect him. The Germans—or the idiots, as he called them—almost murdered him. His sister starved to death in Auschwitz. After his liberation in April 1945 from Dora-Nordhausen camp, where he worked on the V2 rocket, he arrived in Austria. As a 'displaced person,' he was stuck in Austria for ten years."

"Auschwitz, wasn't that one of the Nazis' death camps?"

"A concentration camp and a death camp. My father was there three months. He said very little about it."

"What did he say?"

"I really only know one story, unfortunately. Every day, the camp inmates were sorted by Dr. Mengele, a name that's still infamous, at least among older Jews and historians. Dr. Mengele assigned one group to work, and the other was sent to the gas chambers, murdered. Those who were selected for work got a stamp on their foreheads. One day when he was just sixteen years old, my father was judged 'unfit for work' and was sent to the group to be gassed that day. Across from him stood the group that at least on this day was still allowed to work. It was clear to my father that this was the end. The sorting continued, but was interrupted. Dr. Mengele had to discuss something with someone and left the sorting place. Suddenly someone from the group across from my father ran to him, pressed his forehead with the stamp against my father's, and took him over to the side of those able to work, the survivors. My father didn't know the man who saved his life, and after that event he never saw him again."

The plaza had grown crowded while we were talking, as several thousand people come to eat here in the afternoons. An equal number of bots and drones come to fetch food. Nadine continues puffing on her shan and is visibly irritated by the story. Although it's from so long ago, Germans still seem to have an odd feeling when they hear stories from the concentration camps.

"And your mother?" was the only response that she could manage. But I didn't think she was being coldly distant, I saw in her facial expression what was going on inside her and couldn't be hidden.

"My mother's story casts your homeland in a more flattering light. It's a really incredible story, I'll try to be brief."

It actually begins during World War One with something that happened to my grandfather. My grandfather, or more accurately my Grandpa Herrmann, was fighting in fall 1918 for the Austrian imperial army against the Italians in the Alps near Doberdò. The fighting took place at an altitude of almost 3000 meters. The battles were quite bloody and over the years several thousand soldiers were killed, many by bullets from machine guns, but just as many by cold, lack of nourishment, and avalanches caused by explosions set off by the enemy side.

One day one of his comrades was struck in the head by a bullet and severely wounded. My grandfather threw the man over his shoulders and carried him for hours through the middle of a hail of bullets to a field hospital, where the man was saved. After that my grandfather went back to the front and never saw the man again.

My mother was born in Vienna in September 1938. Not much is known about her family except that they were from the Burgenland and had a house on Czernin Alley in Vienna's second district, where a lot of Jews lived.

On January 30, 1940, when my mother was just a year old, she was deported with her whole family from Vienna to Poland.

It was one of the first transports to the east that the Nazis organized for Jews from Vienna. The transport of around a thousand people, men, women, and children, first went to Opole. They had promised the people that Opole was something like a land where Jews would be able to build up something of their own and wouldn't face persecution anymore.

But actually Opole was a shabby ghetto in Poland dominated by hardship and where Polish Jews, who already had nothing, now had to take care of the Austrian Jews deported by the Nazis. My mother and her family stayed there until early June 1940.

Because transports with Jews from Vienna were constantly arriving in Opole, eventually there was no space left. The Nazis transported my grandfather, my mother, and her family over the Vistula river by ship to Deblin. They were supposed to spend several days at one of the air bases of the German Luftwaffe until they could be taken further east by road, with the ultimate goal of exterminating them. Presumably they were destined for Birkenau.

All the men of the family were drafted to help expand the air base's runway. They were ordered to finish the work by July 23, 1940. It was clear to my grandfather that that would be the end. People already knew about the death camps, Auschwitz, Treblinka, and the others. Many of the Jews in that transport believed my grandfather was a rabbi, and he was regarded as the spokesman for the 400 or so Jews in the camp. On the July 15, he was called before the camp commandant. My grandfather was terribly afraid, not only for his own life but also for the lives of the other Jews.

But the meeting with the commandant would change the fate of all the Jews in that transport. It's hard to believe, but the commandant of the camp was that man my grandfather had saved in 1918 in the Italian Alps.

That commandant[7] and all his personnel at the airbase saved those 400 Jews from destruction for five years. They forged documents, lied to their superiors, did everything to save the group of Jews. Despite that, not all of them made it. My mother's parents didn't survive the poor nourishment, the rampant disease, and the increasing hopelessness of the situation.

My grandfather always said that each day you survived despite the extraordinary situation was a miracle. Grandpa Herrmann and his wife brought my mother with them to Vienna after the war, so I came to know them as my grandparents.

I looked for a document on the display with which every table on the plaza was equipped: "Here's *Acting Under Orders: Another View*, the book my grandfather wrote after the war in 1963. He wanted to explain that it was quite possible for Nazis to do good. In his case, to save Jews from destruction, or at least to make the attempt. But he also tells how

---

[7] Captain Eduard Bromofsky from Vienna, who died in 1945 in the battle of Stalingrad.

those very Nazis who helped the Jews knew already in 1940 that the Jews of Europe were destined for destruction unless they were helped."

By now it had gotten hot on the plaza, and it was time to move on. I wanted to get in an hour of Dynametrics[8] back at the hotel, so we resolve to walk back.

"I never found out what my grandparents did during the war. They avoided my pushy questioning every time I asked and brushed me off with clichés about the war. Eventually I started to think that they were probably ashamed to tell me the truth." Nadine looks at me.

"Yes, maybe... It's important to find out things like that, and most people never even ask...and then the stories go to the grave. Tell me something else. Where were you yesterday?"

"It was a great evening. I was at a wild AICS[9] party. At the Bamboocha Club they have one of those sound systems with a hundred different soundboards.[10] It was really impressive. You feel like you're standing in the middle of the music."

"Do you take drugs along with it?"

"Yeah, I'd recommend it. I had PS7.[11] It's perfect for something like that. They also played an Aphex Twin algorithm by the way. That's from your time, isn't it?"

"It certainly is. I knew him when he was alive, not just now when the poor guy's been turned into an algorithm."

"Better an algo than dead."

---

[8] Dynametrics, a type of sport in which one uses "enhanced reality" and one's movements are controlled by signals to the brain. The movements are automatically executed almost perfectly and are similar to yoga exercises.

[9] Artificial Intelligence Crowd Sensing party, a technology in which artificial intelligence produces the music while sensors and 3-D cameras measure the mood and the movement, gestures, etc. of the public and adapt the music to it in real time.

[10] Unplugged Surround System is a system in which various resonant bodies are directly played. Various drums, trumpets, and string instruments mounted on the ceiling and walls and in the floor generate a direct sound experience that can be located in space.

[11] PS7, an artificial drug named for the Playstation 7 because it came on the market in the same year (2027). The drug's effect is an enormous increase in ability to concentrate along with a slowing and intensifying of thought. If one concentrates on the music and one's own movements, one becomes completely locked on to them for several seconds and cannot form any other thoughts.

"Ha. Let's walk back. I should get in my hour of Dynametrics, and then we'll keep going."

From the Ring, our way takes us to Phayathai Road. I still know the area here a little from 2005 and 2006, when I had an adventure that ended with me in jail. The area has completely changed. The Ring and the district around Rama I up to Asok Montri Road, including the Hyatt Elite hotel where we're staying, belongs to Quarter2.

Quarter2 is an entire city district that belongs to Patricia ML Lim, one of Thailand's richest women. She started developing real estate around 2007 and founded a hotel chain. When the Bangkok city government started privatizing the city in 2034, she and her investment partners acquired this district. It has its own police force and laws, which are among the most permissive in Bangkok.

She permits drugs and prostitution and charges no taxes. The district lives from the proceeds from rentals and fees for drones and SDUs that drive through or fly over it. Traffic on Rama I is completely underground—the Skytrain I rode here in the 90s has disappeared. SDUs made that form of transportation superfluous. A wave of the hand is all you need and an SDU drives up. The trip is extremely cheap and traffic is no longer an issue.

We turn right into Rama I Road, a street lined by restaurants, bars, and various spas. No drones fly over Rama I itself, only a few smaller transport bots and some security bots are driving along the street. Despite all the people, this bustling city is relatively quiet. Between the numerous restaurants, there are clinics for cosmetic interventions, dentists, and bars that offer shans and exotic drinks containing substances for increasing memory, virility, muscle strength, and imagination.

Across from Chit Lom Alley, we come to one of my favorite establishments. The Krabon is a combination of a bar and a combat arena, and like many of the bars, there's also gambling. Krabi-krabong fighting women match up against bots. From outside you can't see much through the dark windows, so I convince Nadine to get a drink. It's a very large, dim space with room for a good thousand people. In the middle, the combat

21

ring raises about a meter above the floor. It's ten meters square and brightly illuminated, and the bar surrounds it.

A giant white industrial robot is installed in the middle of the ring. The robot's arm almost reaches the bar. A metal sword is mounted on the end of the arm.

Whenever a fighter strikes a solid blow against the sword, which consists of metal produced especially for these battles, the sword shatters in a spectacular shower of sparks and the woman wins, and it works the same way in the other direction.

Today a young, pretty—and extremely mobile—Thai woman is fighting. The robot, an ancient industrial model made of solid steel, looks like a monster next to her graceful, barely clothed figure. The robot is loud and moves very quickly, and to a certain extent very oddly. It rotates around its own axis again and again, which appears to be inefficient but looks amazing. The whole thing reminds me of Manga films, and I think the same point is intended here; after all, the Krabon makes its money by selling drinks, drugs, and wagers. In addition, quite a few prostitutes are standing around the already crowded shop. As far as I've heard there haven't been any injuries yet and the robot knows exactly when to stop, but it still looks extremely dangerous. The fight lasts around three minutes, and then there's a few minutes of rest before combat continues. We order two watermelon shakes and watch a few fights. I bet on the robot each time, but the young woman wins all the fights.

Farther east, still on Rama I but close to the hotel, we take a shortcut through the Vote, a shopping mall. A gigantic portrait of Maha Vajiralongkorn, the king of Thailand, graces the entrance. The shops inside are less traditional.

The Vote is considered one of the most modern shopping centers in Asia. Beside the famous fashion and jewelry stores, there are businesses for life-extending treatments, a cosmetic surgery clinic, drones, yachts, analog and digital weapons, vintage cars, and classic and modern art.

Wholegenes[12] opened its Asian flagship store here. We proceed to the Gagosian Gallery in the lower level. There's a permanent installation of Penn and Teller in which three AIs—Vermeer, Correggio, and Jacopo Tintoretto—paint pictures. It's a unique, colossal, grandiosely staged installation.

Three robots are preparing paint from pigments, and one robot is painting with the AI of each of the three masters. You can look at the scenes the AIs are painting through VR, and there are also videos of the masters discussing their current works. When we were there, Vermeer was painting a portrait of a young woman, while Correggio, whose AI had long ago rejected religion, was painting the launch of Starshot.[13] Tintoretto's AI was in turn working on a large-format painting of the new dogessa of Venice. Venice is a favorite subject here, as the Vote belongs to Venetian investors.

One story up, on both sides of the main hall, is the center's actual main attraction. On the left side in the Prada display window, robots are staging a legendary scene from the famous film "Il ponte"[14] in which the envoy of the Italian government hands over the city to the future dogessa.

On the opposite side, in the Hello Kitty display window, robots are staging a scene from the "Kokoro" series.[15] Miko, the heroine of the series, who buys the love of her husband week by week, is declaring to him that she would like to have his love from now on without compensating him for it.

After my training, we meet in my suite. It's now four o'clock in the afternoon and the sun is already hanging low. The view from the 128th

---

[12] Wholegenes, a supermarket specialized in genetically altered products.

[13] Starshot, the first mission to another star, Proxima Centauri. The journey will presumably last more than a thousand years. The launch took place in 2046. A group of private investors financed the mission.

[14] "Il ponte," a film about the detonation in 2040 of the Ponte de la liberta, the bridge connected Venice with the mainland. The subject of the film is the secession of Venice from Italy caused by a secret affair between the Doge and Italy's chief negotiator.

[15] "Kokoro" is a Japanese production about the place of women in Japan. A lack of relationships, frequent childlessness, and infrequent family formation have led to a completely new definition of women in Japanese society.

story is truly impressive in this light. To the north one can see into the interior of the country where the city seems to never want to end. Again and again, isolated sky scrapers can be seen towering over the land. After 2030, Bangkok experienced enormous population growth, from 8 million people at the time to more than 30 million now.

"Should we keep going? IRIS[16] has several questions about the manuscript. Should we check a few of them?"

"For example?"

"The note that the story isn't finished seems fairly helpful. So, how does it continue? Your grandparents went to Vienna after the war, and your mother with them. Your father was liberated from Dora-Nordhausen in Germany, according to IRIS on 11 April 1945. In addition, IRIS tells me that only a single transport went from Auschwitz to Dora-Nordhausen, on January 12, 1945. Are they all in Vienna now?"

My father stayed in Salzburg at first after his liberation and commuted between Salzburg and Vienna. As a 'displaced person,' he could move freely between the zones. The zones were the four different areas that Austria was divided into at the time. The liberating powers—England, France, Russia, and the United States—divided the area among themselves. My father earned his money by smuggling wares from one zone into the others, especially schnapps, whiskey, cigarettes, coffee, medications, and gold. It was a very profitable business, as even normal groceries were smuggled. The economy was dependent on smuggling at that point, since the people were impoverished and dependent on food rations. Whoever wanted more or something else bought smuggled goods.

It was Russian officers above all who imported the wares. My father could speak Romanian, Hungarian, and Russian, and he became the Russian's contact. The Russians were paid in gold but delivered goods of all kinds. The buyers were primarily cafés that offered smuggled goods for

---

[16] IRIS is an artificial intelligence. It understands texts completely and in the context of the author's life. It makes recommendations, researches the background, asks questions, and indicates inconsistencies in the text.

sale in their back rooms. I can still remember one of those coffee shops, Café Grünwald on the Bauernmarkt in Vienna, where poker games were played day and night. Many of Vienna's Jews were there to start new businesses.

I spent a lot of time there as a child. We would run around the tables where our fathers were playing poker, drinking whiskey, and smoking. It was a little like how you imagine the Sicilian mafia, where everyone knows each other, everyone trusts each other. I think that's a very important point. Everyone had been in concentration camps, and those people had an unbelievable lust for life. They felt invincible. I mean, they had truly been in Hell and then came back to life. How afraid of a Viennese cop is a person like that?

At the Café Grünwald, industries and banks were founded. Karl Kahane started trading in citric acid there and later built up a huge industrial sector. Old Moskovic made his first loans at the coffee shop and later owned Austria's biggest private bank.

But the Grünwald was also a place to search for the missing. My parents told me many times how people marked by the war's turmoil had stopped to ask about their relatives at the café.

Despite the awful time my parents had gone through, they describe the following period as a good time, a time of new beginnings. Money was easily earned and there was hardly any governmental influence with business.

My parents married in 1959. Wow, 90 years ago. My sister was born in 1969 and I followed in 1975. My parents were already wealthy at that point. They operated some of the first supermarkets in Vienna at a time when most groceries were still sold in small shops. In 1976, shortly after my birth, they built themselves a stately villa. In addition there were condominiums, bank accounts in Switzerland and all kinds of investments in the companies of friends and family members.

I grew up in Viennese Jewish society, so almost all my parents' friends were Holocaust survivors. The Holocaust was always a subject of conversation. I constantly heard stories about how someone had survived,

25

but above all how the people who didn't make it had relied on the law to protect them. Those people never saw it coming.

My grandfather for example was convinced that nothing could ever happen to him because he had been a highly decorated officer in the First World War. My father's parents trusted that King Michael of Romania would protect the Jews, but in summer 1944 he suddenly switched allegiance and declared Romania a part of the German Reich.

Later, after his liberation, my father wasn't able to obtain an Austria passport so that he could leave. He couldn't visit his parents or the rest of his family, who had all fled to Israel after the war.

And my mother, whose parents had been murdered, couldn't prove that her family had owned an apartment in Vienna's second district, so the apartment remained in possession of the same neighbors who had her parents thrown out of their apartment and deported.

That's how I was raised: the state is the enemy. The Jewish slogan at that time was: never pay any taxes, because taxes feed the beast. Of course you couldn't say that to anybody, so the Jews kept to themselves and created their own way of doing business.

"Why?"

"Why what?"

"Why did you have to keep to yourselves?"

"Everyone had to pay taxes to the government back then under threat of prosecution. It was crazy how many different taxes there were: taxes on every consumer product, income taxes, taxes on rent, on loans—for us today that sounds like some kind of joke—plus fees for building subways, for obtaining health care, for driving, a tax on dancing, a tax on enjoying things, a beer tax, dog taxes, an inheritance tax, a tax on lamps, and there was even a tax on air. It was extremely complicated."

"And people understood how it worked?"

"Not a chance. You needed consultants just to find out which taxes you had to pay, to say nothing of how much you had to pay. I think they could have made it all a lot simpler, but it's a little like with religion or homeopathy. If it's too simple, then you notice more quickly how nonsensical it all is. You don't see the forest for the trees anymore and you're forced to deal with it so much that you slowly start to believe it's actually something important that's been carefully planned."

"Interesting theory, although it presupposes duplicity on the part of the decision makers."

"If you had dared to publicly admit not paying taxes back then, there'd be trouble. So there was a kind of censorship. A lot of people tried to avoid paying taxes, but no one would have ever admitted it, it was too dangerous. So of course there was never a debate about it or even just an honest discussion. The self-employed, who almost always avoided taxes, were too fearful to participate in public life. People would have examined their past and ruined them. As government control increased, the situation got worse and worse. Eventually people gave in, and finally everyone considered paying taxes to be moral. That was completely normal back then. Today you'd call it some kind of collective Stockholm syndrome."

"That's exactly what I learned as a student. But there are still taxes today, aren't there?"

"Yeah, in a lot of countries, mostly very low or even voluntary taxes, but sure, Russia still has real taxes, and France has extremely high taxes, and several African states and parts of the USA and China as well."

"How high were the taxes back then?"

"On average, everyone paid around the half of their earnings. That was the required quota in most countries."

"Really? And for what?"

"Well, with the increasing revenues, countries took over more and more services that today are offered by businesspeople. Although the services were constantly getting worse and more expensive, as they were mostly state monopolies. Naturally it's difficult, or actually impossible, to provide an education that fits everybody, for example. Because education was a governmental monopoly, people had no choice but to cling to the idea of a state that does everything and organizes everything. Worst of all of course was the monopoly on coining money, as it took away people's control over their money. The value of money was always falling, for centuries without end, and even today there are a few countries where that's still going on. It was terrible. You were dependant on a few government-organized currencies that the national states—that were more and more heavily in debt—produced at their own discretion. Of course they produced as much as possible in order to devalue their debts. And along with them the account balances of all those who owned their currency, of course."

"If the governments printed the money, why didn't they just print the money and use it for their expenses? I mean, what was the point of taxes?"

I've got to admit, she's got a good analytical mind. "That was actually the most insidious part about it. The governments actually could have done that, just like China, France, and Australia could do it today. But collecting taxes is also a method of permanently controlling every facet of people's lives.

When I was ten, twelve years old, there weren't any computers in daily use. They only started being used everywhere bit by bit, and with them came more government control: observation of data traffic, surveillance and recording of telephone conversations. Businesses had to share their accounting in real time with the tax authorities. Bank accounts and credit card accounts where you used to keep your money or organize your spending could be examined by government agencies. Since people did all their spending through their accounts, the government always knew exactly what you were doing. And then there was the recording of communications data, security cameras on the streets, automatic recognition of license plates, facial recognition, geographic locating of mobile telephones, travel data, and then DNA and all that.

Just before the collapse, there were ever more rigid regulations. The governments were desperately trying to retain their power and extract more money from their citizens. But there will be more than enough about money later.

My earliest memories of my father are probably from the end of the 70s. You often remember trivial things more than important events. Like with me, it's stayed in my memory how we drove to school one morning with a plastic bag full of money on the passenger seat. Several

28

million shillings. My father said he was going to buy a house with it that day. I was pretty impressed by that. I also watched the first "Star Wars" movie with my father, and then there was the French school I attended and hated, and the synagogue where I was bored.

The house in Vienna with the yard I loved. I grew up there, I played and built things in the yard. My childhood was fantastic. Until my father was diagnosed with cancer and died when I was twelve. A year before my Bar Mitzvah.

When my father died, I was right in the middle of preparations for my Bar Mitzvah. I was still devout back then and studied five times a week with the wife of Vienna's chief rabbi, Paul Eisenberg.

I found it very interesting and wanted to be a good Jew. At the time, Judaism was still very important for me. I prayed, I studied, I was involved with a very conservative Jewish organization—the Bnei Akiva— and was completely convinced of God's existence. I prayed every morning and every evening at home, and every Friday evening and Saturday morning in the synagogue. For the Shabbat I was usually invited over by other Jews in downtown Vienna, since I lived so far away from the city and couldn't drive home for the afternoon.

On Friday evenings and Saturday mornings, I usually walked from the seventeenth district to the first and back, about an hour each way. Sometimes I spent the night with the Birnbaums, who lived on the Kohlmarkt in Vienna, a roofed passage where there are only businesses.

The Birnbaums were a cheerful family. I remember an odd incident that took place at their home. Aaron Birnbaum was a businessman, a tall dashing man with a healthy sense of humor. No one knew exactly what he did. Sometimes they said he traded in coins, sometimes stamps, sometimes diamonds.

One Friday evening I went to the Birnbaums with his daughter, a good friend of mine. Their apartment on the Graben shopping street was huge and there were a lot of people there. Around twenty older Jews were sitting at three tables in the living room and discussing vigorously, most of them in Yiddish. Across from the door to the living room was a safe that stood almost two meters tall. As far as I could make out, the police unit for financial crimes had been there that morning and had been interested in the safe's contents. But Mr. Birnbaum said he had no key to the safe, and so the police sealed it until experts could force it open the following Monday.

The twenty men in the room were discussing what should be done. One could open the safe, clean it out, and simply accept the penalty. One could do nothing. One could try to weld it open from behind, or try to replace the seal; several jewelers were there for that. Or one could simply let the safe disappear and act as if it had never existed.

Among the twenty men discussing the problem were lawyers, jewelers, traders, rabbis, doctors, and scroungers. So something important must have been inside. If they opened it and Mr. Birnbaum had to pay a penalty or even go to prison, it was arranged who would have to compensate him for it and how much.

As it was Friday evening and you couldn't open the safe for religious reasons at that point, let alone touch its contents or take them somewhere else, there was time until Saturday evening. They were confident that the financial crimes police, who were only moderately dedicated to their job, wouldn't show up before Monday to open the safe by force. As far as I remember, they agreed to open the safe and make the contents disappear, and compensate Mr. Birnbaum for any problems.

On other weekends I stayed with the Altmanns. Salomon Altmann, the man of house, had also survived Auschwitz. After his time there, he grew a second skull cap. Salomon Altmann was a merchant. His specialty was trading in all the things that the Americans produced and the Russians weren't allowed to have while the Cold War was going on. It was a risky but highly profitable business. As far as I understood it, the Altmanns founded several businesses in Vienna that produced various electronic parts. These companies ordered components, above all microchips from the USA, and then transferred them to employees of the various Eastern Block embassies in Vienna—Hungary, Czechoslovakia, Romania, and Russia.

The most fun family of all were the Reichs, whose sons were my best friends. The Reichs, as their name suggested, were rich—very, very

30

rich. The Reichs lived in the first district in Himmelpfortgasse. They actually owned a whole house there, which especially in Vienna's first district was more than a little unusual. Every member of the family had their own apartment, and there were a few more apartments for guests. Herschel Reich had come to Austria as a child. His family was from Russia and fled after the October Revolution in 1917 to Graz, where his father worked as an architect. Herschel lived in Vienna after that and studied economics—that was in the time of Mises and Hayek, who he both got to know there.

During the war he fled back to Graz, joined the Austrian resistance movement and fought against the Nazis. Just before the end of the war he ended up in the Donawitz steel factory in Styria; most of the resistance fighters had been workers at this factory. Then the Red Army hired him as a translator, as he spoke Russian, German, and English. As he was an economist, he ended up working in the Austrian oil industry, which had earlier been the Soviet oil industry in Austria, and later the AOM.[17] It doesn't exist anymore in that form, but it used to be Austria's largest oil company.

The Russians took oil as war reparations until the 1960s. But after 1960, the Russians still needed oil, so Herschel founded his own company and continued providing the Russians oil in return for drilling licenses in Russia, as the Russians didn't have foreign currency to pay for the oil. Within a few years, that made him one of the richest Jews in Vienna. Old Reich was entirely consistent in his beliefs against paying taxes, by the way. His sons explained to me that it was at times more expensive to not pay taxes that to pay them: the financial structures that were necessary for that became steadily more complex and opaque, and the organizations that offered these arrangements in turn became steadily more criminal and expensive.

The Braunsteins were also remarkable. My father got to know Dudi Braunstein in Vienna after the war. People say he survived the war as a helper for the SS, a special unit of the German army. The Braunsteins

---

[17] Austrian Oil Management, later simply AOM, was acquired in 2032 by the Chinese company Sinopec.

lived in the Tempel Alley in the second district. Both of them were very short but always dressed with unusual elegance. After the war, Dudi Braunstein opened a language school in Vienna even though he knew no languages except German and Yiddish. When my father asked how that was supposed to work, Braunstein answered that he only needed to be one lesson ahead of his students. He seems to have eventually learned English at least. In the early 80s, he emigrated to Florida in the USA together with his wife. Ten years later he was suddenly back in Vienna again where he organized fundraising trips to Vienna for Talmud Torah schools in New York and Jerusalem. Representatives of the Talmud schools traveled to Vienna and went around the city collecting donations for the schools with Fritzl, Braunstein's partner. Fritzl was a postman in Vienna and knew exactly where Jews lived in the first district, where you had to ring the bell, who would usually donate and how much. Frizl and Braunstein took a thirty percent cut of the donations.

But gradually it came out why Braunstein had returned to Vienna. In 1983, he bought a savings and loan bank in Florida. He financed the purchase for the most part with a loan from another bank, according to rumors around 15 million dollars. After the purchase he took out a loan from his own bank for around 20 million dollars and then transferred the money offshore, somewhere in the Caribbean. Finally he returned to Austria, which had no extradition treaty with the USA for white-collar crimes. He went underground for a few years until bounty hunters hired by the FBI drugged and kidnapped him from his villa in Döbling, an upper-class district of Vienna. He was taken to Hungary in the trunk of a car and flown from there to the USA.

And so I got to know almost all the Jewish families in Vienna's first and second districts during my orthodox phase. It was a parallel world in the middle of Vienna, a Schtetl spread out among a few dozen homes where you prayed, ate kosher, talked about people and the war, and conducted business.

At school, I was primarily interested in mathematics and physics, and a little chemistry. According to my mother, I was a child prodigy. For my eighth birthday I got a Commodore 64, my first computer. That was a thing that you programmed a bit, but when you turned it off, everything was gone. There was no storage at first. And of course no Internet, but I started programming back then when I was eight.

"Really impressive, your resumé," Nadine said with a smile. I decided to accept the compliment.

"In 1988, around two years after my father's death, my mother sold the supermarkets. The proceeds from the sale brought with them a new task that completely preoccupied me: managing our assets. At that point I had already been dealing with securities for some time. Despite my young age, my mother gave me free rein in investing. The timing was perfect, because on October 19, 1987, the markets crashed and people were expecting a recession. Since that didn't happen, the stock indexes quickly climbed again. And then 1989 was the fall of the wall, which especially in Austria led to an economic boom. So more than being smart, I was lucky."

"The fall of the wall? Wasn't that the end of the Soviet Union?"

"You could say that. The economically developed world was divided into two camps at the time. One the one side, the predominately western industrial nations that had installed so-called democracies and could boast of relatively free market economies. On the other side, the nations of the eastern bloc where planned economies dominated and the government organized the economy. The planned economy functioned for a while but then, like always happens when people attempt to rule by force, the Soviet Union and its member states were broke. But the whole thing was pretty good for me. I was fourteen, fifteen years old and spent my free time trading in stocks, options, and bonds. Then I began helping other Jews to manage their wealth. Most of these portfolios were in Switzerland. There were a few smaller blanks where German and Austrian Jews typically kept their accounts. When I was sixteen, I was managing the money of around ten Jewish families in Vienna. All of these families had to constantly transfer money to Switzerland and from Switzerland to Austria. So I started to organize precisely that for them without causing transactions between the countries. So if a family needed 10,000 Swiss

33

francs in Vienna, then I looked for a family who needed 10,000 francs in Switzerland. A wire transfer was made in Switzerland, and I brought the money from one family to another in Vienna. In return I took a five percent commission from both sides. When I was sixteen, I quit school. I was earning a lot of money and saw no point in continuing school any longer. In the years after that I focused on managing wealth and transferring money between Switzerland and Austria. And there we have it, the story of the money in Switzerland."

"Wow. At that age I had completely different things in mind, unfortunately, like going out, for example. But you seem to have made up for lost time in your later years.... Now for something really important: should we get something to eat? I'm starving."

"An accurate observation. Let's go eat and keep going later."

"Great, here at the hotel there's a Puregene,[18] they have the best in vitro meat in the world. Look, it's crazy how many different genes: lamb, crocodile, tuna, buffalo, gazelle. All kinds of different pig varieties, do you like that? Cool, they also grill with lasers or sound, or with charcoal."

"Yeah, charcoal, totally crazy. Let's head up and eat there."

The Puregene is in the 140th story and looks like a Japanese bar from the 030s.[19] The architect is actually an artificial intelligence based on Yoshio Taniguchi, an architect active at the end of the last century.

Especially with business or restaurant chains, it's common to use AIs of architects for the design, as the design of hundreds of stores by talented architects would be much too expensive.

This location has turned out splendidly. It's in an ultramodern simple Japanese style using wood and stone in combination, with an

---

[18] Puregene, a restaurant chain from Singapore that produces meat bred in vitro from their own labs. They breed their own animals as sources for the stem cells. Animals threatened by extinction are kept in nature preserves in order to obtain stem cells for meat production.

[19] "030s" for the 2030s.

34

animated sky and individual sound and climate zones. I find it extremely pleasing. There are no bots here, the orders are taken old school by human waiters. Having the food prepared at your table by a chef comes at a price, of course.

We're welcomed with a set of two drinks and two mini-shans each, all of it perfectly tailored to us. My drinks are based on artificially aged whiskeys, and Nadine's are based on juniper and pine, with shans to match. They recommend Chacoan peccary for us, a pig variety from Latin America that only lives in a few nature preserves that belong to Puregene. Puregene breeds meat from 56 different pig varieties; it's their specialty. The tables are arranged in booths, and every booth has its own cloud of sound in which the music adapts itself to the conversation and activity of the guests.

Nadine tells me about going out the day before, but mostly her thoughts are on an almost perfect match that's come up at OLPA. OLPA is a service that matches up couples based purely on olfactory criteria. There's many similar services now, but OLPA has been around for fifteen years. Data from DNA are combined with current and constantly updated olfactory data. At first I used OLPA often; surprising combinations of people actually come to pass as a result. I'd say ninety percent of the time, you think the person you're matched with is hot and want to hop into bed instantly.

Nadine confirms that the accuracy rate of previous matches is around 100%, although it constantly changes, even with the same partner. The result is a certain time pressure to meet the selected partner quickly and have sex right away if possible. In any case, Nadine seems somewhat disquieted about having to keep working after dinner. I calm her with the suggestion of calling it a day, and in any case I'd rather write the next chapters by myself.

After dinner, Nadine takes another shan, a wild mixture of cocaine, 2CB,[20] and Japanese cedar, in order to get in the mood for her appointment. I order a Japanese beer, and we arrange to meet again tomorrow morning.

---

[20] 2CB is produced synthetically and belongs to the phenylethylamine substance class. The chemical structure displays similarities to mescaline, a component of peyote, which was used by Central American Indians during ritual ceremonies.

CHAPTER 2

Back in my room, I look through the current document. IRIS has a few notes, a few years are off, and certain connections are vague, especially the relationships between people. IRIS is irritating but she's right, and I edit the document. IRIS knows everything, after all. What many people don't know (except people like me who don't have a job in the conventional sense and therefore have time to concern themselves with all kinds of things) is that IRIS was originally developed by the NSA.

The NSA was one of many American intelligence agencies, and for decades it collected all the data it could get its hands on. Telephone call data, e-mails, connection details, GPS coordinates, appointments, pictures, Facebook profiles and so on. The problem was analyzing the data. Whenever it was urgent to establish the connections between people in a particular case, an army of agents had to read through and analyze thousands of document summaries. That could take weeks, months, or even years. Often much too long to achieve any result. So IRIS (Internal Relation Intelligence System) was born. Every person, every organization, in principle every entity that could be identified got their own IRIS. IRIS was like an inner voice for that entity, capable of representing the personality of a person or organization. It knew what was important, what was planned next, how you thought and what you were thinking. Over time, IRIS became more and more clever. Weeks ahead of time, IRIS was able to predict things like depressive episodes, anxiety attacks, peaks and valleys of health, and of course potential criminal acts as well. After the collapse of the NSA, the technology became public domain and was applied in many areas.

IRIS often calls my attention to personality developments that might have negative impacts. For many people, their IRIS has become the most important person in their lives. Sometimes the IRIS of a close friend or relative, often of someone who has died, becomes an important figure in people's lives. These people are called "Iries."

My daughter Sandra asks me if I'd like to see her view. That might be interesting. She works as a biologist for RedBullOceans, an Austrian company that owns and cultivates a large area in the Pacific. I know at the moment that she's in the area of Honiara in the Solomon Islands, where RedBullOceans manages their holdings. It would work best to share the view using contact lenses so that I'd see exactly the same thing she does. But I don't want to wait and decide on a retinal projection instead.

"What do you say?"

" I don't know, is that something to eat?"

"Of course not, that's a Mola Mola, a sunfish. There were two here just a minute ago, which is actually pretty sensational."

"You know I'm clueless about things like that. Where are you, anyway?"

"We're in the Whale[21] at a depth of 650 meters in the Bismarck Archipelago. This is my colleague Susan."

"Hi, Susan."

"Hi, Sandra's dad."

"Call me David."

"So Dad, when are you going to come visit me?"

"I don't know yet. When's a good time?"

"Today, for one. You really need to come here some time, to Honiara. It's so beautiful here. How's it going in Bangkok? Are you writing? Being good? Is everything okay?"

"Yes, yes and no, yes."

"Ha. Will you come? You're not that far away right now."

"We'll see. Sometime I have to go back to Vienna—and you do, too. When will you be in Vienna again?"

---

[21] The Whale is a submarine used by marine biologists. It moves like a fish in water, emits no motor noise, can dive to 10,000 meters, and operates manned or unmanned.

"On May 17. Look, I have to get back to work here, but I'll leave the view on. Look at that—you don't see that every day. We'll talk again tomorrow when I'm back on land. And think about coming out here. The food's great, and the weather's to dream about. It's like something out of the last century here. You'll like it."

"Of course I'll like it."

"Your Watson should find a flight."

"Okay, I'll tell him."

"Talk to you later."

The view really is great. RedBullOceans is only a bit player in the sea business, but they still own a parcel of ocean bigger than Europe.

The next part of the story is my sister's death in 1996. We—my mother, her boyfriend Avi, my friend Ron and I—were sitting at the Shabbat dinner on a Friday evening with some other friends of my mother, like every week. Only my sister didn't show up, and she didn't pick up her phone. There weren't mobile phones back then, so the only way to contact her was calling her at home. We had just started eating, but my mother had a bad feeling. She's normally unexcitable, but she got nervous and insisted that we drive over to see what was going on. Even though it was the Shabbat, Ron and I drove off. My mother had given me a copy of the apartment key. It was dark inside, the television was on, my sister in a chair in front of it. I knew right away that she was dead. Her body was already cold.

For me and my mother, that changed some things. My mother sank into serious depression. She tried to treat it every way she could think of, above all with benzodiazepines.

My sister died in March 1996 of sudden cardiac arrest, in all likelihood caused by a lingering flu. The thought that one's life could simply be snatched away, without any warning or evident danger, from one second to the next—that realization changed my life. And not necessarily for the better. The shock planted these thoughts deep down inside me and even today I'm constantly aware of them.

Before that event, I used to make long and detailed plans. I considered it normal and necessary to accept years of hardship in order to reach goals and obtain success. But then I lost that ability. The fear of dying suddenly was too large. Even when setting long-term plans in motion, there had to be enough time to enjoy life.

In the summer of 1996, I turned over management of client funds to a Jewish co-worker and the money transfer business along with it. I wanted to free myself from as many obligations as I could. I was still devout after my sister's burial and I attended the synagogue more than usual. I even switched to a smaller, more orthodox synagogue. But my sister's death created doubts about my faith for the first time.

As a rule, faith just keeps going all by itself. From my earliest childhood I was used to praying, eating kosher, celebrating holidays, and living and thinking according to Jewish tradition. I would say that I never dealt with my belief on a meta level until I was twenty. It was as natural for me as sleeping or eating. But my sister's death enraged me. I couldn't see any sense in snatching her life away at the age of twenty-nine. I couldn't see any sense in my father's early death, or my mother's losing her whole family. I couldn't find anything remotely divine in the Holocaust and all the rest of the world's suffering. And so a thought process began; in time my doubts grew larger. It took a long time, several months, before I understood: there was no God. I had never actually believed at all, but had only been raised that way and lived in a society where everyone believed in God or at least followed Jewish law.

I kept going to the synagogue and following all the laws, but my faith was gone. If you didn't grow up that way, if you weren't indoctrinated as a child, you can't understand how hard it is to let go of all that. Even if you have already freed yourself from belief, it's another huge step to let go of the rituals. Because when you give up the rituals, in a real sense you're no longer part of the same society. You're an outcast. No longer taking part in a Seder, no longer shaking hands in the synagogue with the certainty that you all belonged to each other, that you formed a community, our people.

I spent the next three years traveling, hiking, and climbing. A stark contrast with managing money, transporting cash, and eating kosher. Instead I spent time in the Atlas Mountains, in the Dolomites, at Joshua Tree and at Red Rock near Las Vegas, where every day I could climb and go to strip clubs.

My Jewishness was gone, at least as far as faith was concerned. What shook me the most was that I had believed that nonsense for so long and invested so much time and so many resources in that religion. What shocked me even more was the thought of how many other intelligent people paid homage to the same nonsense. For the first time it was clear to me how uncritically one accepts faith and how rarely one questions it.

At that point I decided to question everything. That's not a simple thing at all. There are so many levels on which one can question things. After I had gotten over religion, I thought about what other articles of faith I had internalized without really considering them and without evidence. But I often had the impression that on certain subjects I was caught in some kind of aquarium. I wasn't able to question them because I had never truly seen my own imprisonment.

And so after my liberation from religion came my emancipation from my basic socialist outlook. Interestingly, one of the triggers for that was Avi, my mother's boyfriend after my father died. Avi was a veteran of the Socialist Party of Austria, the country's leading party until 2000. Later its popularity dropped sharply until it completely disappeared in 2030.

Avi could take care of everything. He helped me to avoid military service and buy a driver's license. He helped other people to get promotions, work permits, and community housing, to avoid taxes, and so on. You didn't even notice the corruption involved in it. The whole thing felt normal and even Avi didn't make any effort to keep any of it a secret. It was 'business as usual.'

Like all Austrians of my generation, but also many of the later generations, we grew up and were socialized in a socialist, statist system. You have to keep in mind that everything was organized by government agencies: kindergartens, schools, universities, most media, television, health care, pensions, parks, electricity, streets. So it was clear what you'd learn in school and, above all, what you wouldn't learn.

Naturally we were freer than the people in the Soviet Union back then, but we were so happy about that that we only concentrated on the differences between us and not on our similarities to the people of the Soviet Union. And so another thought process started in me that only much later led me to renounce statism.

Ideologically I focused on convincing friends and acquaintances to turn their backs on religion, as in my view it was especially the secularized Jews who formed the basis on which orthodoxy props up all its nonsense and its inhumanity.

The next morning I used retinal projection for a trip to Google Real.[22] In order to conduct research for my book, I took a walk through the Vienna of the 1970s. The area within the beltway was entirely viewable, and at least half of the remaining areas. I walked across the Kohlmarkt of 1975 where both Café Arabia and the Nebehay bookstore still existed, and the Länderbank, my father's principal bank, was still on Am Hof square. Then I went to the Schottentor station. Down to the television monitors, but even here they didn't exist yet; it would take a while longer until the past finds its place in the future. But the old trams run here.

I went back to the Graben shopping street, this time to September 1945. It looks awful. Half the houses have been reduced to rubble. Then to St. Stephen's Cathedral, missing its roof. Unimaginable that people were able to build up a prospering city again within a few years.

I went up into the cathedral. You could see down into the city from the roof timbers that now lay exposed. Someone was there. Ethel Mauskopf. Unbelievable, meeting her here.

"Ethel, hello! How are you?"

---

[22] Google Real is the virtual environment of Google Earth/Google Maps. It became possible by means of an artificial intelligence that reconstructs landscapes and buildings through the interlinking of billions of photos, paintings, maps, etchings, blueprints, and movies. If data are available, the past environment was also reconstructed. By analyzing blueprints, the interior life of most buildings could also be reconstructed.

"David, I can't believe it! What are you doing here?"

"I'm writing a book. Vienna in the 1970s plays a role in it and I wanted to find some inspiration. And you?"

"I miss Vienna. I've been here for two hours. I wandered up here from the second district."

"You miss Vienna in 1945?"

"Of course not, my parents weren't even born then. I wanted to see how it was back then. Really I miss Vienna from 2010 to 2020."

"And where are you now?"

"I've been living in Tel Aviv and sometimes in the Negev for a long time now. I've got a family and children. I'm still singing, but I don't travel much anymore, as I mostly give virtual concerts. A lot of Viennese come."

"Are you still orthodox?"

"That's a difficult question. Yes and no. Me, not so much, but my husband and my whole family are. And my friends. I know what you think about that. At any rate I live kosher. I grew up like that and I'm not changing that now. I take it you didn't turn orthodox?"

"No, to the contrary. But it's funny that we're discussing it here in St. Stephen's, a former church. We would never have imagined it back then in Vienna—St. Stephen's as a restaurant and club."

"Have you been there?"

"Several times. I can highly recommend it. The atmosphere is incredible, especially if you knew the cathedral in the old days. Tourists still come by day, but in the evening the club and restaurant are in business. I also know the manager and owner, Michi Toner."

"Funny that he's the one. He must be ancient by now."

"A Methuselah like me."

"So tell me, where are you? What are you doing now?"

"I'm in Bangkok writing a book."

"About sex?"

"Very funny. No, an autobiography."

"So you're famous?"

"Not yet, but I did something that many people know about, but no one knew for a long time that it was me."

"So you're the Phantom of the Opera?"

"Exactly, that's me. I'll send you the book when it's done. Do you have a moment? Speaking of the opera, should we walk up to the opera house?"

We go down to the St. Stephen's plaza and take Kärntner Street up towards the opera. Rubble is everywhere. Across from the Himmelpfort Alley, almost all the houses are destroyed.

"I don't know what should seem worse: how it looked after a war like that or how incredibly realistic this virtual world is. Incredible that it was possible to rebuild everything so quickly," said Ethel.

"The knowledge of how to build something was still there. There was little to stop you back then. Everyone could conduct any business they wanted. Should we shift times to 2010?"

"Let's go to 2010. Do you miss that time? Would you like to go back?"

"Very much so. I would do some things differently, believe me. But up until 2020 everything was good. After that my life fell apart."

"That sounds dramatic. What happened? You were always doing such interesting things."

"That's just the thing, our world has no need for it. The division of labor keeps marching logically onwards. To be successful, you have to cook noodles for twenty years to reach perfection, and even then there's probably an AI that can do it better than you."

"I know you hate religion and all that, but it gives me a framework in which my life plays out. Like being married or having a job. I imagine that it's strenuous not to have that kind of framework. How do you even know what's okay and what isn't? What is your girlfriend allowed to do, what are you allowed to do? Every day you have to reconsider who you actually are, where your boundaries are, and what you can demand of others. I couldn't live like that...."

"In my opinion, the nucleus of progress and change lies precisely in the reconsideration of these everyday things that often seem trivial. It's not the big ideas that move us forward, but rather the many small, unnoticed changes. That's why I think it's so important to question every little thing, to review them and improve them over and over again. If you don't try something different over and over again, how do you know you're doing the right thing?"

"I think I'm doing the right thing; it just feels good and I'm satisfied with my life."

"My grandmother always said, the worm in the horseradish believes there's nothing sweeter."

"That's mean, but funny. You're just a *shegetz*."[23]

By now we've reached the opera. In 2010, it was still owned by the Republic and operas were performed every evening.

Today the opera is the property of the Novomatic Group and is one of the biggest entertainment venues in Europe. Located in the New Opera are Europe's biggest casino, a jazz club in cooperation with Blue Note, a sports betting lounge, a Nobu restaurant and the Steirereck, a Peruvian and a Ghanaian restaurant, the Roberto Bar, a Japanese cocktail bar, the Establissement Babylon and an adjoining Sans Souci Suites hotel with a spa. There are also diverse luxury brands like Amazon, Sony, Fincantieri,[24] Aurora,[25] Koenigsegg, Airbus,[26] Ehang,[27] Calico,[28] Prada, Adidas, Rolex, and many others.

The grand casino is located on the floor that was once used for the Viennese Opera Ball, which still takes place. The floor can still be cleared for concerts. By and large the Opera Ball, the old opera's only profitable evening, was the model for the opera's massive reorganization.

"Yet another project like this. It's too bad what was done with the opera."

"Have you been to the New Opera?"

---

[23] שֵׁגֶץ, an unbelieving Jew or an apostate from Judaism.

[24] Fincantieri, a business founded in Trieste in 1959 that became one of the leading companies in the area of autonomous yachts in 2050.

[25] Aurora Cannabis Inc. (OTC: ACBFF) is a Canadian firm specialized in the distribution of recreational drugs. Besides marijuana, LSD, cocaine, and heroin, the firm markets hundreds of different natural and artificial drugs in their luxurious stores.

[26] Airbus personal, a company that sells drones for individual use.

[27] Ehang is a Chinese company that offers drones for personal transportat.

[28] Calico is a company belonging to the Google conglomerate that offers anti-aging products.

"No, and you?"

"I go often. It's a cool place, really."

"I'd like it more if one would still perform operas there. That's what it was built for after all."

"Fine, but nobody pays enough for an opera to justify the effort and the location."

"Too bad...."

"And so? Are there any fewer operas today than there used to be because of it?"

"No, there are even more operas performed. But this place was something special."

"This place is even more impressive today! Some time when you're in Vienna again, we'll go out to an African restaurant there, and afterwards to the Roberto Bar in the cellar."

CHAPTER 3

By now it was noon and Nadine was awake. I was able to convince her to go get something to eat right away so we could use the afternoon for writing. We got into an SDU and drove to Sri Nakhon Khuean Khan Park; today's restaurant was supposed to be a surprise for Nadine.

We get out at the park entrance and take the path to Afuri5 at the far end of the park. The park is part of Bangkok's botanical gardens and you see a variety of plants to match.

Afuri5 is housed in a Japanese style country house with a high peaked roof. The outer walls are wood, and inside only wood, bamboo, and stone were used. There are no computers except when you pay for your meal. No bots work here. There's an open fireplace in the middle of the restaurant behind the bar. A copper cauldron around two meters wide with soup bubbling in it hangs over the fireplace. This is the heart of the restaurant, a soup that's been cooking since 1967, if you believe the restaurateurs. It all began in Nakano, Japan, in a small ramen shop. Typically ramen soup base cooks between six and sixty hours. Because the shop in Nakano was too small to hold so many pots, the cooks decided to only prepare one pot of soup, but to leave it simmering continuously. They kept adding new meat and vegetables to the chicken soup depending on how much was sold each day.

After the soup had been cooking for forty years or so, the restaurant was discovered by international gourmets. The third generation of owners then opened numerous franchises by bringing portions of the soup (still simmering) to the new locations, sort of like the Olympic flame, in order to keep cooking it at the new restaurant. Like in computer programming, they call this process "forking" the soup.

Besides the century soup, which is the base of all the dishes here, soy sauces, ramen noodles, various vegetables, and beer are hydroponically produced in Afuri5.

We take a place at the bar in order to watch the cooks. Bustling activity holds sway behind the bar. A lot of things that are taken care of by robots elsewhere are still done by human chefs here. In addition to cooking and the preparation of cocktails, that means cutting up the meat and vegetables and drumming when soup orders are ready to be brought to the customers.

On the way to the toilet, which is in the basement and whose location in the giant wooden structure invariably reminds me of an Alpine ski hut, you can observe the high-tech food production. Where the upper level is arranged traditionally, with the cooks in their Japanese uniforms, the walls of wood and tables of bamboo and stone without any visible computers, the production down here is ultramodern.

A window seven meters wide and three meters tall reveals robots moving around in a completely white and sterile environment full of various equipment. You can see the hydroponic production of vegetables and also the beds where soybeans are fermenting for the production of soy sauces, vessels for the production of miso pastes, and many other boiler kettles, presumably for the production of beer and sake. Japanese cuisine is enormously inventive, but the basis for almost all products always comprises soybeans, rice, and barley.

"How was your appointment?" I ask.

"Oh, it was great."

"And?"

"And what?"

"The details?"

"You think I'll tell you the details?"

"Well, maybe something. Did you like the young man? Did you let him lick your shoes? I know your fetishes."

She grins mischievously. "Sure, but it wasn't a man. We were in a love lounge. Are you familiar with those?"

I try to keep my thoughts under control and not think of how the two spent the night, but it would be too obvious to change the subject suddenly. "Yes, I'm familiar with them. Was it nice?"

"It was totally nice there! You can take the SDU directly to it, and inside there's simply everything. Music, open fireplace, drugs, tools, and a botler[29] who brings drinks and food. It was incredible, your thoughts completely revolve around sex and there's no distraction. You can let yourself completely give in to the lust. We left at four when Christine, that's the young woman's name, unfortunately had to go to the airport, and then back to Norway."

"Oh, that's too bad," was all that I managed to get out.

"Yes, a little, but there are plenty of other matches. As you know, I'm not necessarily unhappy if I don't have to deal with my nighttime companions afterwards. And you were a good boy at home?"

"I was. For one thing, I want to keep going with the book, and besides, with my whiskey drinking, shan smoking, and all that I've reached the limits of my health insurance. In the last few years my premiums have been raised several times because I've been partying more and more. According to the insurance, it's not exactly beneficial at my age. And the new Medicoders[30] can't be tricked like they used to, so I'll have to keep things somewhat quieter the next few days. I can heartily recommend the century soup here, by the way. The chefs here make a classic ramen soup out of it with various natural or artificial meats and with regular or roasted miso."

In the park a few minutes away from Aufuri5, there's a teahouse where everything is completely automated. We get our drinks from the bar that just brewed them and look for a cozy lounge. Using the sound cloud, we block out the noise of the other guests. The table is a workspace and a

---

[29] Botler, a combination of robot and butler.

[30] The Medicoder is a sensor around 5 mm long and 0.2 mm wide that is placed in the body and continuously transmits information about the state of one's health. On the one hand, the information is used to recognize dangers and optimize medications and nutrition, and on the other hand to continuously adapt the price of the current health insurance plan.

monitor at the same time. Nadine reviews what I wrote last evening while I sip on my jasmine shake.

"Cool, you spent years climbing and hiking. Why did you stop?"

"At some point it got monotonous, and I ran out of money. I went back to Vienna."

"I'd like to hear about it. How old were you and what did you do then?"

I was around 23, and back in Vienna I had to look around for something that earned money. I couldn't go back to my old business, and after the wars in Iraq and the financial upheavals after that, my co-worker had lost a lot of customers. And besides, I wasn't really a part of Jewish society any more, people wouldn't have trusted me with their money so readily.

The nation of Austria was heading towards bankruptcy at the time and the tax laws were getting more and more unyielding, so that having bank accounts in Switzerland at all got to be dangerous. A lot of people disclosed their accounts voluntarily and brought the money back to Austria. Slowly but surely, the money transfer business came to a standstill. I had time to enjoy Vienna and I met my first girlfriend, the mother of my first child. Before I knew it, she was pregnant.

My son Rafael was born in early 1999, and now I was really under pressure, I needed money. The next two jobs came about by chance. One of my old customers called me up and wanted to meet with me.

Marco Stern was from a wealthy family. His parents had a chain of clothing stores and whenever they opened a new branch, they astutely bought the building it was located in. Eventually they owned more of a real estate business with fashion ambitions. Marco was the second generation in a row of excellent businessmen, which is pretty rare.

It's actually surprising how difficult it was for the second generation of Viennese Jews to keep pace with the success of their parents. Only very few were able to increase their parents' wealth; most of them had used up their parents' savings after twenty, thirty years. The actual inflation rate kept rising, especially after 2010, which increased the trend even more. Marco was one of the few in any event who added to his parents' fortune several times over. We met up in his stylish villa in the eighteenth district. He got to the point right away: his mother, born in Hungary, had lost her parents in the war, and she herself was one of the few lucky ones who were able to flee to Sweden with a Wallenberg visa.[31]

A distant relative who had died recently had told her he remembered how her parents had brought a considerable amount of money to Switzerland before the Germans invaded. Owing to my contacts with several Swiss banks, Marco was now hoping that I might be able to help find the account. In case of our success, he would pay me twenty-five percent of the money found.

The next day I called up my contact and good friend at Credit Suisse. He was a Jew himself and I thought he would be happy to help me out with the search. But things turned out completely different than expected. He explained to me that the banks simply bled those accounts dry. That means if no one showed up for years, then more and more expensive and less and less comprehensible management fees and other expenses were charged against the account. As proof he sent me a list of 2500 accounts whose owners had not contacted the bank in fifty years, so-called dormant accounts; all together they had deposits of only 20 million francs. He thought the matter was clear: the banks had long ago taken over the actual funds on the basis of provisions in the fine print. "Bankers are like rats," he said, "they look for food, they hoard the food, always more and more; I spend the whole day here in the bank sitting with those rats."

So I could only tell my friend Marco to forget the whole thing about the Swiss bank account, as there would surely be no amount worth mentioning left in the account, and the effort required to obtain such a relatively small amount would presumably be disproportionately high.

---

[31] Raoul Wallenberg, son of rich industrialists from Sweden who in 1944 used his family's influence on the Swedish government to distribute 800 Swedish protective visas in order to save Jews from deportation. All trace of him disappeared in 1947, possibly Russian imprisonment.

But I couldn't let go of the thing with the rats. In my head, I saw rats in a bank. How they trade, buy, and sell. What would happen if rats made good bankers, or at least good traders? I still knew from my own experience that, except for arbitrage, there were in principle only two methods of buying securities or commodity futures for speculating on price gains.

The basic method is this: you look at the company data, the industry, the environment, or in other words at the hard facts and then decide about an investment.

The other method is the so-called technical method. You used to make charts and try to recognize patterns using a pencil and ruler in order to find out how a stock's price would move.

Later you used computers to recognize patterns in the movements of the stock price over time and to make predictions. For a long time I traded using the technical method and earned well, but I always thought that there were hidden patterns in the market that couldn't be detected by algorithms because human intelligence or human feelings, the feelings of the crowd, eluded them. Canetti's *Crowds and Power* won me over to this theory at some point, but I had no I idea how to detect those patterns. My new idea was that the rats were the key to these hidden patterns in the market.

I constructed a type of Skinner box for rats—a small cage in which there were two buttons, one red, one green. One button meant "buy," and the other meant "sell." I took short series of ten stock price movements on the dollar or Euro market and transformed them into pieces of music. If the price went up, there was a high tone, and if the price fell, a low one. According to how strongly it went up or down, the tones became correspondingly higher or lower.

At the pet store on Singerstrasse, right next to St. Stephen's Cathedral, I bought four rats of various varieties, all of them female. Then I played the pieces of music I'd composed for them. If they made the right choice, they received a reward.

After around two weeks of training, one of the rats that I'd named Lehmann was making the right choice with conspicuous frequency. I bought more female brown rats from the pet store and trained them. I generally released the unsuccessful ones at the Danube canal, and I kept training the good ones. Then I kept going with male rats and bred the best rats with each other. Soon I had around a hundred rats in my apartment.

It must have been around the beginning of 1997 when I rented space in an open-plan office that belonged to Russian Jews in Marc Aurelstrasse in Vienna's first district so that I could have more space to conduct my rat experiments.

The dot-com boom was in full swing and I shared the office with four startups, an e-mail portal for children, an Austrian search engine, a portal for text messages, and Toto Wolff's venture capital firm March15.

My rats made me the star of the office. The idea of turning rats into traders was just too crazy. It didn't take long until the first journalists showed up and my rat traders became world famous: interviews with RT, CNN, Fox News, followed by articles in the Financial Times, the Wall Street Journal, and many others. I started getting inquiries from the USA, England, Australia, Singapore, and everyone wanted more information.

At that point I asked some friends if we shouldn't try testing the rats together and risking money on their decisions.

We quickly collected a considerable amount of money and started trading. At first only the Euro against the dollar. The rats were successful and in the first year we had a 17% return. I hired two biology students to take care of the rats. As for myself, I was busy raising capital.

It was the ideal time, with a unique sense of optimism. Everyone wanted to invest in some crazy new thing. Even a somnolent town like Vienna turned into a little Silicon Valley overnight where everyone was involved in a startup. Either as a founder, an employee, or an investor. Even decades-old companies suddenly saw themselves as startups on the launch pad toward becoming global players. It must have been circa 1998 when I founded a fund in the Cayman Islands and deposited the investor capital there. That structure would make it possible to accept further investment, especially from banks and other funds.

Rattraders added three additional new employees at that point, two programmers and a trader. With them we built a system that let us train and trade much more efficiently. Stock prices were transformed in real time into music, and the rats' decisions were passed along to our trader, who looked over them and then initiated the trades.

By this time we had almost a thousand rats in the building on Marc Aurelstrasse, and we could only hope that the building managers or the relevant governmental agency wouldn't get wind of what we had going on there. We couldn't have afforded a professional laboratory with all the legal requirements that went with it.

Then I went on tour through the banking world and visited investment conferences, banks, funds, and investors. I traveled to Munich, London, Luxembourg, Brussels, Paris, Berlin, Helsinki, Frankfurt, and Stockholm. By the end of 1999, we had raised 20 million dollars. Our annual return in the first year as a true investment fund was 11%. But people weren't exactly enthusiastic about that because all around us, investors were multiplying their capital a hundred fold when dot-com domains were sold. We also couldn't avoid noticing that there wasn't much profit for us founders, despite the investment fund's considerable volume.

In order to improve the rate of return, we started having the rats trade stocks as well. In 2000 we earned around 10% and increased the volume to 40 million. Then came 2001. I still clearly remember the day when everything changed. We were negotiating with one of Europe's largest family offices where many families of major European industrialists had investments. Joseph Feingold was the director of the group and there were plans to invest another 50 million dollars in our fund, which would have doubled our assets.

We were sitting in a large conference room at Deloitte Touche, the investors' tax advisor, on Karlsplatz in Vienna, and we were negotiating the very last details. We actually wanted to have the agreement signed at 11:30 AM, but the forty-page contract had to be printed out again and again because here or there some detail didn't fit. Around 1:30 PM the current version of the document seemed perfect, but Feingold had to make a short telephone call. It must have been around 2:00 PM: Feingold apologized for the long conversation, he picked up the most recent version

56

and paraphrased the first page, he went through it page by page, and when Feingold got to page ten, a man came into the room and whispered something in his ear. Feingold and the man left the room for several minutes, and I had a sick feeling; something wasn't right. When he came back, he informed us that they would not be investing any money. He apologized, said he had to go, and that we would soon understand what it was about.

It was September 11, 2001. We knew it would be the end of the dot-com boom, and I already sensed that it would be the end of my investment fund. Nothing happened in the two days after the attack because the American exchanges were closed, and on Friday almost the entire fund was canceled. We tried to convince some investors to stay, but they had to pay out to their own investors and had no choice.

So we had to cancel the remaining investors as well and were forced to sell within a month, which led to a sizable loss. In addition to us, all the other startups vacated the office space. Except for Toto Wolff, who had already made his money, everyone else renting space in the building on Marc Aurelstrasse was bankrupt.

Closing the fund and settling accounts lasted forever. I had to fly to Grand Cayman three times in 2002 in order to make sure that the fund could be closed.

I visited the Cayman office of our auditor, the BDO in the Harbour Centre complex in Georgetown, for the last time toward the end of 2002, it must have been in December. Most people think of the Cayman Islands as an illustrious place where rich people enjoy life in a luxury paradise, but it actually looks a lot different there. There are certainly some nice spots, but overall it looks like a Miami suburb, greatly overpriced and without a trace of glamour. The Cayman Islands are instead a nation of bureaucrats— around the year 2000, a good third of the population were civil servants who made a living by operating just a hair more effectively and economically than their colleagues in Europe and the USA. All of that later came to a sudden end through ICOs[32] and the rise of cryptocurrencies, stocks, bonds, and funds.

To wind up a fund like that is pretty unglamorous business. At every moment you're reminded that you failed in your project. Every day you have to work—without pay, of course—on the burial of your idea.

Down in the café of the auditor's building, I heard a young man speaking German in the line in front of me, and we struck up a conversation right away. Jörg was from Kassell and worked for Frank Schilling, whose office was directly under our auditor. Jörg told me about Frank, who had relocated to Grand Cayman in order to open a casino, but had then registered a million Internet domains within just a year. Jörg invited me to come to a small party the next day with Frank where I could get to know him and other people in the domain business.

The small pre-Christmas party took place at a beach bar. There were about thirty men there and five women at the most, most of them Americans. I got to know Frank Schilling, who was actually German and had registered over a million domain names in the last two years. I also met Markus Schneermann, who had over a hundred thousand German domains. Nat Cohen and Garry Fisher, who already in the 90s had registered hundreds of the most desirable, shortest, and best sounding names. The Vögel brothers, who had inherited a domain name fortune from their father that included domains like oil.com, photo.com, and dubai.com. And Mike Mann, the owner of sex.com.

I immediately felt right at home among these people. Every one of them was an entrepreneur, always on the go and interested in new business. That evening, at least a dozen new business ideas were born. I returned to my hotel afterward with 30 business cards and my head buzzing.

---

[32] Initial Coin Offering, from 2016 on coins were issued, especially in the Ethereum Network but also in other cryptocurrencies, that functioned as replacements for stocks and bonds; within several years, the volume of ICOs was larger than that of IPOs on the classic capital market.

The next day, Markus Schneermann invited me to dinner with a group of German-speaking domain resellers. That's how I met Sebastian Schweizer toward the end of 2002.

Sebastian was a thin, gaunt, small man, around thirty at the time. Always well dressed, only the most expensive brands and conspicuously polite. That should have been a warning sign right away. Whoever is always especially polite can also be especially rude, and I feared polite people. Sebastian was also a domain reseller and was visiting a colleague in Grand Cayman, an arbitrage expert, and he was also determined to meet Frank. Sebastian had a girlfriend in Vienna who he wanted to visit soon, so we made a casual agreement to meet up back there.

A few weeks later he actually was in Vienna, and he explained to me how he had earned an extremely large amount of money through keyword arbitrage. Keyword arbitrage functioned something like this: you bought advertising in the Google Adwords program (that was the advertising on the World Wide Web back then), for example 'hard dick.' Each click on this website would cost us around ten cents. Then you send the person who clicked on it to another page where you've placed an ad from a pharmaceuticals company about 'erectile dysfunction.' Back then this click would get you several dollars. If, let's say, every second person who clicked on 'hard dick' also clicked on 'erectile dysfunction' on the next page, then we earned several dollars per customer.

"I don't entirely understand," Nadine interrupted. "What did the person even want?"

"If he was looking for 'hard dick' on the Internet, our guess was that he suffered from erectile dysfunction. If our guess was right, then he would also click on the second page, where there was an advertisement for a pharmaceuticals company that couldn't use words like 'hard dick' in its advertising, but could definitely use 'erectile dysfunction.'"

"I get it now. That sounds like easy money."

"You buy a cheap keyword and sell an expensive one. Sebastian had made up his mind to work together with me and we started engaging in keyword arbitrage. And at first it really did work beautifully and the money poured in. Since we were working together, I came up with the money, as you have to pay for the advertising up front, and I thought up keyword pairs. Sebastian handled all the technology."

"Keyword pairs?"

"Yes, keyword pairs like tummy ache and appendicitis, dry skin and neurodermatitis, baby tick and tick vaccination, always a cheap keyword and an expensive one as we carried out our keyword arbitrage for months."

But business quickly grew more complex and riskier. Google wasn't stupid, and payment was constantly being held up because according to their agreements it wasn't permitted to send Google's customers on to another Google ad. Or more precisely stated, Google checked the quality of the target pages where the customers landed when they clicked, and Google didn't want them to be low quality. For us, that meant losses. We tried to sneak our way around it by acquiring a constantly updated list of Google bot IP addresses. So if a bot or someone from Google came to our page, then an entirely different page was served up, all clean and informative. But if a normal Google customer came by, all that was shown were five banner advertisements. Another way to avoid Google keeping the proceeds and to improve our performance was forwarding customers on to high-quality domains. At first we used cheaper domains like tickvaccination1000.info, but we discovered that tickvaccination.com worked much better.

Apparently the quality of a domain was a criterion for Google. Pages on nice-sounding, short, high-value and old domains were more likely to be judged as legitimate websites than cheap domains that had just been registered.

So I started buying and registering domains. At first only to get better margins in the arbitrage business. After months I slowly understood how the domain business functioned and bought a domain now and then because I liked it.

The arbitrage business with Sebastian got increasingly more difficult. Firstly, because Google kept getting smarter, and secondly, because I couldn't avoid noticing that Sebastian was a fantasist. He thought that higher and higher returns were possible if you just invested more and traded even more aggressively. Then one day, must have been the middle of 2004, Sebastian was gone, disappeared. And $60,000 with him. And the arbitrage business was over.

But by now I finally understood how the business actually functioned. Back then, around 100,000 domains came available every day because the owners didn't renew them. There were lots of reasons: they didn't plan on pursuing a project and didn't need the domain name anymore, they were distracted by illness or death, or they were simply bankrupt or in prison. Sometimes they reacted a bit too late and the domain had already been bought up.

At any rate, among these 100,000 domains were some really good ones: nice-sounding names or domains that had been previously used for projects and constantly had visitors. Now you could use those domains for advertising. For each click, there was money.

Together with some programmers from Macedonia, I developed algorithms to filter out the best domain names from the 100,000 available ones. At first I only had modest success, but in time the algorithm got better and better, and new data were constantly being used to find the best domains. We found out if the domain was being searched for on Google, if there were links to the domain on the Web, if the words in the domain name were frequently used, if it was used for advertising, how old the domain was and who was the previous owner.

In order to buy the domain names, it was necessary to carry out the registration at exactly the right second when the domain became available. You only had a limited number of registration attempts, and you didn't know the exact time that the domain would be available. So you had to use the most registration attempts for the best domains and somewhat fewer attempts for the less good domains—I wasn't the only one trying to register the domain names, after all. Eventually I got to know most of my competitors by looking up who registered the domains that I didn't get.

One person whose name showed up often was a certain Yun Ye. Never under this name, but instead under various Chinese names and addresses. It was a pattern, and my competitors and I knew that it was Yun Ye. He was the pioneer, maybe the first person who had started domain drop catching.

I only observed his transactions for a short time because he sold his hundred thousand domains in 2005 for 164 million dollars, an incredible amount of money for one person at the time. The interesting thing about it was that no one ever heard from him again, there were no interviews, no address, no e-mail, nothing.

At first I only snagged around ten domain names per day, but after a few months it was up to 200. The proceeds from advertising on these domains brought in up to 3000 dollars per day; business was booming. Over the course of the following years I invested over a million dollars in the development of drop catching software, above all in data collection. That was the most important ingredient for finding valuable domains. With thousands of fake user IDs, I was able to gather data from Google, Alexa, Yahoo, and especially from whois servers.[33]

The industry was still in its infancy in those years. There were maybe twenty other domain snipers out there. Eventually I got to know all of them, at least through online chat. In 2004 I attended a meeting of domain resellers for the first time in Delray Beach in Florida. There was a group of around a hundred people there, some of whom, like Larry Fischer and Richard Lau, I had met in Grand Cayman. I had already heard of most of the others.

What almost all of these people had in common was that they had registered the best domains or keywords during the early days of the Internet. Keywords like sex.com, casino.com, usa.com, newyork.com, insurance.com, health.com, men.com and so on. Every one of them was worth millions back then. In 2002, Yahoo started its domain parking program and suddenly the value of these domains exploded again because the visitors who surfed to these domains could be turned into money.

---

[33] Whois is the public registry of Internet domain names; the owner of each domain is recorded there.

Sex.com had around 50,000 daily visitors at the time, of whom one out of ten made a twenty-cent click....

"Two thousand dollars a day...750,000 thousand per year," calculated Nadine, murmuring.

"Not bad for doing absolutely nothing. All of those people had to do very little work for their money. The second generation of domain resellers specialized in typos—that is, domain names that were typed by accident, like Facebok.com or inm.com, since the *n* is next to the *b* on the keyboard, or Bvlgari.com, because a lot of people believe that it was a *v* and not a *u*. The possibilities were unlimited, and I also registered thousands of typos. Some days I registered 3000 domains, of which around 300 produced revenue as a rule. Within ten months I had earned back my investment. The conferences were highly entertaining. Mostly the participants did what they did best: partying."

"And you?" Nadine asked.

"What about me?"

"Can you party too?"

"Of course I can. Let's just get a few cocktails and a snack, as it's already getting late."

"Maybe a nightmarket? Watson, what about that nightmarket with the moodfood, or whatever they call it here?"

"Nadine and David, what you could try is the nightmarket in Panama Road. It's open until 4:00 AM and offers both moodfood and other dishes. Should I order an SDU?"

Just as we arrive and want to get out of the SDU, a Coconut Gang[34] of fifteen drivers on Cats[35] rides past us. Both the riders, who look

---

[34] Coconut Gang is a group, principally consisting of men, involved in the trade in stolen coins, prostitution, and information, and whose members are mostly former members of the military.
[35] Cats are vehicles from Boston Dynamics modeled after large feline predators that can move up to 180 kilometers per hour. They are mostly ridden under manual control.

like Mexican gangsters, and the Cats are frightening. Panama Road isn't exactly in the best area of Bangkok.

Around twenty street vendors have smaller booths packed together here on a plaza decorated with plants and lights. A highly diverse assortment of people are sitting at the tables. Some of them are curled up in laughter, others sit silently and stare into the emptiness, and then there are families taking a night-time meal and also some Coconuts and members of other gangs. Some farangs[36] are sitting around and smirking. At the food stands there's "normal" street food, moodfood, and smartdrinks. The ingredients of each dish are listed, and there are familiar drugs in the drinks and snacks, above all marijuana, MDA, 2CB, meth, and cocaine. But there are also many natural drugs we've never heard of. Niambog is supposed to have an effect similar to hallucinogenic mushrooms, galangan clears your head, highly concentrated betel nuts are good for upset stomach, monkey rose and pala have an aphrodisiac effect, blue monkshood is calming. There's easily a hundred different psychoactive ingredients processed here including numerous commercial medications in addition to the natural ones. First we order kebabs without any special effects, and then some lightly hallucinogenic mango rice.

Watson notes that we're not impressed. "Nadine, David, I see that you aren't entirely happy. What can I do for you? Would you like more sophisticated smartdrinks in an atmosphere for snobs and the nouveau riche?"

A minute later we're on our way into "Hoffmanns" at Sukkuhmvit 14. The bar is kept in a classic style and essentially consists of a long counter for around fifteen people. Next to flowers and herbs behind the bar, there are hundreds of bottles, flacons, and silver containers. Mirrors and red lamp shades are the bar's other decorative elements; you can have drinks containing drugs of all kinds, but you're not allowed to smoke. The guests are conversing animatedly, and a good half of them are farangs. There was a "normal" cocktail bar here already in the 80s, and after privatization the bar was taken over by new owners and it began to

---

[36] Thai designation for foreigners.

specialize in smartcocktails. We take a place at the bar. The menu is printed old school and there are vast quantities of drinks in five categories: high, smooth, Alice, hot, and confused. We start with the high category and each order a HighSamurai,[37] then a Mexico1905[38] from the Alice category. Behind the bar, seven people are working on the highly complicated mixture of the drinks. Except for a few small appliances, everything here is made by hand. For the next round we try a sacredweed[39] and a 10milehigh[40] from the high category. Two men next to us are drinking cocktails from the smooth category, they ask us how our cocktails are and we strike up a conversation. The two of them are from Saudi Arabia and fled here in 2048.

"Nadine, have you ever been to Saudi Arabia?" one of them asks.

"Not yet, unfortunately."

"It was a beautiful country, beautiful, everything was fine. You know, after the sheikhs, we had a time of freedom. Saudi Arabia was a free country back then, we improved everything: women's rights, freedom, you could drink alcohol and so on. But then after 2040, many foreigners came from Jordan, from Iraq, from Syria. Mainly extremists to get our weapons. Too many weapons in our country attracted too many extremists, and now it's a disaster. Even Afghanistan is better off now. All our money, it's all gone," the younger one explained.

"Well, the Saudis never invested in anything useful and oil got to be so cheap that there was no way to keep earning money," I said. "So what brought you here?" As a Jew, I'm always curious to meet Muslims. I feel positively drawn to them, and they're mostly quite friendly when they find out that I'm a Jew. But of course both sides have had it drummed in to exercise extreme caution.

---

[37] HighSamurai: 1 cl gin, 4 cl sake, 2cl cream, 1 g gyukuro matcha, 0.2 g Bolivian cocaine, 24K gold leaf.
[38] Mexico1905: 1 g peyote powder, 2 cl Fabbri Amarena cherry syrup, 2 cl cream, cinammon, 2 cl pureed dates, 2 cl water.
[39] Sacredweed: 2 cl frankincense extract, mangosteen, 1 cl cannabis sativa extract, juice of one lemon, 4 cl grapefruit juice, mint, rose syrup.
[40] 10milehigh: 1 g Spanish saffron threads, 1 g ground mandrake root, tomato juice, dried green pepper, 1 cl gin.

"What do you know about Saudi Arabia and the invasion in 2048?" the older of the two asked me.

"I know too little, but as far as I understand, most of the remaining Islamists have retreated to Afghanistan and Saudi Arabia after the end of the monarchy and the increasing reform and secularization of many of the surrounding countries like Tunisia, Egypt, Morocco, Pakistan, Bangladesh and so on. The coalition of these secularized countries and western nations want to find the weapons and get rid of them, don't they?"

"You know why I like this bar? No bots, no robots, and the Lander.[41] This drink makes me relaxed. We fled the invasion. I saw the invasion. They came to my town, hundreds of robots, one night, in the middle of the night. They were suddenly there, they stood in front of almost every door in our town. Robots for each house. There was a huge noise, shouting. They ordered us to open the doors. In my house, I was the one who opened the door. You cannot imagine what a beast this robot was, so large, a deep frightening voice, you knew you would do the hell what he told you to do. They ordered us to come out of our house. One of the robots watched over us, we had to wait outside the house, together with our neighbors. They spoke to us in fluent Arabic. They also explained the situation, they were programmed to search our house, then take all weapons to destroy them. The other smaller robot went inside the house and quickly found an old weapon from the 50s, a hunting rifle, a large knife, a magazine from a Kalashnikov. One of us had found it in a field twenty years ago. They took it all, we surely didn't want to argue with them. I think after three hours they left, after the whole town was disarmed. A lot of weapons were found. And do you know what is the most crazy thing? Nobody, I mean absolutely nobody, got shot, not even hurt. Nobody even thought to fight those monsters. We straight out gave up our weapons like that. They left two bots in the town, big ones. Their task was to observe the town, maybe even to protect us, or to control us and report about it. They never spoke again, so we don't have a clue."

---

[41] Lander: 0.2 g raw opium, vintage wine from selected grapes, rose water, lychee juice.

"That's a fucked up story. But why did you leave Saudi Arabia? As far as I can see no harm was done to you and your family."

"True, but around us, there is still a war going on, and the economic situation is a disaster. We were afraid of the extremists. They are much more dangerous than the American and Asian bots. When they leave a town, there is blood everywhere. After the government was overthrown, people who stayed either became extremists or went underground. The others left the country to live in more open societies. We came here to Bangkok where we could buy citizenship. At the moment we are really happy about it."

"How much does it cost, if I may ask?" asked Nadine.

"Citizenship costs 2300 batcoins[42] per person, like a small car now, but it's worth it for us. We also got some amenities for a while, like health insurance, a space to live, some education vouchers. We had to do some training, but the resettlement is very smooth, very well done."

"Did you have the money back then?" Nadine asked.

"Luckily I got a loan. My brother was already too old, but a company here granted it very fast, now I will have to work it off over the years, but it's not so bad for me. We also sold the rights to our organs, but that only got us around 120 batcoins each."

"Only because you smoke too much and have too many of these drinks," interjected the older one with a wink.

"No, because you are old, my brother."

"Ha ha, okay, cheers to that!"

"Cheers."

"Come my friends, take a drink with us, a Lander, or a Rose of Kabul!"[43]

"I'm not sure, we just had some of the High cocktails."

"It will make you more relaxed, it's not strong at all."

---

[42] Batcoins, a cryptocurrency that is very widespread in Thailand. In 2017, 2000 batcoins are worth around 20,000 dollars.

[43] Rose of Kabul: 0.2 g heroin, a pinch of ambergris, a pinch of musk, 2 cl olibanum arak, milk from a fresh coconut.

"Are you guys actually religious?" I asked, unable to resist my curiosity any longer.

"No, not at all, my parents were religious and when I was a child, I was raised religious. But growing up, the monarchy was almost over, so was Islam in Saudi Arabia. And we, the younger generation, we don't care much about that stuff anymore. You'll get only troubles. I am from the Badawi[44] generation, you know, we believe in rights and freedom, no room for religion here."

"And what about the Saudi royal family, they also live here in Bangkok, don't they? What about them now?"

"They are the worst, they still exploit the people in my country. They fight against freedom and pay terrorists. They want to get the country back. Off course it will never happen, but they create troubles wherever they can. They should be in jail, instead they live in the Oberoi Hotel. Anyway, it's a free city, right? Everybody can come here, cheers!"

---

[44] Raif Muhammad Badawi, originally a blogger in Saudi Arabia who was imprisoned for years and later became the icon of the Saudi liberation movement.

CHAPTER 4

Right after breakfast we kept going in my suite. After the mixture last night I had miraculously slept well and was fit for one of my best stories.

"Well, get going," Nadine prompted me impatiently.

I still remember exactly the time someone called me one night in early 2005. Around three o'clock in the morning, I was on my way home and was more expecting a call from a co-worker or from one of the women I was after. But it was someone who asked me if I was interested in a top domain that he wanted to sell very quickly and at a very low price. Porn.com, one of the most expensive domains in the world. I thought that whatever the price was, I'd never be able to pay it. I asked how much he wanted for it, and he said 350,000 dollars. That was low, very low. Too low to believe that the man on the other end of the conversation was actually the owner. I said I was interested and asked if he was prepared to prove that it was his domain by briefly changing the name server. He asked me for the server and around two hours later, at home, the name server had been changed. By this time I had received an e-mail that repeated the offer. But there were a lot of people interested, he said, and I should agree to the deal as soon as possible. I set up an escrow transaction and for all practical purposes confirmed my intention to buy the domain. The next morning things got complicated, and "Donald," as the seller was calling himself, said the transaction could only be made in cash. We could meet either in Sri Lanka or Bangkok, those were the only possibilities.

This category of domain was worth at least a million dollars at the time, and it might even be five million if you were lucky. So letting this deal pass by wasn't an option. Donald said that he and his partners operated schools and kindergartens in Sri Lanka, but it was impossible for him to accept the money except in cash because of the political situation.

There was absolutely no one I could discuss the transaction with, everyone would have done everything they could to keep me from flying to Bangkok. I considered a thousand different ways that I could bring the money to Bangkok halfway safely, and above all how I could make the transfer safely in Bangkok. The domain name was with an extremely small registrar in Bermuda that I wasn't familiar with. I told Donald that the domain had to be transferred to another registrar, and that this might take several days. We would need a creative solution for a secure transaction. He agreed and said that we would undoubtedly think of something. We left it at an agreement to set up a fixed appointment in Bangkok in the following days so that I would have some time for the planning. I withdrew almost everything I had in my account, 280,000 Euros, as a stack of 560 500-Euro notes. Unfortunately that wasn't a small stack, as you could only bring 10,000 dollars into Thailand legally. My stack was around 5 cm high and I had no idea how I could get it through security in Vienna and then through customs in Bangkok.

I resolved to fly to Bangkok the next day, without the money to begin with, and stay for a night before flying back to Vienna in order to see what the situation looked like. Late the next evening, I was on my way to Vienna-Schwechat Airport, booked on an Austrian Airlines flight. The same one that I planned to take to Bangkok in five days with the money. At the airport in Vienna, I naturally had to go through the normal security check. The money would immediately stick out in my suit or in my carry-on. Theoretically I could tape it to my torso, but I didn't know how the metal in the hologram on the 500 Euro note would affect the sensors. Or even just the dense stack of paper. If anyone patted me down, I'd be done for.

The whole flight I thought about how I could make it work. Of course I also couldn't stop thinking about whose business it was how much money I brought somewhere, but that didn't help me. Arriving in Bangkok seemed to be mostly unproblematic; after immigration, where you get a stamp in your passport, there was a customs inspection like everywhere, but those gentlemen didn't seem terribly motivated. But if you did get inspected, there would definitely be a problem, as then all your luggage and probably your clothing as well would be sent through an x-ray scanner.

I was out of the airport around noon and had located three bank branches that I wanted to visit. I was looking for a safe with two keys. In the first bank, located on Taksin Road, someone explained to me that every safe had two keys, but with one for the bank and the other for the customer. It would definitely be possible to leave the customer key in the bank and only grant access when two people who identified themselves to the bank opened the safe together with a bank employee. I decided this variant was the best one and with that, my mission was finished for now.

After that I looked for a hotel, which turned out to be the Grand Swiss Sukhunvit, a quiet hotel with wonderful grounds and a swimming pool. The hotels in Bangkok had a charm all their own because their meticulous cleanliness, the tranquility, and their sterling rooms stood in such stark contrast to the world outside. I was at the hotel around 5:00 PM, so I left my backpack in my room and went out for a stroll.

I was immediately impressed by Bangkok, I loved the damp climate and the city's smell, and there was just so much going on. I spent forever walking around Bangkok, eating street food as I walked. It seemed like every few meters there was something completely new to taste: pineapple with chili, chicken skewers, coffee with copious amounts of condensed milk, Pad Thai, cookies with vast quantities of condensed milk, sweet potato fries, little dumplings with egg yolks inside. After what felt like twenty courses I landed in a typical expat bar, and I spent the end of the evening in a Bed Supperclub. Then I walked back to the hotel by myself and slept.

"No you didn't. I'd never believe that, coming from you!" interrupted Nadine, amused.

"Okay, actually I met a woman named Nonni and then went back to the hotel. The next day it wasn't easy to get rid of this cute Nonni, though, so we also got brunch at MBK, a gigantic department store. Gigantic back then, that is. I don't even know if it still exists. That was one of the best bowls of soup I've ever had, and that's when I fell in love with

73

this city. At MBK I also bought a pair of shoes for Nonni. Otherwise I would never have gotten rid of her, as she wouldn't take any money. Then we exchanged phone numbers and said goodbye."

I went back to the shoe store. The shoes were the solution. I would fit a 2.5 cm stack of money in each shoe, I just had to find shoes with high, wide soles, and then it would work. In Vienna you didn't have to take off your shoes at the security checkpoint, and that wouldn't change in the next few days. Or if it did, I'd just turn around at the last moment. So I bought four pairs of shoes, all of them counterfeits of well-known athletic brands, two Adidas and two Nike models, all of them with a generous sole.

I told Donald I would be in Bangkok on June 4, 2006, where we could meet in the lobby of the Marriott at 1:00 PM. But I was planning to be there already on June 3 and to stay at the Grand Swiss Sukhumvit. I didn't want to stay in the same hotel as Donald under any circumstance.

I was extremely nervous on the way to the airport. It had been anything but simple to fit all the bills into the shoes. I hollowed out the shoes from the inside, vacuum-packed the bills in cellophane, and then hot-glued the whole thing into the shoes. Although the construction looked good, I was constantly afraid that the soles could come loose and the bills would just fall out the bottom.

I didn't have any luggage to check, as I was planning to spend five days at the most in Bangkok. I also planned to buy clothing there. When I finally put my things on the x-ray scanner, my nervousness had already subsided a little. I just assumed the worst and thought about what I would tell the authorities. Although I had emptied everything out of my pockets and laid my belt and telephone on the conveyor belt, the metal detector beeped as I walked through.

I can still remember exactly how a typical unmotivated Austrian official, still chatting with his coworkers, circled me wearily with the metal detector. It beeped when it was close to my shoes, but apparently not strongly enough, and I was waved through.

Everything ran smoothly up until the landing in Bangkok. But at passport control it occurred to me for the first time that I had been here just four days ago, which would certainly seem unusual. I was promptly selected for questioning and a mid-level bureaucrat asked me why I had come to Bangkok twice in such a short time.

"Why did the bureaucrat care? Today no one would bother asking about something like that."
"Those were other times. You can't compare it to today."

These bureaucrats were just waiting to exercise their authority. Anything suspicious was a chance to distinguish themselves. In any case, I explained that my mother had taken ill just after my arrival in Bangkok so that I had needed to return to Vienna. I was proud of my brilliant idea when he asked to see my ticket from the first flight. He didn't believe my story, and of course I didn't have the ticket with me. It got awkward again and he instructed me to wait next to passport control, he had to check something with my passport.

As I was waiting, I toyed with the thought of changing my shoes and hiding the ones with the money somewhere nearby, maybe in a garbage can. But the bureaucrats in the berth next to me never let me out of their sight.

I slowly started to get slightly hysterical, but I couldn't do anything. At the thought of everything that could happen here, real fear set in. After a half hour the man came back and said everything was in order. "Bye bye...."

"How condescending! I wouldn't put up with it."
"It just gets worse, unfortunately."

It was already 1:00 PM, and I wanted to meet Donald at 3:00 PM. There would be just enough time to take care of formalities at the bank. In an airport restroom, I took the money out of my shoes and decided to take a taxi directly to the bank on Taksin Road. When I arrived at Bangkok Bank, I rented a safe under my name. I explained to the bank employee that I would return later and register a second person. I was planning to deposit the safe key at the bank. That was okay in principle, as the bank was open until 7:30 PM. But the following day was a holiday and the bank was only open again on Friday.

I took a taxi to the Marriott for my meeting with the Sri Lankans. I was just in time and looked for a table in the bustling lobby. A quarter hour passed and then I saw the guys, three men, all around thirty. Two of them, pretty fit, athletic, dangerous looking, while the other was lanky. The athletic types were both taller than me and had buzz cuts. The lanky one, a pretty thin guy, had a pointy nose and blotchy skin. He was wearing a yellow turban. There was something shifty about him. Sri Lankans seemed to be darker than most Indians, or at least the ones here were almost black. All three wore dark linen suits. One thing was clear—these were no kindergartners.

"David? Is this you?"

"Yes. Hi, Donald."

"Man, call me Raja, please. These are my assistants, Jagesh and Oojam."

We sat down at the table, and I was glad to have picked out the busiest lobby.

"Michael, I suggest to talk business first, then we can enjoy and celebrate our deal. Is that okay for you?"

That was okay by me. I explained to Raja how I planned to proceed, that we would have to identify ourselves at the bank and could only access the money together. As soon as we had done that, the transfer could be started. As the bank was closing at 7:30 PM and the drive there would last nearly an hour, I pressed them to hurry.

They agreed to my suggestion. Raja gave the two others a sign and they went to retrieve their rental car. Raja said that he had to go up to his room for a moment to retrieve his passport and would be right back.

I remained in the Lobby and googled the names of the three. Their names were Tamil and they also looked Tamil. It was not improbable that they belonged to a wing of the Tamil Tigers. I seriously considered canceling the whole thing. My gut feeling told me not to expect any friendliness from these people.

The Tamil Tigers were considered a terrorist organization by most countries at the time, and doing business with them was generally considered a life-threatening matter, and for good reason.

I tried to find out about the situation in Thailand through Google and if the Tamil Tigers had influence here. And what I could be accused of in the worst case. How would I be able to prove my story? Especially after I had smuggled the money into the country.

I realized what I had gotten myself into. It was absolutely certain that the smallest mistake on my part would lead to catastrophe.

I resolved to abort the operation at once. Right at the moment I was standing up to make my escape, the three of them showed up right in front of me. My bad luck....

We drove as a foursome back to Bangkok Bank on Taksin Road. We got there around 6:00 PM. The guy from that afternoon was still there. Raja, the bank clerk, one of his coworkers, and I went down to the safe. Raja was evidently experienced dealing with cash but counted the bills leisurely.

"Okay, let's do it!" he said.

Raja registered himself as a second owner of the safe, so that now we could only open the safe together; in case one of us died, two additional people were registered. Raja listed his two colleagues who were back in the car, and I lifted my business partner Davies and my son, who was eight years old at the time.

We drove back to the Marriott, as we wanted to start the transfer as quickly as possible. Back in the lobby, I initiated the transfer of the domain to my registrar. Then we had to wait until Raja could respond to the transfer request.

It was nice to log in for a moment, but the request wasn't showing up yet, and it can take hours or even days, depending on the registrar. And with the tiny registrar that he was using, it would definitely last even longer.

Raja suggested going to get something to eat before we logged in again.

The Le Normandie Bangkok at the Oriental Hotel was one of the most expensive restaurants in Bangkok. I found it a bit odd to go out for French food, but the establishment was a fitting backdrop for signing off on a shaky deal between a Jew from Vienna and three members of the Tamil Tigers.

While we ate, we talked a little about Internet domains. Raja wasn't a major expert, but he knew his way around a bit. He claimed that he owned only a few domains, but very valuable ones. According to him, he had purchased porn.com three years ago under his organization's name. But now the organization that he said operated schools and kindergartens was in a financial squeeze because of the tsunami. Since they were Tamils, it would be too dangerous to transfer the money by bank to Sri Lanka. That didn't explain why it couldn't have been wired to Bangkok, for example, but I really didn't want to know all the details.

At that time, domain names were an ideal commodity for moving money from one country to another. Nobody had any idea of their value, and the domains could be transferred from one person to another, switching at the same time from one country to the next, without filling out customs paperwork and without an invoice or any other record.

After we'd eaten, Raja suggested driving to a club. It wasn't close, but I'd definitely like it, he said. Only a few people knew about it.

We caught a taxi in front of the Oriental and took it back to the Marriott, where we got back into the rental car. I didn't like that at all, but I didn't want to let them notice how nervous I was and didn't protest. After all, the three of them had behaved very hospitably until now and, I thought, they probably wouldn't murder me without their money.

The drive took a long time. In the back seat of the car, Raja and I talked about restaurants, fishing, and prostitutes. The area around us was quite spacious, alternating between housing projects, shopping centers, and fields. After around an hour, we drove through a large gateway, for a few more minutes through a park, and then reached the "B." The cars in the parking lot suggested that it must be a pricey establishment.

From outside, the "B" appeared inconspicuous. The building was a plain, newly built, quite large villa surrounded by palm trees and exotic bushes. The palm trees were lighted from below, which cast a mild light on the villa. All the windows were shaded, with only the entryway illuminated by two torches in cast iron holders attached to the stone wall.

First of all, we were searched for weapons in the entry hall. There were several pretty women at the front desk, but exclusively eastern Europeans and not a single Thai. After this procedure we were registered, but the car key stayed at the front desk.

An exceptionally cute Russian led us into the main room. It was like an enormous oriental tent. Directly in front of us was an expansive bar with a DJ. At the edges of the tent, booths had been created with large cushions, and Persian rugs had been laid out to cushion the floor. Thai statues stood everywhere, in addition to scantily to entirely unclothed women. It smelled of a mixture of incense, perfume, and marijuana.

Of the five women tending the bar, three were busy mixing cocktails, while the others were stuffing chillons, preparing small bongs for smoking crystal meth, and folding intricate origami spoons out of aluminum foil for smoking heroin. Around thirty women were waiting around the bar to be invited over to a booth.

There are many different ways to look someone in the eyes. In a bordello, looking into someone's eyes is comparable to a wifi connection with another person; within a fraction of a second you know if you fit together or not. The more you rely on this look in the eyes the better, in my experience.

My gaze fixed on a short woman with black hair who was wearing nothing but high heels and a fishnet stole around her neck. I nodded briefly to her, then Raja finished his order and the cute Russian led us to our booth.

If we were interested in a girl, then we should please let her know, she told us. Right away I point to the short black-haired woman, while Raja and his colleagues haven't made up their minds yet.

Delia is from Romania, just like my father, which I tell her right away. We both have to laugh about how we had to travel to a luxury whorehouse in Thailand in order to meet each other.

Delia likes gin and tonics but asks if I like cocaine, as the Russian woman could bring us some. I've only tried it two or three times in my life, mostly for New Year's Eve, but why not.

While drinks and cocaine are being served, my three business partners are smoking heroin out of the origami spoons. By now another three women are sitting in our booth and are heating the spoons with matches while Raja, Jagesh, and Oojam inhale the smoke through silver pipettes. On a black glass tablet, Delia keeps laying down new lines of coke. The others are now combining their heroin with cocaine, and the Russian keeps bringing new drinks. At this point I'm everything: stoned, drunk, high, my confidence only stops short of the heroin. A small bowl of blue pills was served to us along with the last round of drinks, my first Viagra. At least Delia was nice enough to recommend that I start with a half pill. We went up to our room.

After around five hours of screwing and doing coke, the Russian came to the room. Politely but resolutely, she said that I had to leave. "Sir, sorry, we are closing now, I must ask you to leave, thank you very much."

She didn't sound as friendly as earlier when we were still down in the circus tent. I could forget about the orgasm that I had been saving up for so long. Completely wiped out, I dragged myself with Delia down to the front desk. Delia said on our way down that "B" never closed, so there must be a problem of some kind.

The three Tamils were at the front desk and there was an argument going on. Jagesh or Oojam—there was no way to tell the two apart—had some kind of problem with one of the girls.

"I did not ask you and you did not ask me, so fuck you!"

"I asked you, for sure, but you are drunk and you do not know what you are doing!"

"I did not ask you and…."

So it went, back and forth. I don't think anybody knew exactly what it was about, but finally Raja asked what the bickering was about. He thought the matter could be settled with money, but it wasn't about that. Raja paid for the drinks, girls, and drugs, and we were all led rather impolitely out of the establishment.

"I'll tell you the rest after we eat or tomorrow, either way. Are you hungry, too?"

"Of course I am! That's a crazy story, you can't just stop telling it now. Where do you want to go? Have you ever been to THM?"[45]

"What's that?"

"The Human League, with the animal films."

"Oh, no. I think that's more than a little odd. I mean, I don't want to see the childhood movies of the animal that I'm currently eating. Here's a suggestion from IRIS[46]—Sea Shepherd, space is available, it's not stupid, what do you think?"

"Sure, great, but that's insanely expensive, isn't it?"

"Yes, but I have a 25% discount because I donated thirty years ago, back when they still hunted whalers."

"Hunted whalers?"

"Sea Shepherd was an organization that hindered the Japanese whaling fleet during their hunt, it was really impressive. They ended the whale catch and then, I think after the Searush in 2034,[47] they acquired a large area in the Pacific. Today they run these restaurants and the fish that you buy...."

After Nadine had changed, we drove off from my room. The Sea Shepherd is quite close to the Hyatt Elite on Witthayu Road in the 152nd story of the new Plaza Athene Needle.[48]

---

[45] THM, The Human League, was earlier a charity organization for animal rights. Now a restaurant chain that offers meat from animals that were accompanied throughout their lives and observed by drones to guarantee that they had a species-appropriate life. The films can be downloaded in the restaurant.

[46] IRIS is fed by information-collecting devices, Watson among others, and predicts events and other things based on this data.

[47] Searush: In 2034, the USA, China, and India ratified the "Law of the Sea Treaty" in a last attempt to preserve their relative power on the high seas. The reaction to that was the Searush under the leadership of the "International Seabed Authority" in which private organizations brought large parts of the oceans under their control.

[48] Plaza Athene Needle, finished in 2042, is the most modern hotel in Bangkok. The 155-story hotel was almost completely created through a 3D-printing process and thus consists of a

Sea Shepherd controls the area east of Japan from Sakhalin to Papua New Guinea and uses an ultramodern network of autonomous submarines, drones, satellites, and underwater microphones to protect its fish stocks. Beside selling fish, Sea Shepherd earns money from overflight rights, ship traffic, wave and wind energy, as well as licenses for mining sand. They don't permit drilling for oil or digging for minerals.

The restaurant is done all in light wood, and the ceiling is a projection of a starry night in the Pacific. The menu is projected onto the table, and there's an enormous selection of fish, certainly over a hundred types, all from the Pacific. We decide to accept the recommendation, based as it is on 2200 of our prior restaurant visits after all, and they bring us ten different dishes made from fish and sea creatures, side dishes, and a Chinese Chardonnay.

"Should we eat something healthy tomorrow?" asks Nadine.

"Do I look so unhealthy? Do you know somewhere good?"

"Ha. That wasn't supposed to be an insinuation.... The Yoofoo,[49] for example, that would definitely do us some good, and it would reassure our insurance company. Tomorrow during the day I'm planning a temple tour. I saw that in the evening there's a Zire[50] at a mosque. Have you ever been to one?"

"To a mosque? Yes, I've been, but a Zire? No idea what that's supposed to be...."

"It's a kind of trans-traditional dance event, very interesting. Around a thousand people move in a circle accompanied by singing. You fall into a trance. Come on, I'm sure you'll like it."

---

single casting. Among other things in the hotel are a cosmetic surgery clinic and a zeppelin landing field.

[49] Yoofoo is one of numerous "personal food" restaurants that arrange food and drink on the basis of the customers' DNA and/or blood values and/or psychic condition. As a rule you share the data from your medicoder and the food is automatically selected. Many athletes, among others, live exclusively on "personal food."

[50] Zire is the modern form of the Zikhr, a tradition originally from Chechnya attributed to the Sufis. In the traditional form, suras from the Koran are sung and only men dance in the circle. The new version is open to women as well and modern texts from the new secular Islam are sung.

"Let's make up our minds tomorrow. I think I'm too old for something like that."

"I don't think so, but whatever you think. So, keep going with the story!"

"As you say, boss. There was the argument between the Tamils and the girl, we had that already...."

Then we were asked to leave and were just about to go to the car when it occurred to Raja that the car key was still inside. So we went back. Inside they told us that we were all drunk and that for our own safety and because they didn't want any problems with the police, we would only get the car key back the next day. That's when Raja got enraged.

"This is one fucking hour from the city, it's my car, my key, fuck you! Give me the key now or I call the police!"

"If you continue speaking in this way, it is up to us to call the police."

"Fuck, fuck, fuck!"

Raja was really furious. He went to the car, the three of them talked briefly, and then one of his two assistants took a rock and smashed one of the back windows. He climbed into the car, evidently knowing just what he was doing. As I looked shocked, Raja tried to calm me: "Jagesh is a mechanic, he can fix, we will replace the window tomorrow. We are not gonna walk back, it would take us hours and we are all tired, right?" Yes, we're all tired, I thought to myself, but we're all up to our gills in drugs of some kind along with Viagra and alcohol as well.

After a few minutes the car started, the power locks opened and we drove off. Just after we had left the gate, I saw the red lights of a police car behind us. My first thought was that the police would drive past us, as we hadn't done anything, after all. Only when I could register the motor sounds and the speed of the two police cars, the feeling crept over me that it might get unpleasant soon.

One of the police cars passed us and slowed us down, and the other one stopped behind us. Five or six police officers got out of the two cars, but because of the blinding flashlights I could see almost nothing.

They motioned for us to get out with our hands up. We were searched for weapons and then they wanted to see passports, and we all didn't have ours with us. One of the police inspected the broken window.

"Stolen car?"

"No, we lost our key."

He shone his flashlight directly into Jagesh's eyes, probably to see how quickly his pupils contracted.

"Ah, yes, you cocaine? Heroin? Alcohol?"

„No, nothing" responded Jagesh, who was in the driver's seat.

The officers talked on their radios for a while and then brought us to the police station. I was out of my mind with fear, but I had no idea that drug consumption was a big deal. I was sure that there'd be some way to wangle things with a little money.

At the station, first everything in my pockets was taken from me, and then I was asked to piss in a jar. I waited in one room for the next steps. Although I was extremely tired, there was no way I could sleep. After waiting three hours a new official appeared. He led me to his office and we sat at a desk across from each other.

"Mr. Wenkart, you are in trouble. In your test sample we found traces of THC. Smoking weed, as you surely know, is illegal in this country and we must keep you here to appear in front of a judge for further proceedings."

I expected that I would be told an amount that I could pay in order to spare myself the trouble. But no offer came, and in my mouth I could taste my tears. What's funny is that I can remember thinking that at least I could finally sleep.

I demanded that the Austrian embassy be informed; the official said it would happen later at the prison. After another two hours, an official came to me with all my things. He took me to another room and said that if I were ready to give up the 400 dollars that I had on me, he would transfer me and my three colleagues to a better prison. I agreed at once. That was a good decision, as it turned out, as the Thonbury Prison where we were sent was according to all descriptions the best option for a prison stay in Bangkok.

Late that afternoon we were all driven together to Thonbury Prison. It was torture, thousands of thoughts were clamoring in my head, but we weren't allowed to speak a word with each other. After our arrival inside the prison we were removed from the vehicle one by one.

The prison is one of the smaller ones, but it still seemed gigantic to me. Over 3000 men were incarcerated there.

I ended up in a cell with twenty other foreigners, but no trace of the Tamils. My cellmates were primarily English and Australians, plus two Nigerians and a Pole. All of them were here because of minor offenses, most of them because of drug consumption or possession, a few because of theft. With twenty of us, the cell was quite full and sleep was torturous. We slept on the bare floor, and it gets fairly cold at night in Bangkok. Now and again a cockroach would run around, but because there was so little to eat, the amount of vermin was limited. The light stayed on the whole night and normal sleep was impossible. What made the stay bearable was that we spent the whole day in the gigantic prison courtyard, from 6:30 AM to 6:30 PM. We had to organize everything ourselves there and assume responsibility for cooking and washing.

My good fortune was that I was escorted to an ATM on my second day and was able to withdraw money. So I bought myself some things for comfort: showers, t-shirts, fruit, vegetables, juice, and access to a telephone. I contacted the Austrian embassy, who had already been informed and would soon send someone. I notified my hotel that I'd only be able to come in a few weeks. I didn't tell anyone in Austria about my situation at first.

Even after a few days had passed, I still couldn't find the Tamils. I slowly made friends with my cellmates, who liked me most of all because I was continuously escorted to the ATM and the prison shop. Most of them were young men who had come to Bangkok for partying or sex and then run into problems of some kind with the police. Some of them were in prison for the second time. They thought that you'd stay here around a month for smoking a little grass. But some of them had spent a considerable time in other prisons in Thailand and had only been transferred to Thonbury Prison a short time before their release in order to be near to their embassy.

Thonbury is known for its Thai boxers. Around 300 men train Thai boxing every day in the yard, and they spend the whole day fighting in the ring. That was a welcome diversion.

The first days for me weren't half so bad, I saw the whole thing as a kind of extreme experience. Plus I was sure that I'd be out again in a few days. I spent the time with my fellow inmates. I especially liked two Australians, Simon and Dennis. The two of them had been transferred here after four years in the Bangkok Hilton, Bankwang, known as the Tiger. Bankwang is one of the worst prisons in Bangkok, with 12,000 inmates. Abuse from the guards and fights between the inmates are the order of the day. Their stories weren't always easy to digest.

On the third or fourth day, a stuck-up employee of the Austrian embassy came by for a conversation. A Matthias Kerschbaumer, around twenty-three years old. He gave me a lecture about how the embassy took no pleasure in Austrian citizens in Thailand not behaving in a manner suitable to their station, and that he very, very rarely had to visit an Austrian in prison. I found that more than a little astonishing in light of the Austrians I knew who frequently traveled to Thailand, but whatever. He further explained that too much interference by the embassy was counterproductive, and he urgently advised me to hire a local attorney. If I could afford it, the lawyer would then "take care" of everything else. He didn't want to give me too much hope, but with enough money, one could get fairly good help here. He promised to send me a list of attorneys and I asked him to just send one from his list as soon as possible. After he had promised me the best one from the list, he left.

"Now we're coming to the actual climax of the whole story. It's one of my favorite stories. You'll definitely like it too."

"I'm curious how you plan to top this story. Your stories sound so crazy and amazing, one might think that you're just inventing everything...."

Nadine grabbed a fresh coffee made from jungle beans from the kitchen and sat down across from me, an intent expression on her face. Telling a story was really fun like this.

A week had already passed in prison. My Thai lawyer hadn't shown up yet and my mood was starting to deteriorate. You can somehow put up with anything, bad food, boredom, cockroaches, no women, no cigarettes, no alcohol, no newspaper, no Internet. But to be locked up, not being able to leave, that wipes you out.

Simon and Dennis, the two Australians from the Bangkok Hilton, were cooking on one of the stoves in the yard for our group. Simon asked me if I had already heard the story of the Chinese man, Mr. Woo. I hadn't heard of him.

By now he's a legend, Simon informed me. He must have been an extraordinary man. So Dennis and Simon told me the story of Mr. Woo.

Around the year 2002, two young Chinese men were arrested in Bangkok. The official explanation was that they had murdered a Thai man, but it was never proved. The rumor was that money was really the reason.

The two Chinese were wealthy and had large amounts of cash with them in Bangkok. People said that they had traveled to Thailand on behalf of corrupt government officials or businessmen in order to invest the money in real estate. When criminals heard about the two Chinese men, a murder was pinned on them. They were arrested and their money was stolen....

They were sent to Bankwang and it took until summer 2004 for their trial to finally start. During their stay in Bankwang, they were badly mistreated. They were constantly locked in solitary confinement, beaten, and tortured. According to Simon and Dennis, many of their fellow inmates could confirm that. As they had been in Bankwang at the same time as the Chinese men for several months, they heard the story first hand, but they never talked to the two Chinese men themselves.

It was also known which guards took part in the abuse. At that time, according to Simon, circumstances in Bankwang were bad, but torture and mistreatment of such a rough kind were nevertheless rare and were therefore the subject of conversation among the inmates.

It was in July or August 2004 when the two Chinese men were acquitted on appeal, but the prosecuting attorney objected and they stayed in prison. A few months later, in November 2004, they were murdered.

The exact circumstances remained unknown, but from what the other inmates said, they were taken from their cells in the middle of the night. The next morning, the official statement was that they had made an escape attempt and had fallen to the street from the outer wall, and both had died instantly.

"Wow, a real cops and robbers story...but I believe you, of course!" she said, smiling, and stretched herself across the sofa.

Too bad that I'm no longer young.... "Well, I should hope so! Should we go get a bite to eat? For a change of pace."

She giggled. Then she seemed to realize something. "But we wanted to go to the Zire.... Come on, let's go take a look, and then we can go to that giant casino."

It took some persuasion, but I was finally able to convince Nadine that I was too old for the Chechen ethno-dance. I wanted to see a little of the Apollonian Games[51] instead that were currently taking place in Gurgaon in India. We decided to go to F&P, one of the largest and most modern of Bangkok's casinos, where the games could be watched via 3-D projection.

The F&P isn't in Quarter2 but rather in Noi, close to Thonbury Hospital. That's not a problem in Bangkok, you can travel to all the city's districts, but it's not like that in other cities. There are private districts that aren't so simple to gain entry to like Holmby Hills or Bel Air in Los Angeles.

---

[51] The Apollonian Games were introduced in 2026 as a counter event to the Olympic Games, after they had been informally held some years previously. Doping is legal, but the form of doping must be revealed. In almost all disciplines similar to those of the Olympic Games, better marks are achieved and more world records are set. This quickly made the Apollonian Games more popular than the Olympic Games.

Watson chimes in immediately when he hears that we want to go to F&P: "Nadine, David, I recommend that you take a boat or drone to the casino. A drone is fastest, but the boat trip is the most scenic option."

We follow Watson's recommendation and take the boat, which takes us directly to the casino. The F&P is one of the most modern casinos in the world, seven stories tall. In the middle there's a kind of oval court where sporting events are broadcast live, full size, and in 3-D. You really see each event right in front of you. When we arrive, we see women's archery. An imposing woman from Gangwon[52] was taking her turn, sponsored by Merck, who provided her performance-enhancing drugs. Next to her is a woman from Seoul sponsored by Celltrion. Both women's doping programs are excessive, with blood doping, cell doping, DNA doping, and hormone doping. In addition there are stress-reducing medications, pain medications, and much more. Despite that, the life expectancy of participants in the Apollonian Games is higher and their marks are better than those of the traditional Olympic Games.

After archery we watch the men's crawl, women's rowing, and lightweight boxing. Sometimes we place bets, but we don't have much luck. We also don't have much of an idea about all the various sports, which is why we return to our hotel around 1:00 AM a few ccoins poorer.

---

[52] Gangwon, a private province in South Korea that belongs to the Hyundai concern and is among the wealthiest Korean provinces.

CHAPTER 5

"Good morning, David," Watson's voice reverberates from my suite's perfect sound system. "You seem to be well rested. It's May 24. It's rainy today and the temperature will rise to 27 degrees Celsius. Since you want to fly to Vienna on Monday, should I book a flight for you?"

"Hold off for a moment, maybe we'll fly a bit later. Set up something with Steve, dinner if possible."

"Okay, I'll do that. Your health insurance premium was raised by 4.2 ccoin per month. Please drink a lot of water..."

"Spare me all that!"

"Okay. Ccoin is at 231.99, Belgium has opened its Congo archives from 1892 to 1907, NATO has deployed an additional 200 4Fbots[53] in West Brussels for increased security, and in Japan the last remaining section of street was privatized."

"Thank you."

"I've ordered breakfast to your room. Nadine will be here soon with her friend Natalie, so you should get ready."

"Thanks very much, Watson. Thanks." He must have heard my sarcastic tone. He stayed quiet in any case.

The suite's ceiling is a Hi-Power high-resolution screen that not only simulates any kind of sky, view, or color, but also provides the warmth of the sunbeams and the breeze and the scent of the scenery along with it. We select morning in the Alps.

---

[53] 4Fbots are fighters on four feet based on the Big Dog concept from Boston Dynamics and see frequent military use.

Natalie is an enchanting young woman from France who is visiting her brother in Bangkok. Nadine and Natalie were introduced to each other by an AI through a kind of proactive networking.

"Natalie is studying history. I told her about your book project, and she really wanted to meet you. Maybe you can keep telling both of us a bit more. I think she'd be especially interested in the China story, and I've already told her the Bangkok story."

"Sure, just my thing. Story time for two young women, with pleasure."

Nadine smiles, amused.

"What are you doing in Bangkok, Natalie?" I ask her pretty companion.

After a side glance at Nadine, Natalie says, "I'll be a student here. I'll have more peace and quiet and less stress than in France at the moment."

"I'm not surprised."

"What doesn't surprise you?"

"That it's impossible to be a student in France. And please, call me David."

"Agreed. It's possible to be a student in France, but it's just not so simple. The universities are out of date, and teachers on the basis of AI aren't standard. And I wanted out of France in any case. It wouldn't be so easy for my parents to leave the country, but they encouraged me and my brother to move away."

"France was always problematic, and it doesn't surprise me that political developments there have gone so badly. A good friend of mine, Felix Marquart, was advising French young people to move away forty years ago."

"David, before we get lost in political discussions, let's keep going," interrupted Nadine.

"Sure thing, we can talk about France some other time. I value such discussions highly, and the story I'm about to tell you, one of my favorite stories, actually has a little bit to do with the French Revolution. We'll see how far we get. So we were at the part about the two Chinese men who were apparently murdered in prison by guards; that was April 2005. My two friends Simon and Dennis were also in Bangwank at the time. That seemed to be the end of things."

But in summer 2005 in Bankwang, this Mr. Woo showed up, a friendly, high educated Chinese man who spoke perfect Thai. He quickly made himself very popular with Dennis and Simon, and really could become equally popular with anybody. He got the guards to grant him extraordinary perks, like better food and more frequent washing, and he also had money and could always buy himself fresh fruit and vegetables that he often shared with the other prisoners. What stuck out about Mr. Woo was that he asked surprisingly often about the murdered Chinese men. He raised the subject at every opportunity, and his fellow prisoners were eager to share information with him. There were rumors about which guards had probably been involved in the torture and murders. In the course of a week, Mr. Woo made friends with the guards, especially with the ones who were suspected of murdering the Chinese young men. It went like that for a few weeks. Most of the guards had side jobs like driving a taxi or running small shops, so-called mama and papa shops. According to the other inmates, three guards had taken part in the murders, although the order to kill had probably come from someone else, an official higher up in the Thai justice system. The guards were apparently paid for the torture and murder. After around three months in Bangwank, Mr. Woo was released. Then some very unusual events took place.

One of the guards, a man around 50 who worked evenings as a taxi driver, suddenly and without any warning signs to his family took his own life by overdosing on heroin. A few days later, the second guard hanged himself in a toilet in Bangwank. Then the third one set up a meeting at a hotel with the person who had ordered the murders. He overpowered the man, tied up the government official, blindfolded his eyes, and beat him with a truncheon for hours. At least five hours passed before someone called the police. The man was still alive, while the guard sat at a desk impassively next to the beaten man and was arrested without resisting. The man who had ordered the murders died several days later.

In the prison these stories spread like wildfire, and people started to fear the always friendly Mr. Woo. Some people ascribed dark magic powers to him, while others saw in him a benevolent avenger. Supposedly the Thai police even looked for Mr. Woo, but he was nowhere to be found by this point.

Sitting on the ground in the Thonbury Prison yard, Dennis and Simon waited for my reaction. I too found the mysterious story about Mr. Woo compelling and I wanted to learn more about this person.

They leaned in close to me and told me quietly that of all the people in Thailand, they alone knew how to find Mr. Woo. They wanted to visit him as soon as they were released in order to find out what had really happened.

I think it was on the tenth day of my career as a jailbird when they brought me to the visitation room. My lawyer Chatchai was finally there. He reassured me that things weren't all that bad. If I was prepared to assume the trial costs of around 2000 dollars—that would be about 200 ccoin—then I could get a trial very quickly. In a few months I'd be out, but I'd never be allowed to enter Thailand again. The circumstances, he thought, were favorable for me just then, because things outside were quite chaotic. The Thaksin government was coming to an end and people were afraid a military junta would assume power; now was a good time for a "sin nam jai," as they call it here, a generous donation.

Never visiting Thailand again didn't sound appealing to me, as I still needed to get to my money in the safe somehow. It was already difficult enough that I had not the faintest clue where the Tamils were. And I'd never survive months in prison. After ten days my nerve and my strength were completely used up. Fortunately my lawyer thought that things could go faster for more money.

That same day I arranged to transfer 12,000 dollars via Western Union from Austria to my lawyer in Bangkok, and on the next day, eleven days after my arrest, I really was free again.

It was indescribable, one of the best days of my life. At 7:30 AM, right after the morning routine, I was released along with the things I had been wearing at "B." I took a taxi to the Swiss Hotel, immediately got a room, and took a shower for the first time in twelve days. Then food, then alcohol, and then I called Nonni, the girl from my first visit.

In Bangkok, all hell had broken loose just then. Tahksin's supporters and opponents were demonstrating in the streets, traffic was blocked, and everyone was afraid the military would seize power. The mood in the city was strange, both exuberant and tense at the same time, an atmosphere of doom.

With the help of my lawyer Chatchai, I managed to get my computer back from the impounded car. The porn.com domain hadn't been transferred. So now I had to find the Tamils again, otherwise I was out all my money. I explained the situation to Chatchai, and in less than an hour he found the three of them, they were also in Thonbury Prison.

In order to visit a prison, the most important thing is to look well dressed and groomed. In Thailand, clothes still make the man. So I had an elegant suit tailored for me, I shaved, and the next day I set out for Thonbury Prison. The bureaucratic formalities took over two hours, and then I was brought to the visitation room. There were about ten windows for ten visitors. You could only talk through the glass, and it was extremely loud in the room, a confusion of adults and children who screamed and wept.

Raja was in a bad state. He was barely able to talk loud enough for me to understand him. He was only allowed out an hour a day in a small courtyard, and he was sharing his cell with forty other men. He had money and could get food and other small things for himself and even a lawyer, but his lawyer seemed to be not especially talented. Raja couldn't believe how quickly I had been released and I promised to send Chatchai to him. At my request to give me the login to the registrar in order to transfer the domain to me, he just said: "I am not stupid my friend, first you get me out of here, then we talk."

Chatchai explained to me that Raja thought I would pay for legal representation for him and also for his two friends. Jagesh and Oojam's case was more sensitive, however, because heroin was involved in addition to marijuana. And Jagesh's case was even more difficult because he was

95

the driver. Chatchai estimated that it would cost around fifty thousand dollars and last several weeks in order to fix things up.

I gave Chatchai an advance of ten thousand dollars, but now my personal reserves were slowly reaching the end and I had to think about where I could borrow the remaining forty thousand dollars. In any case, it was clear that my stay in Bangkok would last a while longer. In order to avoid overstaying my visa, I flew back to Vienna after two weeks.

Back in Vienna I stayed in contact with Chatchai, who kept me informed about the progress of negotiations with the authorities. My mother loaned me twenty thousand dollars so that I could pay Chatchai again. Shortly after my arrival in Vienna, there was another domain resellers' conference, this time in Las Vegas. I thought it would be a good opportunity to seek out a discrete broker for porn.com or even a buyer.

I held some appointments with domain brokers, and each one immediately wanted to broker the deal, offering up to 5 million dollars. Even for a quick sale to another domain reseller, 1-1.5 million was offered.

I had planned to fly back to Vienna in the evening on the third and last day of the conference, but within an hour I received two interesting calls. First from Simon, the Australian from my time in Thonbury; he said he had been released yesterday and wanted to know if I was still in Bangkok. He had to take care of something for Mr. Woo, the Chinese man, so he couldn't return to Australia yet. The other call came from Chatchai, who said there was a chance the three Tamils would be released early the next week. As I still had all my money in a safe in Bangkok, I didn't want to miss the three Tamils under any circumstances, so I flew that same evening to Bangkok via Los Angeles.

Soon after my arrival, however, it turned out that it would take another one to two weeks until the three of them were finally out. The reason was that just at that moment, the constitutional court of Thailand had annulled April's election and the justice system, in fact the whole country, came to a halt. They were expecting Thaksin's new swearing-in around the middle of May, but the Tamils' release couldn't be expected until then.

The two Australians had spent the last few days in a cheap hotel on Khao San Road, and on Monday they would get their passports back. They wanted to leave for Australia as soon as possible, but since they had promised Mr. Woo a visit in order to tell him what had happened after his departure, they had to postpone the journey home. As far as I understood it, the two of them were expecting a generous reward for it.

They wanted me to come along at all cost. Their time in prison had left them skittish and they had the feeling that having me there would keep them safe. They said Mr. Woo would certainly not object if I came along. I was extraordinarily interested in the story, and since they promised that you would never get a second chance to meet someone like that, I took advantage of the unique opportunity.

The two didn't have a direct telephone number for Mr. Woo. They had only a memorized address: Wa Yao, Gejuma, near Lincang.

In Gejuma, they thought, everyone would know Mr. Woo, and they would find him there somehow. He had promised to stay there after his release. The place couldn't be found on any map on the Internet, but in a shop in Bangkok we found a map of China on which the town was marked.

So the next day we flew to Lincang. Hypothetically Wa Yao is around five hours by car north of Lincang, but there was practically no one who spoke a word of English in Lincang, and no taxi drivers to speak of, which delayed the whole trip.

After we had tried in vain for four hours to find a way to Wa Yao from the airport, we had to check into a hotel. With the help of the receptionist and another hotel guest, the next morning we succeeded in arranging for a driver who would bring us to Wa Yao. The drive actually lasted nine hours, which was especially burdensome because our driver didn't want to stop for any reason, whether we wanted something to drink, something to eat, or a stop at a restroom. At some point we started pissing in the empty plastic bottles we'd drunk out of.

It was already dark when we finally arrived in Wa Yao after several detours (the driver had to keep turning around because roads were blocked). Our driver got out, placed our luggage on the street, asked us politely to get out, and immediately drove away.

Wa Yao is small, really small, the whole village consists of around fifteen houses. After a few minutes, pretty much the whole village was standing around us. We were something like aliens from Mars there, children touched us cautiously, the adults conversing with each other excitedly. A Chinese young woman asked us to follow her and a few minutes later we were standing in front of Mr. Woo's house.

"Dennis, Simon, you are heroes, you did it! And you are?" asked Mr. Woo.

"David, David Wenkart."

"Hello, David, it is an honor to met you. Come in, you're surely hungry. How was the trip?"

Ju, Mr. Woo's assistant, or girlfriend, it wasn't possible to figure out exactly which, cooked for us. We talked about Bangkok and China, but we avoided the subject of prison.

"David, you look as if you have experienced something out of the ordinary for you."

"You could say that."

"You are from Europe. Are you a Jew?"

"Well, yes, yes I am. How can you tell?"

"Why have you parted from the traditions of your religion?"

"At some point I lost my belief in God. How do you know that?"

He only nodded sympathetically to me. After we had gotten something to eat and drink, we all went into the study.

"Should we talk now? Or would tomorrow be better?"

"Now would be great," I said.

"Very good. I'm also a friend of the night. That's the best time, awake, fully concentrating. That's how it is at night. That's how one is at night. So, Simon, Dennis, I promised you a reward if you would tell me what happened after my release. If you tell me, I will give each of you 2500 dollars. My assistant will summarize your story. If you sign her summary, you will receive an additional reward. Not money, but a journey. For this journey we will not need to leave the room, as it's a trip into ancient China.

98

Knowledge of this story holds great value. Because David was so kind as to accompany you, I will reimburse him for his expenses and bring him along on this journey. Dennis, come to me for a moment, give me your hand."

Mr. Woo took Dennis's arm in his left hand, and with his right hand he touched his shoulder, and at the same time he looked into his eyes. Without breaking eye contact, the two went back to Dennis's chair. Mr. Woo sat down across from Dennis, who now appeared to be completely relaxed.

"Dennis, tell me exactly what happened."

"It was after morning roll-call on September 23, 2005, around 8:00 AM. There was suddenly a flurry of activity in the yard as we were still at roll-call. Eleven guards ran over to the guards' offices in sector B. We had to remain standing until around 9:40, and then we were ordered back into our cells. We weren't allowed out for the whole day. I heard from Sammy, the Nigerian, what happed. Ram, the skinny guard in block F, where we were, had hanged himself in the toilet next to his office over night, it must have been after midnight. On October 2, 2005, we heard about Sunan's death. A prisoner, a Thai whose name I don't know, told me about it. Sunan was driving his taxi one night like almost every night. The next morning, he was found dead in his taxi near Bangwank. He had taken an overdose of heroin. Allegedly he had a heroin problem many years ago, but hadn't had any heroin in the last few years. Finally, on October 5, 2005, Dusit was arrested for the murder of Akara. I heard the story from Francois, one of the older prisoners, who had good contacts. Dusit had lured Akara to a meeting at a hotel, then tied him up, gagged and blindfolded him, then bludgeoned him with a truncheon for hours. When the police arrived, Akara was still alive but unconscious. He was taken to Bumrungrad Hospital, one of the best in Bangkok, and died the evening of October 7, 2005. Many rumors arose after this event. All four of them, that is, the three guards and Akara, the justice ministry official, were somehow involved in the deaths of the two Chinese young men. People thought that someone had avenged their deaths, and others claimed that you, Mr. Woo, were behind it. Especially some of the Thais, who all believe in ghosts, thought that you had summoned evil spirits against them. Others said that

God had taken the fate of those men into his hands. The fate of the four men was discussed for months in prison. Some of the guards also believed the ghost stories, and I think I can say that our treatment by the guards became somewhat better after these events."

Mr. Woo scratched something on a piece of paper and pressed it into Simon's hand. He closed Simon's hand in his own and indicated that he should listen carefully: "Thank you, Dennis. Think back briefly to that day when the thin guard came into our cell to search it with his colleagues. Remember how he looked when he explained in Thai what they would do and which punishments we could expect. How he stood in front of us with his truncheon. Think of his shirt, the buttons on his shirt, and the loops. Visualize the shirt in front of you and look at the number on the shirt. What is the number?"

Like a shot from a pistol, Dennis replied "9376726."

Simon opened the piece of paper in his hand, and on it was the same number: 9376726. He was visibly irritated and showed me the piece of paper. I was astonished. David wasn't the brightest guy out there, it has to be said. I had wondered in any case why he had asked Dennis to tell the story. It was inexplicable how he could remember all of these dates and even the guard's number.

Mr. Woo touched Dennis on the shoulder and stood. Dennis looked as if he had just woken up. He rubbed his eyes, took his bearings, and looked much more cheerful than before.

"That is the way of Do. I will explain it to you later. Ju, are you finished with the summary?" said Mr. Woo resolutely.

Simon and Dennis signed the summary, and Ju brought us pu-erh tea.

"Let's go now on a journey. I will tell you a story that you cannot read anywhere. I tell it to my pupils, and in some cases to friends like you who have earned it."

Our journey begins in China around the year 600. Fujian, one of China's southern provinces traversed by the Silk Road, experienced a considerable economic revival under the Tang Dynasty. Until the year

1400, Quanzhou's harbor was one of the largest, maybe even the largest in the world. Around the year 900, the Shaolin established a cloister in Quanzhou. The Shaolin nuns and monks were long known as warriors and the city hoped the Shaolin would provide protection against the numerous pirates. Later, under the Ming dynasty, the cloister experienced its golden age. Countless varieties of martial art were practiced and developed there. The Shaolin monks trained hard, up to sixteen hours every day, most of them from childhood on.

It was the year 1644. China was in a period of upheaval. The rebel leader Li Zicheng mobilized twenty thousand men in the northern provinces and marched with his army on Beijing. He sealed the end of the Ming dynasty, which had already been seriously weakened by corruption, numerous revolts, and the fight against the Manchu in the north. He founded the Shun dynasty. His time in the palace in Beijing barely lasted a year, and then the Manchu took over the country and founded the Qing dynasty.

The Qing wanted to establish themselves as China's ultimate rulers and bring an end to the many revolts and rebellions. Their goal was to unify the land and make it strong. China's many cloisters had previously been spared by the rulers and remained independent, but now the Qing also wanted power and control over the spiritual China as well.

One cloister, the Shaolin cloister in Quanzhou, was especially a thorn in their side. It had always been financially supported by the Ming, and in return the Shaolin nuns and monks had repeatedly served the Ming by participating in secret military operations, for which they were supremely well qualified by their martial arts.

After the Qing seized power in 1645, some of the generals of the Ming dynasty had also found protection in this cloister.

Around the year 1670, Emperor Kangxi of the Manchu dynasty sent his son Yinzhen, who he would later name as his successor, to the cloister under a false name as a spy. Yinzhen recognized some of the former Ming generals and was back in Beijing a few months later to report what was going on in the cloister.

In March 1673, Emperor Kangxi sent his army, over 2500 soldiers, to destroy the cloister and arrest the generals. To their surprise, the 128 monks of the cloister succeeded in beating back the Qing army without taking even a single loss on their side. In the following years, the cloister was considered impregnable and it became a symbol of resistance against the Qing. Everywhere in China, people knew the deeds of the Shaolin monks.

On December 20, 1722, Emperor Kangxi died. On his deathbed, he decided that Yinzhen would succeed him and be known as Emperor Yongzheng. Yongzheng determined to take vengeance as soon as possible for the disgrace that the Shaolin had inflicted on the Qing army and his father. Already on February 12, 1723, only 54 days after taking office, the Qing army attacked the Shaolin cloister together with Tibetan mercenaries.

Before the break of day, the soldiers began bombarding the cloister for hours with burning spears and arrows, cannons, and firearms. In one day, 110 of the 128 monks in the cloister were killed. Eighteen of the monks were able to flee, and the Qing soldiers hunted them in the forests for another seventy days. During these seventy days, they killed another thirteen of the monks.

It is known that five of them survived. Jee Sin, Ng Mui, Bak Mei, Fung Dou Dak, and Miu Hin. Two years after the destruction of the cloister, these five regrouped and were able to go into hiding on Mt. Emei in Szechuan province, where there are many cloisters. They planned to infiltrate the Qing dynasty and destroy it from inside. These five became famous because each of them had developed several fighting styles, of which many are still practiced today. These five are considered the origin of modern martial arts and their story can be found in many variations in books, movies, and comics.

The story of Hi Liangyu is less well known. She was one of the nuns of the Shaolin cloister. For hundreds of years, the nuns in the cloister had been divided between the uncompromising pacifism of Buddhism and the development of martial arts, and during all those year the contradiction could never be entirely resolved. The teachings of Buddhism were always more important to Hi Liangyu than the principles of martial arts. Despite that, she belonged to the inner circle of martial arts teachers and she developed her own fighting style. People say that Hi Liangyu was a granddaughter of Qin Liangyu, a famous and highly decorated Ming general, and that she was always interested in political developments for this reason. Because of her lineage, she always had to be especially watchful, as she was aware of how the worldly events in distant Beijing could also affect life in the cloister.

When the monks in the cloister heard of Emperor Kangxi's death in 1722 and the swearing in of young Yinzhen as the new emperor, Hi Liangyu immediately grew alarmed. She understood that the old Emperor Kangxi wouldn't attack the cloister a second time because he would lose face completely in the case of a repeated defeat. But it was just as clear to her that the new emperor would soon attempt to wage war on the cloister.

In the years since the last attack on the cloister, the army had been equipped with improved cannons, firearms, and other weapons. In the meantime the troops and officers had also become more experienced in the many battles against the rebels and more effectively organized. Defeating the imperial army appeared unlikely to her. Victory over the cloister would be an important signal to the opponents of the young emperor.

Hi Liangyu attempted to convince the other 127 monks and nuns to leave the cloister quickly and seek shelter in the mountains. She explained to them that the world had changed; fifteen hundred years ago, a thousand years ago, even fifty years ago it would have been possible to oppose a gigantic army through perfect knowledge of the martial arts, just as had happened in 1673. But those times were past. No martial art could defy the firepower of the cannons. The cloister would fall, and soon. The cloister, said Hi, would be easy prey for the young emperor to distinguish himself and prove his superiority over his father, with whom he had had a strained relationship.

But the Shaolin nuns and monks weren't convinced. Instead of recognizing the danger, they saw in Hi Liangyu a risk, as she was descended from a prominent Ming family. She was expelled from the cloister and told never to return. Hi Liangyu departed already in early 1723 for Mt. Emei, where in March 1725 she met the five survivors of the battle for the cloister again: Jee Sin, Ng Mui, Bak Mei, Fung Dou Dak and Miu Hin. All of them were determined to continue teaching the martial arts they had developed in other cloisters. But Hi Liangyu had other plans, as martial arts in her view had lost their original value.

For over a thousand years, the cloister had been able to defend itself with their help against bandits, against revolts, and also against the every-changing rulers and princes. But now martial arts had become pure artifice. Hedonism and an end unto themselves—that's what the martial arts really were. The monks boasted about their muscles and highly trained bodies, but it all stood in stark contrast to what Buddhism taught. The development of the martial arts was always justified by the necessity of defending the cloister, but now that the cloister would need no more defense, the justification was no longer valid.

For many years she had been planning to create a completely new fighting style, and in the last few years on Mt. Emei she had already started to develop it. The nuns and monks of the cloister should learn from the history of the original Shaolin cloister—from its founder Batuo, who came to China from India over a thousand years ago and founded the first Shaolin cloister in Luoyang. Batuo was a master of Dhyana, the Buddhist art of meditation, and precisely this, according to Hi, provided the key to rebuilding the cloister and continuing it in good conscience.

Her martial art was to fight without weapons and without hands: the art of fighting with the mind. By placing oneself and the opponent in a trance, one could gain power over the enemy and influence or change his thoughts, his plans, and even his beliefs.

Of the five survivors from the cloister, Ng Mui and Bak Mei were especially interested in the new technique, but Hi had to be careful, because the five had also repeated the accusation that Hi and other former protégés of the Ming dynasty shared blame for the cloister's destruction. Hi withdrew to the Fuhu Si cloister on Mt. Emei.

The cloister lay at an altitude of 3000 meters near the mountain's peak and in those days was in its golden age. It was expanding and numerous new buildings were being built, including a hall with 4700 Buddha statues. The new facility comprised a good hundred buildings in the middle of a forest and was lined with basins, benches, and paths. Many of the monks also practiced various fighting styles in the six large courtyards. Hi was welcomed by the nuns and monks, as she knew a few new fighting styles, for which there was keen interest at the cloister.

But Hi wanted to study the "Way of Do," as she called her spiritual martial art. She would teach some of the monks new fighting techniques, and in return they would help her with the development of her new method. Hi selected six suitable students, two nuns and four monks. The cloister provided them their own small building for training on the outskirts of the cloister. She was experienced in the development of martial arts and approached this new form of martial art with the same process. She tried things out, organized them, and practiced.

After several months, two fundamental directions, which today we call hypnosis and mass hypnosis, emerged from this teaching. Hypnosis targets an individual. The disciples of Do studied the fastest way to put someone under hypnosis, first within minutes, then within a few seconds. How to give someone orders, influence their opinion, and learn things under hypnosis that the person themselves often wasn't even aware of knowing as they were so deeply buried.

"Like Dennis, who probably can't remember the thin guard's number any more, am I right? Dennis?"

Dennis sat up and thought hard. "954...934, crap, no, I don't know it anymore."

Because of their decades-long training in the martial arts and meditation, Hi and her apprentices were able to put themselves into a deep trance state. They recognized this as the prerequisite for putting others into trances. They could bring about such deep hypnotic states that needles could be pushed through the hands of the hypnotized people.

They took a strictly methodical approach to developing Do. As in the classic martial arts, they built a system with various tactics and perfected it over the years. With Do, they could bring about a deep trance within seconds, erase or change their opponents' memories or create new memories. They could give orders that would only be carried out in the distant future, and in the state of hypnosis they could learn secrets, or change them, or make people forget them. They could prevent pain or cause pain. They could possess an incredible power over a person.

They developed various deep techniques, and some were purely for conversation: a story from the past, for example, or a dream that was specially invented in order to attain a specific goal, or in order to change a person's thoughts and attitudes. The hypnotized person was to be brought to a particular form of behavior. Deeper techniques had the goal of causing personal changes more rapidly.

The arsenal of techniques grew over the years and the seven masters of Do perfected them by practicing up to sixteen hours each day. The nuns and monks of the Fuhu Si cloister were often a part of the exercises that Hi and her students conducted.

In one such exercise where a monk was being hypnotized, she noted that some other monks also fell into a trance. This was how Hi discovered mass hypnosis. In the early years she hadn't been aware that it was possible to hypnotize many people simultaneously. She feared the possible uses of mass hypnosis. After just a few years with her students, she recognized how much power she could obtain over a single person with the help of hypnosis. She observed that the larger the number of people was, the easier it was to induce mass hypnosis

Hi understood that this technique in the wrong hands could put large groups of people into trances. It wasn't even necessary to cause an especially deep trance. In the case of mass hypnosis, language was the ultimate key. Hypnotic messages could also be transmitted in writing. Through the mass production of writing, one could hypnotize thousands of people, even entire nations.

Mass hypnosis draws its power from the living language of the sentences that the listener must interpret, as their sense only results from their interpretation, which will be different for each person. In a crowd, however, it produces its effect as if everyone shared the same ideas.

Presuppositions are an additional means of hypnosis; one assumes that something has been completely proved in order to build another hypothesis on top of it. Most people then concentrate on the hypothesis without ever questioning the presupposition.

Simon appeared to be overburdened by this and wrinkled his brow.

"Okay, if I say that pu-erh tea is healthy and it would be shame to mix it with sugar, then at first glance it all comes down to the question of whether or not you should add sugar to your tea. But actually a presupposition is being slipped past us, namely that pu-erh tea is healthy. But who says that? How do you know it? How do you even prove it? We find presuppositions everywhere today, in advertisements, in political debates, at universities, in daily conversation."

Hi and her students developed an entire arsenal of hypnotic techniques. Flash hypnosis for putting the enemy in a trance in seconds. For that, you had to be able to exactly imitate the other person's blinking and breathing and each of their smallest movements. A very effective long-term technique was what we know today as post-hypnotic suggestion, a suggestion that continues working in the subconscious mind for years after the trance. Then there was the tactic of giving the opponent small commands, completely trivial things, like holding an object for a short time, or helping out with something. With time, over minutes or months, the commands would become more complex and elaborate, but the greater number of small commands that were carried out, the more servile the person became.

The disciples of Do especially valued developing the voice and body language. They knew exactly which words and movements would trigger which reactions. The environment could also help to induce a trance; the Do understood that the design of cloisters, temples, and palaces pursued certain aims. Architecture, fashion, paintings, flags—all of it affects the subconscious and we take it in subconsciously.

Three times a day, before sunrise, at noon, and in the evening, all two thousand inhabitants of the cloister gathered in the great hall of 4700 Buddha statues. The hall must have been incredibly impressive. Just the roof by itself was a unique construction made only of bamboo formed in a complex, interconnected manner. The air was heavy and impregnated with the smoke of countless thousands of incense sticks, which veiled the room in numbing fog. A fire burned in the middle of the room. During the ceremony that often lasted several hours, the nuns and monks meditated to the accompaniment of music. At the same time, one of the monks sang mantras in Sanskrit, his voice reciting at an irregular pace while giant double-skin drums constantly beat the same tempo. The singing was supported by a choir that monotonously intoned deep syllables using their characteristic laryngeal technique. In addition, the singing and drumming were accentuated by bells and meter-long trumpets, with several in use at the same time so that others could keep playing while one caught his breath. Other instruments for the ceremony were made out of human bones. These ceremonies utilized the human capacity for attentiveness to its full extent so that every sense was overwhelmed in the accompanying meditation and everyone in the room inevitably fell into a trance. The crowd of hypnotized people strengthened the process, resulting in a deep mass hypnosis. So all inhabitants of the cloister were in a permanent trance state, which helped them to overcome their deprivations: cold, hunger, monotony, and for many, sexual abstinence for years at a time. When the Do wanted to practice with other members of the order, they first had to break them out of the existing trance, and often themselves as well.

Through their knowledge of the function and working methods of hypnosis and mass hypnosis, the students of Do became immune to occultism and transcendentalism, and their minds were protected against every form of magic, miracle healing, and fortune telling, practices that were deeply rooted in Chinese culture.

It was clear to the Do how these occult techniques functioned. They saw that the fortune tellers, healers, and magicians were themselves masters of hypnosis, often without knowing it. Many of these "magicians" were so good at hypnosis that they themselves believed in their extrasensory abilities.

There were many fortune tellers in China. Today as well, many people still use the technique of "cold reading." For that, one reads information about a person from features such as clothing, posture, language, appearance, scent, breathing, movement, and many more. In addition one pays exact attention to the person's reaction when one talks about these details. Someone who is experienced, for example a fortune teller, can bring to light astonishing things about a person's past in this way, and of course build up trust at the same time, so that one can prophecy about the future as well.

"I performed a cold reading of David in this way before dinner. I though your name sounded Jewish, and everything else about you was easy to recognize."

"That explains some things," I said.

Hi exposed many magical techniques and deprived the fortune tellers and miracle healers of their magic. There were constant conflicts with other nuns and monks when she tried to encourage them to take their fates into their own hands instead of relying on fortune tellers.

Control over language was a prerequisite for their hypnotic martial art, so the Do usually put themselves in a trance every morning in order to get to know and to better control this state of mind.

For inducing a trance, one uses formulations that are as ambivalent as possible. The meaning of these statements is ascribed to them only by the listener. Typical formulations are: you can learn that; you know what you need; everyone knows; one does this or that; and so on. These sayings have no meaning, so that each person will have to give these sentences their own meaning.

For that, it helps that it is in the nature of language to constantly have to interpret the meaning of words and sentences. Every word can have several meanings. Especially phonetically, it's often only possible to determine the sense of a word in context, and even then a decision must be made about the meaning. The more meaningless the sentences become, the more decisions and attribution of meaning we have to undertake for ourselves, and this deepens a trance, as it increasingly turns our attention inward.

When the Do weren't in a trance, they used a type of language they had developed for themselves. It was strictly cleansed from any trace of hypnotism. It helped them to reach a state of absolute wakefulness, the state that they also saw as the key to Buddhism.

Their language was free from adjectives and from indefinite words like *life, learning, happiness, love, experience, worry*. They used no verbs that described vague activities like *change, think, feel, remember, experience*. In their language usage, they renounced all forms of meaninglessness, for example generalization and presuppositions. This kind of language required a high degree of discipline because casual speech is full of vague sentences and generalizations, and even with the highest degree of discipline, dealing with language still always requires extensive interpretation. One can never defend yourself completely against a trance.

For Hi and her students, this systematic, utilitarian analysis of hypnosis led to a completely new understanding of Buddhism. Hi interpreted the "awakening" that Siddhartha Gautama, the founder of Buddhism, experienced as the waking from a trance.

The four paths of Buddhism are the recognition: life is typically suffering that is caused by greed, hate, and blindness. Suffering can be avoided by preventing these causes so that one attains a happy state through a just life and meditation.

Hi saw in this a guideline for recognizing and preventing hypnoses, especially mass hypnoses. The teaching of meditation, which is nothing else than a form of hypnosis, makes it possible to recognize if one is in a trance. It also arms one against attempts at hypnotization. Anyone who is experienced in hypnosis knows exactly when he is and is not in a trance.

From now on, the Do had their own interpretation of the history of Buddhism and they discussed it with other nuns and monks. But in so doing they lost the favor of the older nuns and monks of Fuhu Si. While they completely shared the Do's view that Buddha had recognized the trance and the terrible consequences of mass hypnosis and had found a way to arm people against them, they couldn't countenance the idea that the Do were planning to develop a strategy or even a weapon out of this recognition in order to use it against others.

Even when the Do argued that the cloister itself used the trance in its ceremonies, in the architecture, the clothing, the organization and complexity of belief, they couldn't convince the elders. In addition, stories about the Do on Mt. Emei and about the power they could gain over others were multiplying. The cloister elders were afraid of falling under the control of the Do. It was the first rift between the Do and the cloister. Hi knew that her days in the cloister were numbered.

It was in the winter of 1732 when Bak Mei, one of the five Shaolin survivors, appeared at the cloister. Soon after the destruction of the cloister, Bak Mei resolved to travel to Beijing, as he had joined the rebels and wanted to take part in the battle against the Qing for the restoration of the Ming dynasty. But after eight years in Beijing, he gave up the fight. Many people were seeking to kill him, however, including some of the other four survivors.

Bak Mei reported that in Beijing he had met a member of Hi's family, Miaoyu, a young woman close to the Jian clan who had lived in a cloister for a long time herself. Her uncle, Ju-long, remembered Hi as a young girl and was very sad not to have heard from her in so long. Unfortunately Bak Mei had to report that her parents were no longer alive. But the Liangyus were a large family who had very good contacts in Beijing all the way to the emperor, and Hi would be welcome at any time.

By now Hi was 32 years old. She had been living for 25 years in cloisters, and only in the last few years had she left the cloister frequently with her students to try out her new methods in villages. She wanted to get out, to test her technique. Hi wanted another life.

So after a discussion, it came to a separation between the cloister and the Do. The cloister gave the Do 4000 candareens at their departure, or around fifty ounces of silver. The Do promised for their part to represent the cloister worthily in the future, and also to support the cloister financially if they entered worldly society. In 1733, the seven of them reached Beijing, China's new capital.

Beijing counted over a million inhabitants at the time. In the preceding decades the city had experienced an economic upswing and it was growing at a rapid pace.

The Liangyus were a well-situated family with an estate near the Forbidden City. The estate included two large houses and a garden with numerous small pagodas and four smaller houses. Hi truly got to know her family here for the first time: her brother Biming, her niece Chen, and numerous uncles and aunts. The head of the family was Ju-long, a merchant who especially traded in silver that the court bought from him, and he exported tea, silk, spices, and porcelain. He imported the silver from South America. The Qing court bought great amounts of it from him so that Ju-long became wealthy from the trade within a few years and visited the court frequently.

Hi and her six students settled into one of the small houses in the garden, where they continued to pursue their studies. Hi explained at first that they were practicing Kung fu. At that time, a Min dialect was still spoken on Mt. Emei and it took several months before they perfected the Mandarin spoken at court. Ju-long talked about Hi at court and finally arranged a meeting between a high court official and Hi. Hi wanted to persuade the emperor to spare the Shaolin cloister in the future.

This meeting was the first time that Hi would deliberately use her Do art outside of the cloister and for her own ends. The official afterward showed great interest in advocating for the cloister, and Emperor Yongzhen actually issued a personal decree in 1735 to rebuild the cloister.

Hi recognized in her dealings with her family and the officials at court that she had completely internalized her own teachings. On the one hand she took pride in the many new techniques that she had mastered, but on the other hand she noted a change in her personality. Her vocal pitch and body language, her manner of formulating and intonating were different than before, and the reactions of the environment to her had long since changed. Hi had the feeling that she could attain anything;

everyone would gladly do something for her and fulfill her deepest wishes."

I look at the projected starry sky. It's already dark. "With that, Mr. Woo ended the evening and we went to bed lost in thought. Are you two hungry? We could go outside and get a little to eat."

"Gladly, but I definitely still want to hear the rest of the story," Natalie persists.

"Let's do that after we eat. Where should we go? I'd like to eat something healthy, either one of those DNA/blood places, or should we get shakes?"

"David, I made reservations for you at KLD[54] nine days ago, but for four people," chimes in Watson, who's listening to us.

"Oh yeah, exactly, that's the restaurant with the robots and drones. They have a herd of robots that comb through the jungle and collect and harvest thousands of wild plants, roots, mushrooms, and fish. Then the drones fly it to Bangkok and they make the most unbelievable dishes out of it."

"Does lusting after food just come with age?" asks Nadine, amused.

"No, it's always been like that. It's part of my hedonistic lifestyle. Almost everyone goes out to eat these days, though. The food is in any case one of the main reasons why I keep coming back to Bangkok. And I've seen through you already. You like to eat as much as I do...."

The fourth person ends up being Claude, a friend of Natalie who works in the French embassy. She seems to have something going on with him.

---

[54] KLD, Khao Laem Diversity Restaurant, obtains its foodstuffs from Kaho Laem National Park, the jungle around 800 km north of Bangkok. Robots comb through the jungle there day and night in the search for specialties. The KLD restaurants belong to a Thai investment group that also bought the national park.

At 140 stories, the Baiyoke Horizon hotel is one of the tallest buildings in Bangkok and also one of the most luxurious. There are numerous bars and clubs in the hotel and the ultra-rich of Bangkok pass through here every day.

On the ramp there's a Rolls Royce RW, the absolute top-end vehicle. It's an ultra-modern, windowless coach that inside and outside consists of a single seamless high-resolution monitor. On this one, you can see gentle patters that react to the environment, wind, temperature, and sound. The coach can be turned into a convertible and is pulled by six four-legged robotic horses arranged like the horses of a royal coach. A crowd has gathered around the vehicle and admires it. Although the coach appears to be empty, the robotic horses are not still. The horses formed from chrome-plated black metal and curved monitors have enormous expressive eyes that sluggishly alter the direction of their gaze in sync with their bodies. Some of the admirers stroke the curved monitors on the robot horses' backs and necks, which is acknowledged by the horses with approving movements and sounds. The whole thing has an unbelievably impressive appearance; it's not only a form of transportation, but also an orchestrated scene that aroused sympathy and admiration among viewers despite the coach's ostentatious appearance. In buying the coach, the owner obtained not only a vehicle, but also the public's favor, much like kings had done earlier.

The people around were discussing who the owner was, and it seemed as if it were Vorayuth Yoovidhya, a colorful personality in Bangkok society. His family owns numerous companies, hospitals, and pharmaceutical concerns, and he is also the main owner of Red Bull. Borayuth had gone underground for twenty years after he had been condemned for the murder of a police officer. He could only surface again after Bangkok's privatization and a settlement with the officer's family. Since then, he's been living the life of a philanthropist, art collector, and high tech investor here in Bangkok.

The KLD is housed in an outlying building. One of the elevators that slides both vertically and horizontally along the outside wall brings us directly to the restaurant. We are automatically recognized and an illuminated path on the floor leads us to our table. The restaurant is quite large and rather dimly lit. All the tables are arranged in a circle around a large rectangular court that is brightly illuminated and open toward the upper end. In the courtyard there's a garden with exotic plants. You can see bamboo, palm trees, carnivorous plants, agaves, and large ferns. The second part of the court is roofed and has four marked landing pads for giant drones, where two are parked at the moment. The drones look like a mixture of helicopter and quadcopter and are a good three meters long. We sit down at the table, and it's raining. The atmosphere is strange, but interesting in any case. It reminds you of the landing pad of the Death Star from Star Wars.

Claude is already there, as the French embassy is right around the corner. Bamboo water is served to us before we focus on the rather complex menu.

KLD works with the owners of nature parks in Thailand, one of them around 800 km north of Bangkok, two others around 500 km to the south. Various robots trawl the primeval forest there, some of them searching close to the ground, mostly along bodies of water, where they gather fish, shrimp, mussels, and other creatures. Others comb through the tree tops. Over fourteen thousand different species of plants, fruit, fungi, roots, fish, crabs, mussels, and snails have been flown in and offered to customers by KLD in the past five years. The robots test the edibility, quality, and ripeness on site in the jungle through spectroscopy and other methods, and then they reap. Every two to three hours, one of the drones brings the harvest to Bangkok, where chefs process the deliveries into eccentric creations.

Among other things, sauces, chutney, tea, schnapps, marmalade, and snacks, which can be purchased in the shop right next to the elevator, are produced here from the fruits of the jungle.

In addition to food dishes, drinks, teas, and cocktails, KLD also offers plants for smoking as well as psychoactive substances that one can ingest in a lounge after the meal.

In the middle of the table there's a small basin in which water splashes and various jungle plants are growing. I'm no expert, but I think

115

they're various kinds of orchid. I don't see a single thing that I've ever eaten before on today's menu, and I haven't even heard of most of them except for wild pineapple. The menu consists of a good twenty dishes, and we decide on a variety of fern salads. One consists of bawang, a kind of jungle garlic, the oil of wild almonds, and asam paya vinegar with dogfruit, which resembles a potato but tastes like bitter physalis. The other is a fern salad with kembayau, something like a wild olive at least in appearance, and mangosteen, a rather sweet fruit, with the juice of wild lemons and chili. In addition to the salads, they bring us gourami, a type of fish, and then a walking catfish with brati, a type of nut, along with pesto made of plants identified on the menu only by their Latin names, as any other name for them has disappeared.

Claude is a very nice young man from Paris. He's working temporarily in the embassy as an IT security expert because the French embassy is having problems with hacker attacks. His actual interest is anthropology; he's studied the field, but there's hardly any money to be made with it. A few years ago he had a few performances as an anthropologist on shows in France, England, and the USA after he developed a wild theory about circumcision, but after there was no more money to be made that way, he specialized in cybersecurity.

"I had my son circumcised, but I regret that now. At that point I was no longer devout, but my dislike of religion was still weaker than my respect for my Jewish cultural heritage. I definitely wouldn't do it today. But how did you land on that topic?" I asked him.

"Much like you did, I think. I'm also from a Jewish family and was circumcised. We weren't ever religious, so I couldn't understand why I was circumcised at all."

"I don't think it's so bad," Natalie interjected.

"Sure, most women like it because it's hygienic and you can screw forever. But it's also arduous to always have control and never be able to experience true ecstasy," I explained to her.

Claude nodded in agreement.

"Personally, I don't find it so bad, either," Nadine remarked.

"Great, so at least the ladies don't have anything against it.... So, what did you discover? Sorry, I didn't catch your performances."

"Circumcision of both sexes has been known for thousands of years. There are many theories for why people started: as a sacrificial ritual, for presumed medical reasons, to prevent masturbation.... But in the end there's hardly any way to prove any of them, and medically it makes no sense. Many people even used to die from it. You can halfway make sense of it as a ritual, but that's mostly only camouflage for other motivations. My thought at the time was to investigate the voluminous DNA data currently available to see if I could find out anything with the help of IRIS and Watson. That's how I learned that until around five thousand years ago, women always conceived children from different men. Today we have an excessive amount of DNA data available, and it tells us which people are attracted to each other. It turned out that back then many children were produced by people who would never have sex with each other voluntarily today because genetically they wouldn't find each other attractive, let alone have children together. And that all happened long before arranged marriages or other kinds of alliances, so that's significant as well. The statistical data combined with the DNA data point instead to village communities constantly having sex with each other whenever they were in the mood. Now there's an unusual phenomenon that when women live with each other, and even more so when they share sexual partners, their menstrual cycles adjust to each other. That's not to synchronize the days of menstruation, but instead the days of ovulation."

"Interesting, I've heard that before. What result does that have, exactly?" asked Nadine and took a large bite of her fern salad.

"It raises the chances of less attractive women obtaining the genetic material of the best men. If all the women ovulate on the same day and there are no inhibitions or other obstacles, then there would have been a lot going on in a village like that five thousand years ago."

"I would like to have been there," said Nadine, almost choking on her fern salad.

"As almost everyone is doing it with everyone else, genetic material collects in the foreskin and is then distributed among almost the

117

entire active village community. In that way the best genetic material asserts itself, and that's apparently how children were born to people who according to modern understanding wouldn't normally have screwed each other."

"Sperm collects in the foreskin and can survive there for one or more hours if it doesn't come into contact with air. Appetizing thought, isn't it?" said Natalie. She seemed to be already familiar with the story.

"The problems started with the agricultural revolution. Suddenly people had farmsteads, a field, a hut, tools, and possibly livestock as well. That's when people began to understand that children were their descendants and not the offspring of some magical deities. The analysis of DNA, bones, and city ruins suggests that life expectancy rose rapidly and mobility increased at this time five thousand years ago. So people from various parts of the world, with different skin color as well, came together and formed larger communities. These processes probably led to understanding of the sexual act."

While Claude is still talking about his theory, the second course arrives:

Risotto of wild rice with strangler figs and thickened juice of wild mango.

Dysoxylum cauliflorum, a seed of the mahogany tree, sharply roasted, with three different kinds of pepper.

Basket clams, a freshwater mussel, with cooked Glochidion hylandii[55] and a pesto made from Cooper's Puzzle.[56]

Juice of Tribus Globbeae, a species of wild ginger.

"And then how did circumcision come about?" I wanted to know, still chewing. It really tasted good!

"Circumcision was just one element of the catalog of measures taken to ensure that your own child is your heir. Additional measures from the catalog included: only impregnate a virgin; only the firstborn child

---

[55] From the Phyllanthaceae family.
[56] A plant from the soapberry family; the capsule fruits often open explosively and contain large seeds that one can cook and eat.

inherits; circumcise all men so that no foreign sperm can be smuggled in; control and/or circumcise a woman so that she experiences no lust and has no chance to sleep with another man while one man is trying to impregnate her. With these steps it was possible to ensure that only your own child would inherit the property you'd worked for. Today we take for granted that our biological children will be our heirs. Through the spread of DNA information, it's almost 100% certain today. Of course you have to ask yourself why it was originally so important and why it's still so important now, or if it's perhaps a natural human predisposition. Maybe there were alternative cultures in which the topic of natural inheritance played no role and they perished because of it.... It's a topic that raises many questions, but also some uncomfortable answers."

"What would the uncomfortable answers be?" Nadine enquired.

"All cultures that exist today bequeath wealth according to succession, so only to their own DNA. In an economic sense, what's taking place is a 'survival of the fittest.' A wealthy family passes its wealth on to its children, with the same DNA, who in turn start life with a financial advantage. It appears that this was and is a recipe for success. If we deviate from this principle and distribute wealth according to other principles, then according to this theory, that part of society would possibly become weaker."

"I think that's a pretty bold theory," answered Nadine. "Have you already gone around talking about it in France?"

"Not that part," Claude responded. "It wouldn't be well received."

During the meal, drones are constantly arriving from the primeval jungle and are unloaded in the courtyard. The whole restaurant is an experience, definitely a highlight for gourmets. Information about the dishes and the restaurant constantly appear on the table, and I read that an AI decides how the food is prepared, and that the database includes ten thousand of its own recipes.

Another AI—and a shameless one—appears to set the prices, and I almost have a heart attack when I see the bill. Still, our host, a young Thai woman, informs us that we are invited to have a cup of tea with a mild euphoric effect. In the restaurant lounge, this mild euphoric effect turned out to be a sizable load of psilocybin fresh from the jungle. That reminds me of my younger years in Austria, where every fall we looked for the little mushroom with psilocybin among the cow patties on the Wechsel, a mountain range near Vienna.

It was highly entertaining in the lounge, and for the next two hours I more than anyone else could barely stop laughing. At the end of the mushroom trip, we were provided with another friendly gift of various jungle snacks, chiefly unfamiliar fruit whose look and taste caused further laughing fits. In addition there was a VR trip where you experienced the robots' walk through the night-time jungle live, which was a unique experience while on a mushroom trip.

Only late in the evening are we clear enough in the head to keep going. I tie back in to my trip with Mr. Woo and tell its conclusion.

"So, back to China and Mr. Woo in 2006. The next morning, congee was prepared for us along with jasmine tea. Mr. Woo had already been awake for a while and suggested that we take a walk along one of the small lakes next to the rice fields, and during the walk he would tell us the rest of the story."

Ju-long was the first person outside of the cloister who heard from Hi what she was actually teaching her students. The audiences at court had gone so well that Ju-long had already assumed that something uncanny was at work. In the following years, Hi repeatedly helped Ju-long with his business and Ju-long paid good money to have Hi instruct him and some of his trusted associates. So the circle of initiates continued to grow and in 1745, Hi already had over fifty students, including court officials. The disciples of the Do moved to their own house and Hi taught there until 1773. In that year she disappeared on a trip to Mt Emei, and no one knows where she ended up. One assume that she was murdered by bandits or by Ju-long's adversaries. Her closest students from Mt. Emei continued her teaching, and some of them went abroad.

Already in 1750, Chen had departed for Macao, and from there he traveled to Spain. It was said that he taught at the Spanish court, but all trace of him is lost and it's not known if he had students in Spain. Suota traveled to France after Hi's death and continued to teach there in a secret organization. Armand de Puységur is said to have once been a student in the organization, but there is no credible evidence for that. But in any case, various schools of hypnosis appeared in France in the middle of the nineteenth century. I presume that they can be traced back to the teachings of the Do. In China, Feng established contact with the English and set out in 1755 at the request of the British for Calcutta, where he taught numerous students. Around the year 1840, the trail of this school reappears when Dr. James Esdaile, a well-known English surgeon, carried out the first operation under hypnosis in 1845 in Calcutta, even before the discovery of chloroform. Jiao and Liling remained in China and they and their students continued to work at the Qing court until 1912. After that the school was divided between those who joined the communists—none of whom survived—and those who went underground or fled to Hong Kong.

I myself am from Hong Kong and learned the way of the Do there. I only moved here a few years ago. With the invention and rapid spread of mass media, first newspapers, then radio and television, governments have often made targeted use of mass hypnosis with the Do's counsel. It was nation states who controlled all forms of mass media in the beginning. This was so even in the freest countries on earth. Only in the last fifty years has direct access to the masses become possible for everyone through technological developments. Mass hypnosis is so omnipresent today and so normal that it is difficult to escape its influence. The consumption of many different forms of media at least has the advantage that one does not subject oneself to a single hypnosis, but instead many different ones exert their influence. In this way the effect is weakened. But the dogmas that are anchored deep in our society are constantly nourished by numerous presuppositions and they make it difficult to free people from the effects of mass hypnosis.

"Are you claiming that we are consciously being controlled by other powers? I'd consider that rather improbable," replied Simon.

"I think that would be an exaggerated claim. No one has sufficient control over enough communications channels to control an entire people. But those who have power over definitions, who can make their voices heard, whose ideas and doctrines are propagated the most.... The mass media in themselves, that is to say their structural composition, build on generating attention as simply and playfully as possible. As a rule this is accomplished through various forms of mass hypnosis. Even the very stylistic device of repetition leads to us believing in something, and the combination of images and music do so as well. The Buddha taught that long ago. In any case it's just as important today as at that time to wake up from hypnosis and become conscious of it."

"I still have a question," said Simon. "Why did you have us come the whole way here to you to describe the events after your release?"

"I thought that you would come back to that. I needed your statement as a confirmation for the one who gave me the assignment. I was supposed to avenge my two unjustly murdered countrymen.... As I had to leave the country after my release, I needed you to confirm the events."

"So there was something true about the rumors. It was no ghost, it was Mr. Woo! The way of the Do.... Now I understand everything...."

"So that was it, the story of Mr. Woo. After this conversation we set out on the return journey to Bangkok."

"I honestly don't know what I should think of the whole story. If I believe it, it would mean that we're all in a hypnotic state right now...."

She seemed to be lost in thought.... When she looked up to me again, I continued talking.

"We drove back to Bangkok; Simon and Dennis kept going to Australia. I wanted to wait a few more days until the Tamils would be released from prison. But soon their situation got more complicated. It turned out that one or more of the Tamils' passports were counterfeits and that started the ball rolling. There was no talk of a quick release after that. To make it short: I never saw those guys again. At that point I got scared of contacting them, the whole thing seemed spooky and I didn't want to have anything to do with it anymore. Luckily I wasn't contacted again by the authorities in Bangkok on account of our little trip."

"And the money and the domain?"

"All came to nothing. The money is worthless by now, and it's probably still sitting in the safe in Bangkok. Apparently the registrar took over the domain for himself after the transfer didn't go through and no one paid the registration fees. I never heard anything about the three Tamils again, maybe they're still sitting in prison. Who knows? In any case, at that point I had lost all my money."

"What did you do then?"

"I could still keep drop catching and registering domains that became available, but the payments for domain parking became unprofitable for me within a very short time. Yahoo was no longer available as an advertising partner and Google paid much worse, so I had to look around for a business model in that sector that didn't require me to invest anything, but where I could make money very quickly. I started marketing domain names with mass e-mails. After all, I had the list of all domains that would likely become available in the next thirty days, and the list of all the owners of the domains along with their names, addresses, e-mail, and telephone numbers, as well as the list of domains they owned. So I had a new tool built that compared these data against each other. If the domain luftburg.com was going to drop in a few days, for example, then I checked who owned a similar domain, like luftburg24.com or luft-burg.com or luftburg.de or had the e-mail address luftburg@ibm.com or owned the firm Luftburg ltd. or had a domain with a website that mentioned the word *luftburg*, and so on. I offered to sell all those people the domain. For that I had to send out around 600,000 e-mails per day, which isn't that easy."

"Because it's spam?"

"That's a matter of definition."

"Well, you could call 600,000 e-mails per day spam, couldn't you?"

"Look, to send that volume of e-mails, you needed a lot of know-how, you needed servers in the USA or Europe that permitted it, you needed clean IP addresses, and a lot of them. Data centers often billed thirty times the normal price for that kind of infrastructure, and often they wanted to be paid in bitcoin, so without an official invoice. In short, this business was in a legal gray zone. But there was a demand for it. My business was only possible like that, I had no other way to advertise those domains, and after all everyone was free to install filters in their e-mail programs to block my e-mails and any similar ones. But because it all got to be more and more illegal, the active participants got to be more and more criminal and the spam increased and became inferior in quality. Spam turned into a matter of ideology: system administrators worked for anti-spam companies for free because they thought they would save the Internet that way, but in fact the exact opposite happened. Precisely the same people who fought against spam, at least the foot soldiers, were angry that Google had become so powerful. But Google was the company that was behind the anti-spam efforts, because if you couldn't advertise by e-mail any longer, which was inexpensive and effective, then Google was left as almost the only advertiser on the Internet.

"And how does the situation look today?"

"At the time there was a whole e-mail-ecosystem. Firms who traded, assessed, laundered, and parked IP addresses and controlled the e-mail servers and what went in and out. In part that was genuine highway robbery, because if you only paid enough money, then the e-mails went through. Today that's unnecessary because of Watson and company, as messages are typically read first or answered right away by our assistants. Plus it officially costs coin today to send mass e-mails, so that it doesn't pay to send millions of them senselessly. But back then business went along for a while quite well. From 600,000 e-mails each day, around twenty domains were sold, and a team in the Philippines handled interactions with the customers. That was a very relaxing time for me and I got a little capital together in order to build something new.

"And that would be?"

"I traded in domain names and sent spam until 2012, and in addition I started collecting and making art and trading in string instruments. Then the spam business got harder because the spam filters got more and more clever. In addition, over all those years we only had one system administrator who set up servers for us. Kaustuva from New Delhi. I only new Kaustuva from Skype text chats, where he was only available afternoons New Delhi time, which always disturbed us. Before and after that we couldn't reach him, and he never wanted to talk by phone. But around twenty people made a living with our business and Kaustuva was, technologically speaking, the sun around which we all rotated. Sometime in early 2012, all the servers were detected by Spamfarm[57] after a short time and had to be reinstalled. This time I wasn't prepared to discuss it via chat, so I forced Kaustuva into a video conference. And at that point we determined that the sun we were rotating around was an eleven-year old boy from New Delhi who went to school in the mornings and was in bed in the evenings. That was the moment when we gave up...."

---

[57] Spamfarm.org, one of the largest anti-spam organizations, whose owners are a secret, but in the course of time has established its software on almost 50% of e-mail servers. In 2027 the managers of the company were arrested after their connection to the "Deathcoin" project was proved. In 2025, a truck was parked in the middle of Times Square and when the police arrived, they found a diesel generator and dozens of servers that were mining deathcoins. An encoded message revealed that deathcoins would be required in order to prevent the outbreak of a virus installed on millions of servers. The deathcoins produced in this way would then be fed to the viruses in order to prevent the virus from paralyzing its host. Experts were able to prove that Spamfarm software made possible the spreading of the deathcoin virus, so the entire Spamfarm management was convicted.

CHAPTER 6

At KDL, Natalie had invited us to a party at the French embassy to celebrate the national holiday. She thought all the expats would be going and it would definitely be fun. Philippe from the embassy had put us on the guest list.

It was clear to me that this was a bad idea. I mean, what do the French have to celebrate? The country is a complete catastrophe, the economy is ruined, and the crime rate is extremely high. The reason they were having a gigantic party in Bangkok was that any Frenchman with a brain had left the country long ago.

I would have really like to send my regrets, but Nadine pushed me to go, and the thought of holding a serious debate with the expats of the *Grande Nation* also had its attractions.

The party is held on the terrace of Porsche Tower, which seems to me like a stark contrast to the ideological foundation of all Frenchmen, but unfortunately there's no Citroën Tower. The terrace is on the 88th floor. By SDU, you arrive directly at the level underneath the terrace. The terrace lobby is packed full with people wearing Tricolore hats. Several women are wearing dresses made from glittering screens that alternately light up in *bleu*, *blanc*, and *rouge* like a flag blowing in the wind and show video clips from the revolution, like the storming of the Bastille or the *Fête de la Fédération*. Glowing sashes in the national colors hang from the shoulders of most of the men, and people are resolutely speaking only in French.

Nadine tries to reassure me and says that at least the buffet is really good. When we emerge into the open, a sea of people stretches before us, all of them adorned with the French flag in some form. The terrace itself is surrounded by three-dimensional projections of the flag. Even the music is French, but at least it's a Daft Punk algorithm. We make our way as quickly as possible to the bar where the drinks are poured by automated dispensers, but there are bartenders who take your order and set the glass from the dispenser on the bar for you. Rather pointless, but it looked a bit more festive that way.

Natalie introduces us to Praline and Paul, a young couple from Paris; they've been running a French bakery in Bangkok for a few months. Praline is small but has a great figure, although her face gives the impression of fatigue and exhaustion. Paul also seems rather tired. He has dark features, maybe an Algerian or similar. Soon another couple join in, both of them also around 35: Catrine, an elegant lady who is busy with a toddler at the moment, and Philippe, her boyfriend, who arranged the invitation for us. He works in the trade section of the French embassy.

Nadine and Natalie have already gotten their drinks, Nadine a "Danton" that looks more like a classic martini, and Natalie a "Champs Élysées" that tastes like a Moscow Mule. After a little small talk about the buffet, the drinks, Bangkok, and French bread, conversation turns as you would expect to French cuisine.

Catrine remarks that people in France cook at home much more often than in most countries of Europe or Asia, and that it is a sign of high culture when so many people are able to cook. I can't just let that stand; in most countries, people don't cook because the economy is more developed. Cooking is part of the division of labor too, and in most civilized countries people go out to eat because it's cheaper and more economical than spending their time cooking. In most of these countries, people often don't even have their own kitchens anymore. French people cook at home because of their economic problems. Philippe refuses to accept this thesis.

The problems in France, so he says, are not so bad. For the most part, the end of the EU was to blame, as it had hit France the hardest and led to a long recession, in which the state had to take control of many businesses. Now they only needed the political will to get the country back into shape again.

I interject that with an economy that is 70% in the public sector, you could assume that the entire country would soon be led only by political will in any case.

Philippe sees matters differently. Capitalists, or better stated capitalist foreign countries, were making life difficult for France, in his opinion.

I comment that I find it odd that that people here are celebrating the freedom the revolution was supposed to have brought, while France itself is becoming more and more totalitarian.

At that point Natalie wants to lighten the somewhat tense atmosphere a little and suggests we raise our glasses to make a toast, to which Philippe provocatively wants to drink to the revolution. I hold off while the rest of the group politely takes a sip.

"You won't drink to the revolution?" asks Philippe, almost excited by my refusal.

"No, I'd rather not."

"Do you think France would have been better off without the revolution?"

"Perhaps. The revolution did put an end to some highly problematic things like guilds and private tax collectors, but otherwise the revolutionaries got the state hopelessly in debt and caused an inflation of a few thousand percent. Oh, and they brutally murdered thousands and thousands of people. But in their defense, that's completely normal for republics. Theft and murder is just daily business for such nations," I add. I'm really in a fighting mood now. Nadine lured me into coming here after all by telling me I'd be able to hold some interesting conversations.

"What's your book actually about?" asks Philippe, attempting to soothe me. Maybe he didn't want to cause a scandal at his own party after all.

"Funny you ask. It's about money, the old forms of money like gold, silver, and platinum, and the national currencies like the dollar, euro, or yuan, and the new present-day currencies, especially ccoin. The freedom and economic rebound they led to, and how society was changed by it. You might say it's about money as the foundation of our society and the source of change."

"Source of change? I rather think that money is the root of all evil," responds Philippe.

"So you think that money is the root of all evil?"

"I think Philippe's right, money is the root of all evil," adds Paul, now getting into the mood.

"Have you ever asked yourself what the root of money is? Money is only a medium of exchange. It exists because there are goods and people who produce them. The foundation of money is that people who want to trade with each other can exchange valuable objects with each other by means of money. Money is made possible by people who produce things. Would you call that an evil?"

"What I call evil are the producers, the corporations who pick money from people's pockets and enrich themselves in the process!" replies Paul.

"But if you accept money as payment for your services, you do it in the belief that you can exchange it for the services of other people. It's not the beggars and thieves who give money its value. Neither a sea of tears nor all the drones in the world can transform the coins in your bank account into the bread that you need to live on tomorrow. The coins represent a promise—your claim to the activity of productive people. Your money represents the hope that there are people somewhere in the world around you who obey the moral principle that constitutes the root of money."

"Fine words, and maybe you're right, but it's always the powerful, the producers, and corporations that accumulate money. The free market is ruled by the law of the jungle. The strong eat the weak."

"And what is the root of production? Look at a microchip, do you think that it was created purely by the muscle power of idiots? Try obtaining your nourishment only through physical exertion and you'll see that intelligence is the root of all products and all wealth."

"That's not what I mean. I think we'd all be better off without money, especially the poor, but also the entire society. Money produces greed and greed produces sorrow. The rich get richer and the poor get poorer."

"You say that money is made by the strong at the expense of the poor? What strength to do you mean? It's not the strength of weapons or muscles. Wealth is the production of intelligence and knowledge. Is money made by the person who invents a microchip at the expense of those who didn't invent it? Is money made by intelligent people at the expense of the idiots?"

"You're twisting my words. It's simply the case that corporations set prices for their products that gain them the maximum profit. As a consumer you're at their mercy. Whatever it costs, you have to pay it. The corporations don't care if you can afford it or not. And so they get more and more rich and powerful," responds Philippe.

"Money allows everyone to receive as a reward for their products and their work what they are worth to the customer, but not more than that. Money prevents any business from being conducted except that which profits both sides. Money requires everyone to work to their own advantage, not to their disadvantage, for their profit, not their loss. When people engage in trade, then reason decides and not violence. The best product, the best service wins and a person's productivity determines the level of their wages."

"Come on, most rich people have produced nothing at all for their money. They inherited it or swindled others out of it. They've done absolutely nothing for it. Money is in the hands of a bunch of decadent men who buy women and drugs and luxury with it, pay no taxes, and do nothing for society," says Paul, joining the conversation again.

"If an heir is master of his money, it serves him; if not, it destroys him. You would say the money ruined him. But did it? Or did he ruin the money? Don't envy a worthless heir; his wealth doesn't belong to you, and you wouldn't have done anything better with it. Do you think that it should have been distributed among you? Burdening the world with fifty parasites instead of one wouldn't bring back the wasted potential that the wealth represents."

By now the conversation has attracted a larger group. In addition to the two couples from France, Natalie, and Nadine, an older, aristocratic, tanned couple in their sixties and two young men have joined the group.

"Money has always brought misery to people. How many people do you think earn their money dishonestly or are forced into jobs that they hate?" the tanned older gentleman says.

"Let me give you an hint about how someone reveals their character: he who condemns money has obtained it dishonorably; the person who respects it has earned it. Run away from anyone who tells you that money is evil. By this statement you can recognize that a looter is approaching. As long as people are living together on earth and need a medium of exchange, the only replacement for money is the muzzle of a gun."

"I earned my wealth quite honestly, but I don't think that I should enjoy more of it, as you put it, than necessary. I'm glad to make my contribution so that other people can also gain a livelihood, and everyone should do their part for the common good in similar fashion!" the older man argues.

"People who apologize for being rich will not remain rich for long. They're the natural prey of looters who stay hidden until they meet a person who begs for forgiveness for the sin of possessing wealth. They will quickly relieve him of his guilt. These looters consider it certain that they will rob defenseless people as soon as they pass a law that disarms them. But their prey then becomes bait for other looters who snatch it away from them in the same way that they got their hands on it in the first place. Then the race belongs not to those with the greatest productive wealth, but to those who use violence the most ruthlessly. If violence is the standard, then the murderer is victorious over the purse snatcher. And such a society will inevitably decline."

That seems to have struck a nerve at least with Philippe, who correctly recognizes his role as a government official in my description. "David, what are you saying? Who are the looters here? Perhaps the state? Politicians?"

"Philippe, please don't take it personally, but when you see that business deals no longer come about through mutual agreement but rather by force, when you see that in order to be allowed to produce something you have to obtain the permission of those who produce nothing, when you see that money flows to people who don't trade in goods but in favors, when you see that people get rich through deception and connections instead of through work and your laws don't protect you from them but rather the other way around, when you see that corruption is rewarded and honesty is self-sacrifice—then you know that your society has a problem. Money doesn't compete with weapons. It doesn't make compromises with brutality."

"I'm afraid there won't be ideological agreement between us this evening, but I don't want to keep quarreling. *Santé!*" Paul raises his glass.

"*Santé*, it was nevertheless a pleasure," and my own belligerence has now run dry. I feel tired.

Later I discover to my own amusement via openDNA[58] that I was related to Paul, although the connection was eight generations back. Oh well, you can't pick who you're related to.

---

[58] In 2049, the DNA of over a billion people has been decoded and openDNA indicates when people with related DNA are nearby.

CHAPTER 7

"We're going to shut IRIS out of the document for a bit in order to DNA-encrypt it."

"Okay, but why?"

"You'll see in just a moment. We're now getting to the real reason why I'm writing this book, and to the problem that I'm struggling with. I have to really be able to trust you now. No one can find out about this before the book is published. The good thing about it is that if you tell someone this story, no one would believe you...."

"Then let me hear it!"

In 2016 I kept focusing on blockchain technology and trading in bitcoin. Of course there were constantly setbacks, sometimes painful ones, because coin were stolen or the organizations holding my bitcoin went bankrupt, but I could live quite well from my coin. I was interested in advancing the state of bitcoin, however. The rising living expenses and the constantly climbing actual inflation rate led the savings my father had left us to continually decrease in value. It was clear that with inflation continuing to rise, the money would be gone within a few years. As the central banks back then were producing so much money, the demand for money declined, and interest rates along with it, until there were even negative interest rates. In order to earn money with your capital, you had to take higher and higher risks.

You have to think of it like this: all the money in the world was organized by some country's government, and every currency was the monopoly of the corresponding central bank. Europe had the euro, the USA had the dollar, the English had the pound, and so on. Every nation went further and further into debt and it was very much in their interest to inflate their currencies.

So the national states printed more and more of their currency, and in effect they dispossessed peopled who saved money and rewarded everyone else who had gone into debt.

The result was a kind of culture of inflation that made those people rich who were able to go heavily into debt. Those who possessed capital were punished because their savings constantly lost value and they were actually the ones who bore the risk for those who were able to take out loans.

In addition, the central banks also controlled interest rates. And, no surprise, after a while they settled around 0% and at times, as I mentioned, there were even negative interest rates. The inflation that resulted didn't fall on everyone equally for two reasons:

First, because constantly rising prices, especially for real estate, were simply regarded as a rise in value or an increase in demand, although it was actually only the result of inflation.

Second, because the economy was functioning despite the use of fiat currencies and productivity kept increasing, masking the rise in prices due to inflation.

Actually all prices should have kept sinking in relation to income because we were all becoming more productive, but currency inflation nullified this effect in many areas of the economy.

Bitcoin, the first digital currency, was invented in 2008 by a certain Satoshi Nakamoto. No one ever discovered for sure who he actually was. Now, bitcoin and the many other digital currencies were like gold—or at least similar to it, since recently gold started being consumed...."

"Wait, what?"

"For a few decades now, the amount of gold in industrial use has become so minimal that recycling it no longer pays, and so gold is lost. It wasn't like that earlier. That's also the difference with bitcoin and the other cryptocurrencies, because gold would be used more if it were less expensive, in contrast to bitcoin and other currencies of the early years.

Many of these first currencies are still around: litecoin, dash, darkcoin, nucoin, Monero. They were all like money, you mined it digitally and were rewarded for maintaining the network or, more precisely stated, the blockchain."

"I think you should explain that briefly for your future readers."

"Fair enough."

With the original bitcoin, it worked like this: in order to conduct a transaction you needed a wallet where the bitcoins were kept, and then you could move bitcoins from wallet to wallet. The transactions were collected around every ten minutes and recorded in a document, the so-called block.

The bitcoin network is a peer-to-peer network, which means that everyone is cordially invited to participate in verifying the validity of these transactions. These participants operate the cores with special bitcoin software, and these then check the transaction and solve a mathematical riddle, in essence the encryption of the block, under certain conditions. The first one who produces the desired encryption receives a reward for it in the form of a newly-created bitcoin. You have to imagine that when the concept became known in 2009, there was no other possibility for making electronic payments anonymously. Back then you had accounts with banks or similar institutions that were all licensed by the government and only allowed currencies from governmental central banks.

A short time after bitcoin was invented, the first Internet drug markets were formed. The Tor network, the first of the dark webs back then, functioned through a combination of bitcoin and anonymous access, and in this way you could reach various resources through the Internet. As with most ideas, at least ones that are technical in nature, there was a huge media hype surrounding digital currencies. At least at first, and then they were forgotten or only bad news was published. The media mostly slept through the rise and rapid spread of digital currencies and the blockchain technology they were founded on. That also had its good side, as politics wasn't expecting it when it was hit by the power of blockchain technology.

Over the years, cryptocurrencies actually did get more and more popular, and besides drugs they were increasingly used for paying for work and consumption, and for almost everything in countries with hyperinflation. The step-by-step elimination of paper money further helped these currencies, as everything that you didn't want documented like prostitution, betting, gambling, alcohol, undocumented employment, or simply a vacation somewhere was paid in digital currency. But there were two problems.

The first was economy of scale. Since every bitcoin was just as good as another and production in larger units is always less expensive than in smaller ones, a concentration of power resulted. Fewer and fewer cores had more and more capacity and the originally democratic organization of the various blockchains turned into an oligarchy.

But I found the second problem even more concerning. It was a problem that gold already had.

It's very difficult to estimate how much gold there is in the world. Gold has been mined for thousands of years, and estimates back then assumed there was around 170,000 tons available. It's actually kind of funny, but some of the gold that we wear today as jewelry may have been mined by the ancient Romans. In any case, back in 2016, all the gold in the world constituted less than 1% of the total money supply.

The most widespread money at that point—and today too, by the way—was credit money. It made up around 90% of the money supply. Credit money is created when someone borrows money, just like what used to happen with banks. If you want to buy an apartment, for example, that let's say costs one million euro in the national currency back then, then the bank loaned you 700,000 euro, and in return it had a lien on your residence. If you didn't pay off the loan as agreed, then the bank would take away the apartment, sell it, and serve the loan with the proceeds.

This leads to the second problem that all the digital currencies had back then. Without credit money, the value of the currency had to rise to absurd heights in order to cover the worldwide demand for financing. Gold would have had to rise in price a hundred times over, not to mention bitcoin, a thousand times over....

But the fundamental problem, which most people didn't understand back then, was something completely different. Credit money has an extraordinary characteristic, although only in connection with a functioning registration of assets. If you own a piece of property, for example, and you can demonstrate ownership, then you can turn it into money by means of credit money. In particular, you can use it as collateral for a loan and develop it and make it more valuable through agriculture or construction.

But the most important thing is to demonstrably own the property in the first place. In Europe, the USA, and Japan, that had been possible for a long time. The ownership of real estate and land could be verified going back centuries. But in most countries of the world this wasn't the case. In South America, Africa, and many countries in Asia, it was completely unclear what belonged to whom. Families often lived for hundreds of years on a piece of land without appearing in a title register. Because of that, there was no interest in developing or investing in the parcel of land. In addition, there was a lack of trust that extended beyond the family, perhaps even because of the unclear ownership situation. In these conditions, it was very difficult to undertake anything on a large scale.

Of course it would have been theoretically possible at the time to replace credit money with gold. But I wanted to go further. I wanted to clarify the land titles and ownership relationships. I thought it would be best if all the land parcels and buildings that people could use as loan collateral were securely registered.

It actually is legitimate and possible to create money from an unencumbered property just with the intent of destroying the money again when the loan is repaid. And that's faster and simpler than having to find someone with enough gold or bitcoin to loan you the gold or the coin, particularly when you already have the asset in question.

That's why I considered credit money an entirely practical solution, as it disappears after repaying the loan. The way it works with credit money is that the money is created when the loan is made, and it's destroyed again when the loan is paid back.

Essentially, credit money represents a way to transform everything of value into a liquid asset, typically money, without exchanging it immediately for money, that is to say, selling it.

Let's say I have some real estate, and with the value of the real estate I guarantee repayment of a loan that you want so you can buy a car. For that we use credit money.

My friends and ideological wayfarers at the time from the Austrian school of economics didn't look at all kindly on credit money, they were more of the gold bug type who longed for the restoration of the gold standard. I myself was more of a pragmatist, or open to any currency that the market selected. In addition, it was perhaps not yet clear to them how much trust between people could be established through blockchain technology, which would release unforeseen potential.

I thought that the reason credit money had such a poor reputation back then was the enormous lack of transparency. Nobody knew what assets backed a bank's loans, so there were constantly bank failures; the whole system rested on feet of clay. Basically, everyone constantly feared a collapse of the entire system.

What was needed was a credit money system that was transparent. You would always know what the total value of all assets was because the assets themselves were reliably registered. Ideally there would be several credit money systems at the same time so that a competitive environment would develop.

I had the urgent need to create something that would privatize the money market again. Everyone should be able to use the money that they liked. In addition, whatever you thought of credit money, the success would be undeniable. My plan was that the best way to beat the nation states was with their own weapons, with credit money in a public ledger.

That's how I hit on the idea of ccoin.

"So ccoin really was your invention?"

"It was my project for sure, but to be fair it must be said that there were already other technologies, other currencies, in which you could have created credit money among other things, but everything would have become insanely complicated and cumbersome. I wanted to create something completely simple, so I made ccoin."

"Cool, let's drink on it!" Nadine rocks excitedly back and forth on her chair.

"I don't really have anything to celebrate because of it, but okay."

"Is that why you have so much money? I mean, you don't really work at all, do you?"

"Let's check our drinks and then we'll continue. I'm glad you find the story interesting in any case," I say, in an obvious attempt to distract from her question.

But she understands the hint and goes over to the refrigerator. There's a drink maker on the front of the refrigerator. The suggestion for Nadine is a Campari Mineral. She points upward, for something stronger, and Negroni is the next suggestion. Another wave, Blood and Sand, and that seems to please her. A press of a button and the device starts production. You can recognize the silhouette of a martini glass whose upper funnel is made of red glass and whose lower section is transparent. A bull is etched into the red glass, and a grid structure lies over the red liquid that smells of lemon.

"Awesome appliance, it's mind-blowing! It looks great, doesn't it? Plus the glass is stylish. What will you have?"

"I don't know. It's still so early...."

"Come on, we have to celebrate this!"

"Believe me, I've been celebrating it for decades...."

"Ha, fine, but not with me." She smiles because she knows she's won.

"Fine, make me a Singapore Sling. It comes in a really unusual cup, I've tried it already."

The Singapore Sling is served in a small statue: the head of a lion, the body of a fish. The material feels like marble, and the drink is located in the lion's mouth.

"That's so kitschy!"

"But it tastes fine," I said, defending my drink.

"Okay then. But come on, keep telling the story!"

Back then there were two trends in the digital currency circus. Those on the one side wanted to create digital currencies and gain their acceptance by nations and government offices. The wanted to move nations to accept and authorize their private currencies, as they believed in a democratic process that would allow other currencies to exist alongside the monopolistic currency. In their opinion peaceful coexistence would have been possible, but I thought the idea was naive.

The other, more radical side, in which I included myself, was rather revolutionary in temperament. For us, the state was the enemy and we saw in digital currency a realistic possibility to finally break the omnipresence and omnipotence of the nation states and the major banks associated with them.

"I have to explain briefly how the system functioned because it's important for the rest of the story, okay?"

"Sounds good, professor."

"In the ccoin system there were various participants, on the one hand the borrowers who wanted to finance something, let's say an excavator. So to the process is that the producer of the excavator, who also has control over the excavator through remote management, transfers control over ownership of the excavator to the blockchain. In the next step the guarantor comes into play. Let's say he transfers 20% of the price of the excavator as a guarantee to the ccoin blockchain, for example using a cryptocurrency or gold. The borrower then receives ccoin in the amount of the excavator's value, pays the producer, and receives the excavator. Now the borrower pays off the monthly installments. When he has paid all the installments, the excavator belongs to him and the ccoin that were borrowed are destroyed, or they're already destroyed with each installment."

"And if he doesn't pay?"

"Then the guarantor steps in with his 20% liability, or sells the excavator, which at this point actually belongs to the blockchain, and pays back the loan."

"Why does the guarantor do that?"

"Right, sorry, the guarantor receives interest. If we assume that the annual interest comes to 5%, then the guarantor earns 25% from his capital in the first year, which is quite a good deal. Because all the information about every contract is always available, you can verify the intrinsic value of the entire currency, or ccoin in this case, against the mortgaged assets. In addition, you can verify who the owner of the mortgaged property is even after the loan was repaid. So ccoin also developed into an international property register. That was of course the main problem back then when banks still managed this business. Nobody could say how valuable the loans actually were that the banks were making. National states were always stepping in and bailing banks out of their messes with tax revenues."

"That really doesn't sound so complicated."

"Generally speaking it isn't, but the devil's naturally in the details. There are still strategic reserves and things like that.... Notaries play an important role in the system as well because they often act as trustees who integrate assets into the blockchain and monitor the ownership structure. But it's actually relatively simple to understand. Following the example of Satoshi, the inventor of bitcoin, I wrote a white paper in which I explained the whole thing and published it in early 2016 under the pseudonym Hongli."

"How sweet!"

"Hongli was the birth name of Qianlong, the sixth Chinese emperor of the Qing dynasty and the most successful of all emperors, and for several years the ruler over a third of the world's population."

"Got it. So just your normal everyday megalomania."

"Exactly...."

I wanted to stay secret for many reasons, firstly because governments would cause trouble for me if my idea worked, and secondly because I didn't want to tie the idea to one person. And also because this secretive approach works well, as the participants would more easily identify with the technology and more readily accept it. If a specific person is behind it, then the users would have to declare themselves in agreement with this person and his ideology. After publication of the white paper,[59] the idea was generally well received, but it was strictly rejected by many people for ideological reasons because they were simply against the credit money system. In any case, the enthusiasm wasn't large enough that third parties stepped up to program the system I had thought up. Especially since there were already systems in which credit money could theoretically be produced, some of them even developed by respectable companies. In summer 2016 I set out to find programmers with knowledge in this area, that is to say in cryptology and blockchain technology.

As I wanted to remain anonymous, I relied on the dark web, which was already functioning quite well at the time. I found two programmers from Moscow. Alexander was an assistant professor for information technology on the faculty for system security and supercomputing at Lomonosov Moscow State University and an expert in cryptology. Mikhail was his acquaintance and supposedly one of his best students.

In summer 2016, when the university had its summer break, we started work. We handled everything online. I was never in Moscow and the two of them never visited me in Vienna. We never even had a video conference. I took care not to reveal my identity as far as was possible. By the end of the summer holidays we were almost done, at the end of the year we were still testing, and then in early 2017 we had a stable version.

Our software was simple to manage for the customer who wanted a loan and also for whoever wanted to act as a lender. We had created the basis software, the actual blockchain, and a program to manage the blockchain as well. Anyone who wanted could write a program like it. But to get things rolling, we thought it would be important to have one to start off with. That was "ccoinet." I paid the two of them the last installment for their work in bitcoin and left it open to them if they wanted to keep working on "ccoinet." With that their job as such was finished.

Then I made two crucial mistakes.

---

[59] The white paper can be found in the appendix in the original English.

"Oh dear. What was it this time?"

I had spent around 60,000 euro for the programming at that point, that would be around 5,000 ccoin today. I wanted to have a way to earn back the money somehow if the project was successful. With normal digital currencies, you could mostly produce currency very simply and inexpensively at the beginning and then hope that they would become more valuable in time so that you could make a profit. That wasn't possible in this case. I installed the ccoin blockchain and also the first five nodes and made the first transactions. For that I used various bitcoin and ether accounts that I mortgaged to create ccoin. I did that for a few days until a small exception occurred.

I opened a loan without a repayment date that was guaranteed by an internal account.

The account was an internal system account, a virtual account in which all ccoin that had ever existed in the system were recorded, including those that had already been destroyed when a loan was repaid. With this I was theoretically able to borrow an amount many times greater than the existing ccoin and would never have to pay it back.

In order to install this exception, I created a new version of the blockchain that allowed the exception. I used my own five nodes to authorize the transaction, created a new version of the software and closed the security flaw. That was in block55. I thought that if one day the whole thing went big then I would at least get my 60,000 euro back. If there were millions or even billions of ccoin, then no one would notice. Then I enacted many more transactions that were relatively meaningless. At first I didn't borrow anything. That would only happen much, much later.

"That sounds like a nice crime story. I mean, does it still work? Is that how you earn your dough?"
"I'll answer all that later."

The problems also came later. Strictly speaking, I was still calling it problem55. There were more and more crypto freaks who found the idea interesting and wanted to increase the amount of bitcoin that they had or just wanted ccoin. At the end of 2017 there were 120 nodes, 2000 wallets, and 800,000 ccoin, which came to 8 million euro at the time.

In order to promote my own invention as Hongli, I acted as a consultant for digital currencies, principally for ccoin actually. Back then I didn't tell anyone that I was behind the project. Only the two Russians knew about me, but they didn't know my real name. I founded a consulting firm for digital currencies and contacted companies to convince them to design their projects so that they could be controlled through the ccoin blockchain. To make loans possible, it was of course necessary to control the collateral. With a bitcoin wallet that was simple, the password was just changed through the ccoin blockchain. But with a car, for example, it was quite a bit more complicated. The stated goal of ccoin was to register assets that previously could not be registered, land parcels in particular, so that the owners would finally have security and be able to borrow against it without being dependent on banks. That's where the notaries came into play, especially for real estate. Many companies already had control over their products through remote management, for example with construction equipment, diagnostic instruments, motors, excavators, cranes, airplanes, ships, and much more. With the continued progress of the Internet of Things, more and more property could be controlled and then used as collateral for taking out a loan.

So I was constantly flying around the world to congresses, meet-ups, seminars, and cryptocurrency expos. I convinced Bitstamp,[60] Kraken,[61] and other cryptocurrency exchanges as well as other companies to integrate ccoin. In 2018, the first step out of the digital domain was taken when we convinced two online gold traders, who for their part were managing their holdings through a blockchain, to integrate the ccoin technology. So then you were able to mortgage your gold holdings and

---

[60] A cryptocurrency exchange based in Luxembourg.
[61] A cryptocurrency exchange based in the USA.

either take out a loan against it or make loans to others. Because the value of ccoin was bound to the assets on which it was based, the currency remained relatively stable—in contrast to the other digital currencies that were always quite volatile. Ultimately the total value of ccoin generally corresponds to the value of all the foundational assets.

I spent the following years continuing to collect art and promote ccoin. I also worked on various artworks. Back then I bought pieces by Mario Neugebauer, Erwin Wurm, Björn Segscheider, Konstantin Luser, Michael Marcovici, and many others.

CHAPTER 8

By the beginning of 2019, there were already 220 nodes, 8000 wallets, and 3 million ccoin. Most assets in the ccoin blockchain at the time were bitcoin, Monero, ether, iota, and gold. In summer 2019, the first vehicle, a Tesla X, was financed with ccoin. The buyer and also the financier were friends of mine. We made it into the international news media in any event, and for the first time there was wider interest in the currency. Several journalists even understood how the currency functioned. Some of them warned their readers right away against the currency, which was the best advertising we could wish for. During the course of 2019, another fifty cars were financed, some earth-moving equipment, and around ten larger machines. In 2020 there were already 10 million ccoin, the thing just grew and grew. The first house was financed, over 200 cars were integrated into the blockchain, and around 150 other machines. A small infrastructure grew up around the currency. More and more notaries were interested in the system, and especially certain industries were suddenly interested in it: the aircraft industry for leasing airplanes, the paper industry so that printing plants could finance new machinery, stock brokers, commodity traders, and many more.

I can still remember January 1, 2020 precisely. I had spent New Year's Eve with my friend Martin Bernegger, the publisher of Austria's second-largest online newspaper. There was champagne in abundance and even a little cocaine in the bedroom, but all in all it was a quiet evening. The children had their fun, and around midnight you could enjoy a panoramic view over Vienna and the fireworks from the terrace.

After midnight I retreated off somewhere like I always do to avoid having to waltz to the "Blue Danube," a horrible Viennese tradition. The conversations centered on Europe's and Austria's economic problems and on the upcoming secessions in Germany, Belgium, and Italy. Because of high inflation and generally bad economic conditions, I had assumed that

149

there would be fewer fireworks, but people's celebratory mood appeared to be undeterred.

Around two o'clock I drove home to Färber Alley with my daughter. While people were still partying wildly in the streets around me, I checked in on the ccoin world. There were 621 nodes, 49,203 active wallets, and 34,920,344 ccoin.

The project had definitely taken off. Because of inflation and all the new taxes on real estate and capital, my savings had evaporated. I was in a financial vice, I had two children in private schools, two ex-wives, relatively high living expenses, and hardly any income. The amounts I was planning to steal were minimal compared to the total supply of ccoin, so it would increase the money supply each year only by a thousandth of a percent, but the risk I was taking was enormous.

Somebody could find out what I was doing and blackmail me, or the whole thing might be made public and inflict harm on the project or even cause it to collapse. On top of that, many countries had already declared ccoin illegal and were fighting against it. A security flaw like this one that let an unknown person fatally inflate an entire currency that was considered impossible to counterfeit—it would mean giving the enemies of ccoin the best gift they could ask for.

But in the end I had no choice. I justified my intervention with the fact that ccoin was my creation, that I had worked hard for it, and that I was to a certain degree entitled to the money. I had spent a significant amount to advertise the currency, after all, and had invested a lot of time in it. In hindsight, what really astonishes me is that I as the founder didn't just officially take a dividend of a thousandth of the money supply every year. If I had built that in from the beginning, I'm now convinced, no one would have taken offense. But back then I chose a much riskier alternative instead, an alternative that could have landed me and all other ccoin creditors in serious trouble.

"I agree, no one would have complained if you had been officially paid as the founder. Work is rewarded with money after all, so why should it be any different for you?"

"I've often thought about that. It must have something to do with my personality—a part of my personality that I really don't like. I seem to lack self-esteem. I didn't feel like I was allowed to ask for it. At the same time, it was all the more clear to me that I was completely entitled to it. Schizophrenic, somehow."

"Poor David."

The password was the one I used for several other accounts. I applied for a 10,000 ccoin loan to the contract that I had embedded in Block55, and gave my approval with the five nodes that I still managed. The money was transferred to one of my wallets. Then I repeated the whole thing a few times until I had collected 100,000 ccoin. So in a half hour I had as much money as I had spent in the last five years.

It took a few days and required several acts of obfuscation in order to exchange the ccoin anonymously for Monero,[62] and then finally for euros. But the money wasn't like other money I had earned. It somehow felt like it was stolen. I had the urge to spend it as quickly as possible. On the day it became available, I ordered dozens of things from OpenBazaar, where I could pay in bitcoin, AliExpress, and Amazon. Clothing, computers, toys, delicacies, bed sheets, furniture, lamps, a washing machine. The same day I bought an art piece by Michael Marcovici, a steel sculpture of a heart studded with slivers of glass that was defending itself that I'd had my eye on for some time. In order to get even more money, I bought cash on the dark web, chiefly euro notes and gold coins. And, since I was already there, some weed, Viagra, and cocaine as well.

The cocaine came a week later by mail. I hadn't touched cocaine in years, and I'd actually done coke maybe five times in my life, but on New Year's Eve I'd somehow thought it was cool and wanted to at least have a

---

[62] Monero, a cryptocurrency that has existed since 2014 in which money flows cannot be followed and is therefore a currency perfectly suited for concealed transactions. After 2020, Monero and some other currencies surpassed the first cryptocurrency, Bitcoin, which was technologically unable to keep up with the newer currencies.

little at home in case I felt the urge to take some. The urge hit a few hours later, and the urge for alcohol and sex along with the cocaine. And so my favorite evening routine took shape, consisting of around a gram of the finest cocaine, a quarter liter of vodka, and seven hours with prostitutes.

Unfortunately we have to stop at precisely this point. Nadine has to go, as she still wants to meet people, and I go to bed. In the night I have an odd dream in which I suddenly realize that Block55 would come to an end one day. I still wanted to enjoy as many things as possible and stuff my whole life into the time I still had left. In my dream I consumed vast quantities of food, alcohol, and drugs. I bought huge machines, airplanes, and I transferred enormous sums of money out of Block55 again and again, billions in ccoin. People pleaded with me to stop but I had to keep going, no sense of responsibility or prick of conscience could stop me, my goal was the destruction of ccoin and with it my own destruction.

The next morning, we continued with the writing on the terrace of the 128th floor.

The year 2021 saw numerous political and economic changes. No major ones, but signs of decay in Europe were unavoidable. For one thing, as already mentioned, a culture of inflation had spread. Everyone tried to take on as much debt as possible, because by this point it was clear to everyone that the major fiat currencies, the euro and the dollar, were approaching their end. And in fact an unusual shifting of wealth was taking place. Those who were able to borrow money—large companies, but also lawyers and other high earners with good contacts in the financial and political worlds—went into debt beyond all measure. The central banks kept printing money and bought up much of the debt directly in the form of bonds.

It was similar to the crisis of 2008. Back then all the banks had bought mortgage-backed securities on a grand scale in the assumption that home mortgages were completely safe. But the mortgages were in fact in miserable condition, the borrowers paid irregularly, and the houses were unsellable. Despite that, business went well for years.

With the major currencies, the dollar and the euro, things were similar. The only assets backing the currency was loan collateral. But interest rates had been stuck at zero or even negative for years, so people took on more and more loans with higher and higher risk. They bought real estate at horrendous prices with returns of only 1%, so that if interest rates rose even a little, no one would be able to pay off their loans. That risk was now part of the currency, but not many people realized it.

By now there were 770 nodes, 50,000 wallets, and 120 million ccoin, and thousands of vehicles and hundreds of real estate properties had been financed. Some shipping firms, first and foremost the Weiss brothers, permitted the integration of shipping containers and warehouse goods into the block chain so that the financing of consumer goods and machinery also become possible.

Some things started to happen on the financial side, too. There were attempts to repackage and resell loans from the blockchain, whether packets of auto loans or small shares in several different loans. There was also an attempt to take out a loan against securities. That required a circuitous route at first, however, because banks refused to cooperate. Even the first insurance policies were replicated in the blockchain.

The political situation in Europe and the USA was becoming increasingly tense. In Europe, France was experiencing the outbreak of severe unrest that was soon christened the "Intifada française." Only after the unrest had broken out and two police officers had been killed, the mayor of Marseille admitted to having lost control over some districts of the city years earlier. The national guard was called to Marseille to restore order, but after weeks of fighting where youths pelted the police and national guard with Molotov cocktails, home-built rockets, and rocks, the security forces withdrew and something like a ghetto took shape in the city.

No one could enter or exit from the Camas, Noailles, and Belsunce districts without passing through checkpoints. In the following weeks it came out that the checkpoints had actually already existed, but the checkpoints to these neighborhoods had been set up by the residents themselves, who were almost entirely foreigners. In order to prevent the situation from escalating further, the checkpoints remained in place. Belsunce, Camas, and Noailles were now ruled by Sharia law or by no law at all, and other French cities were heading toward similar conditions.

For me personally, it was an unusual time. My access to Block55 was not entirely healthy for me. I looked at it as stolen money, and it was difficult to buy anything useful because that would have attracted the authorities' attention. I saved a little, especially ether, dash, and Monero. I used the money that I could withdraw in euros or dollars above all for my pleasures: food, drugs, women. At first only once every one or two months, but eventually more and more often, soon weekly, then daily. I didn't have to work or think about my income. Then again, I couldn't tell anybody that I had money, let alone where it was from, so I kept taking drugs and enjoying myself.

In this way I gathered a group of friends: pretty girls, artists, night owls, prostitutes, authors. I can't complain about this period. My health was in a pitiful state, and I had practically lost my ability to remember things, but I had a lot of fun. It went on like that without interruption for around two years.

In 2022 there were already 200 million ccoin and over 1000 nodes. In the media and Internet forums, people had puzzled for a long time over who was behind ccoin, and they usually guessed someone Chinese due to the Hongli pseudonym. Sometimes it was Craig Steven Wright, an Australian already nominated as the inventor of bitcoin. But I was too busy partying to follow what was going on too closely. Apart from going out, getting money from Block55 was my chief occupation.

It must have been around February 2022, the time of year when Vienna is a sad gray city. In order to console myself about this fact, I had spent almost the whole night at a sauna club.

Finally around noon, I came home completely wasted, with around six hours to sleep before I had to take care of my daughter. The phone rang while I was in the hall, and I hurried into the apartment and saw it was an unknown number, so I thought it was one of the girls who I had given my number to and didn't pick up. A minute later it rang again, and again. My head hurt and I was tired, but also curious. Maybe I had left something like money or coke somewhere. On the other end was a man who spoke English.

"David, how are you? You don't remember me, do you?"

"Oh hi, well not really. Who are you?"

"Mikhail, your programmer. Remember?"

My heart, that beat too fast to be healthy as it was, almost leaped out of my chest. I knew immediately that this meant nothing good. It was more than an evil premonition.

"I am in Vienna. Let's go for a coffee."

"I can't right now, I'm sorry, what about tomorrow?"

"David, come down now. I know where you are and what you do. Better we talk now. I will wait for you at the Café Naber on Wipplinger Street in ten minutes."

I took a big swig of water and tried to freshen up somehow, changed my shirt quickly and looked for my sunglasses. I was too tired to think up an excuse. I knew it was a mistake to meet him now in my wretched condition, but I didn't have the strength to avoid it. So I went down to Café Naber, only a hundred meters away. Mikhail was in the back room. I had never seen him, but he must have researched my appearance, as he recognized me right away.

"Hey Hongli. Looks like you had a funny night, my friend."

"Yes, somewhat. So what brings you to Vienna?"

"What do you think?"

"I have no idea, it's a very popular destination for tourists, maybe the heritage of the Habsburgs? Or the Prater, if you like roller coasters."

"You used to have more imagination when we talked the last time."

"Look, just tell me, as you must have put some effort into finding me. I don't assume you came here only to chat with me about old times, especially since I prefer to stay anonymous."

"Ccoin is doing well. Aren't you happy?"

"Yes, it's doing very well. Sure I'm happy, and amazed as well."

"Me too, but I am only amazed and not happy like you. It seems you have forgotten me."

"I'm not sure what you mean...."

"Ha ha. Yes, I think you know exactly what I mean. Look, David, I want my share of the deal, my friend. I know what you do. I know that some code was removed in version 0.94 and that it was put back in place in 0.96. It's very obvious to me why you did this."

"You think so? Why?"

"Because in one of the blocks between 12 and 87, there is one block where you made some shady deal with the blockchain. A leak, a flaw, a hole in the treasury box. You borrow against the wall."

"That's new to me."

"Don't bullshit me. I want my share. Now."

"I really don't know what you mean. This hypothetical event is now almost ten years in the past. There's no flaw or anything today. And even if there were, it's none of your business. This is a public ledger and not a business partnership."

"It was exactly five years ago. But good point. It's a public ledger. So I guess this flaw should be made public too, right? Look, I did my homework. I found you. I checked the versions that you manipulated back then. I am not stupid. Don't mess with me. How much did you take?"

Mikhail was fast and direct, and in my condition I wasn't up to it. I could only think about bed and wanting to never see the guy again. Maybe there would have been a chance to keep myself out of it, but in my moment of weakness I wasn't capable of it.

"About 80,000 ccoin so far."

"From now on we are partners. When you take one coin, I get one coin, understood? I am not stupid and I am not greedy. I want 80,000 now and then at least 10,000 every month. I will send you the details where to store them."

"And if I don't comply?"

"No problem for me. But you know, my friends don't like that. I know your name. I know where you live and I do not need to elaborate on all the possible troubles I could create for you and ccoin. When you pay me I will work with you to keep this a secret. And help you to avoid troubles. From now on we are partners!"

I thought that the 10,000 per month might be the basis for negotiations, since after all it's as much as a small car every month. And I still had some questions of my own, as it appeared that the Boy Scout super student had changed from a programming genius into a small-time criminal, but just at the moment he finished talking, he stood up and left the café without saying goodbye and without paying.

I paid for his coffee, went back to the apartment, and tried to sleep.

I paid from now on. In the final analysis it hardly mattered in comparison to the total supply of ccoin, and I didn't want even more problems than I already had. But of course it was totally unpleasant, as I didn't know what the next step would be. Taking the password from me? Demanding more? Mikhail had me completely under his control.

In the following months our deal ran quite unproblematically, however. Mikhail was actually quite a nice guy, so I always withdrew the double amount and sent him half via various cryptocurrencies that we had prearranged. We never saw each other again in person, but we chatted almost weakly and discussed new currencies and blockchain projects, especially ccoin. In time, Mikhail became a good friend, certainly also because he was the only one who I could discuss ccoin with. For a whole year I had some peace and quiet again and everything ran as usual.

The year 2024 was an especially successful one for ccoin. There was a gigantic leap upward in the money supply, from 350 million at the beginning of 2023 to over 800 million ccoin in summer 2024. The reason was that two international stock brokers, Interactive Brokers and Swissquote, allowed their customers to mortgage their balances or bonds to the ccoin blockchain. That set off a boom, as everyone who had an account with one of those banks could now leverage their investments, which had been impossible for private customers before that point. The money supply tripled within a few months after the announcement, and others followed, and it seemed to be heading for a turning point for ccoin.

There were even more developments concerning ccoin, including one that was particularly interesting and unexpected. Especially in emerging markets, in the Congo, Zimbabwe, Ecuador, Venezuela, and

Ghana, the blockchain started being used as a property registry. The official registries in these countries were highly unreliable, changes weren't recorded for years or simply forgotten, and corrupt officials changed property registry entries arbitrarily. The ccoin blockchain solved this problem. The entry in the property registry could serve for borrowing money against real estate, which encouraged investment in these countries in order to increase the value of the land parcels. An interesting symbiosis arose between local property owners, national and international investors, and local and sometimes even international security forces that now guarded the properties in order to protect their investments. This created for the first time in these areas the possibility of borrowing money, investing, and enjoying security. People drew confidence from this. Their possibilities were suddenly expanded, and a better future seemed to be possible.

Ccoin was not yet regarded as a threat in Europe, but steadily declining currency values, lack of economic growth, and high taxes led to more and more political upheaval and massive efforts toward secession. After England, France, and the Netherlands, now Germany, Italy, and Spain wanted to separate from the EU or renegotiate their membership. Wallonia wanted to separate from Belgium, Wales from England, and Venice from Italy. South Tyrol prepared for a referendum, Bavaria wanted out of the Euro completely, and Brittany and Catalonia considered introducing their own currencies.

But the year still had some surprises in store for me. In the fall of 2024, I received a call from Moscow. It was Alexander, Mikhail's professor, who had programmed ccoin for me. He wanted me to come to Moscow to discuss something. He said it was important and I had nothing to fear. I guessed that Mikhail was behind it and contacted him immediately after my discussion with Alexander. I sent him an e-mail: "Mikhail, we need to talk ASAP, can you call now? It's urgent!"

His answer came at one: "Yes, call me on telegram."

"Mikhail, what is your current relation to Alexander?"

"I have not heard from him in a long time. Maybe five years, maybe more."

"He contacted me today!"

"That sounds like bad news."

"Yes, he says there is some problem and we need to talk and I should come to Moscow to talk to him."

"And?"

"And of course I am not going to Moscow."

"That's a wise decision, David."

"Look, I think it's clear that he knows something."

"Yes, that's possible. Sounds like he does."

"Do you know what his job is at the moment?"

"I think he is a security expert at Kaspersky."

"No, he is a security expert for the Russian government."

"That's bad. That's very bad."

"Yes, that's bad."

"So what did you say?"

"I told him if he wants to meet, we can meet in Vienna. He told me he will get back to me. He will come here for sure, so it looks like he wants his share, too."

"I don't think so. It's not his style. He is a true believer. Believes in the state. But you will see. There's not much I can do for you."

A week later I got a message from Alexander: "We meet at Hotel 25, Vienna Airport, Suite 221, eleven o'clock. Only you and me."

I answered: "We can meet in the lobby."

Alexander was already there when I entered the lobby of Hotel 25 near the airport. The lobby was small, with around ten tables, and I could easily see all of it. Alexander was tall and half bald, with a high forehead. He was wearing a metallic blue suit, and on the table in front of him was an Nvidia Titanium, an ultra-high end smart phone. It consisted for all purposes of a single block of Titanium in which all the components were fused with each other: the screen, the battery, and the quantum computer were housed within the one homogenous part. The whole thing was at the same time a screen and a sensor, transmitter, and receiver. It was the absolute top of the line model on the market.

"David, great to see you finally."

159

"Hi, Alexander."

"It's great to finally meet you in person. I was curious, after so many years."

"How was your flight?"

"Fine, went good. Come have a seat. Would you like to drink something?"

"I'm fine, thanks."

"Should we get to the point immediately?"

"Sure, why not?"

"Does Block55 mean anything to you?"

"Nothing."

"David, what does Block55 contain? If you can tell me."

"I don't know, I don't even know what you're referring to."

"David, I am not here for my own pleasure. I am here because I work for the Russian government and we would like some answers. Otherwise I am forced to make public that ccoin was your idea, and on top that there is a major issue in Block55."

"Alexander, I don't know what you are talking about, but here in this setting with your super phone on the table, we will not have a private conversation. If you want to talk privately with me, we can do it in the *onsen* of the ANA airport hotel at Terminal 4."

Alexander was anything but enthusiastic, but I didn't want someone else recording me talking about Block55 like Mikhail had presumably done two years ago. He agreed to keep talking in the *onsen*, although as it turned out he had no idea that an *onsen* is a traditional Japanese bath.

The *onsen* is on the top floor of the ANA hotel at the new Terminal 4. In the changing room, you remove all your clothing. In the next room you wash while sitting on a small wooden stool. In front of you there's a shower hose, shampoo, soap, razor, toothbrush, dental wipes, and shaving cream.

After we both washed—and after I shaved, in order to gain more time to think about my strategy—we went out to the baths. There were four different baths on the terrace with a view over the forests and the airport: a large warm bath, a cold bath, and two baths with green tea. We found a place in one of the green tea baths where the temperature was a bearable 34 degrees Celsius. There were six other people in the *onsen*, all of them Asians, and I felt some degree of safety here.

Alexander was amused by my caution. He laughed about the whole operation: "I really did not expect to end up here all naked with you in a Japanese bathtub. But I like it, it's beautiful. I hope you have answers fast. It's pretty hot in here and I mean the temperature. Ha ha. So look, I know something is wrong in Block55. I don't know exactly what it is, but I could research it. I have lots of capacities. I just thought we both save each other time, nerves, and money."

"What do you think is wrong?"

"Someone borrows ccoin out of the block, probably against the wall. And it seems you made two more versions of the software after we finished our job in 2017. But the second version is exactly identical to the version we handed over to you and the source code for the version before is not available. It wasn't audited well. This stinks a lot."

"Well, okay."

"You are obviously borrowing against some internal resource or some imaginary resource from the chain, probably without intention to ever pay it back and without any underlying asset."

"I have only taken back my investment."

"How much can you borrow, what is the limit?"

"I don't know."

"David, I work for my government, not for a Montessori kindergarten."

I had to interpret that as a threat, as my daughter went to a Montessori kindergarten. In the hot pool, I suddenly felt hotter, and an unpleasant feeling spread inside me.

"I can borrow."

"David, I will make it simple for you. We want control over the blockchain and the nodes. We are ready to compensate you for this, but we want the absolute control."

"I'd rather close the bug."

"I said we want control over it. Ccoin is becoming a threat to established currencies. It's a powerful instrument for us. And don't bullshit me because you cannot close the bug. I know at least that."

"Alexander, when we developed ccoin, it was clear that the intention was to develop a currency that would compete with fiat currencies. A money for the people so everybody can lend and borrow, not controlled by states. If I give you control now, it will destroy the whole project. People will stop using it and in the end, nobody gains anything. Why doesn't your wonderful government come up with its own currency in order to provide a better one than ccoin? Compete with it. That's the normal way to do business."

"Sure, David, keep on dreaming. Look, we want the control. Nobody will know it. It will be a secret."

"Maybe other governments have already contacted me. Maybe I've granted control to another government already."

"Did you?"

"Maybe."

"David, you are a fool. You believe you can fight all governments with ccoin? What you do is dangerous. If you think it through, governments will lose control over the money and will lose power and control over other important aspects of life. Who will provide security when the government cannot do it anymore?"

"Governments provide security? The last time I checked, governments killed 400 million people in the last two hundred years alone. I think humankind will be much better off without governments."

"You are being polemic now. You know that the world needs law and order and strong governments to maintain order and stability. And security and to steer the economy."

"I can't believe you actually believe that, I mean, just look at countries today, and especially the history of your own nation. The more a government is in charge, the poorer the country ends up. If there is less government, the people are better off. The whole world is moving in a new direction where centralized entities are becoming decentralized and self-managed. Public ledgers are taking over government organizations. What you do is just a last attempt to get some power back for your criminal government."

"I doubt we will convince each other here in this discussion. What are your options, anyway?"

"Alexander, for me there are three possible outcomes to the situation. The first one is that I actually do convince you that you will harm people by giving your government power over the ccoin blockchain. The second is that I offer you a bribe. The third, of course, is that I could close the bug or, more precisely, destroy my password and lose my income. The last option is to make a deal and hand over to you the power you believe I have."

"Option number five: we publish documents that will prove the bug exists and destroy ccoin."

"I doubt that information would destroy it. I could respond to the accusations and then we'll see what people believe. Perhaps they trust me more than your government. I would have a good chance, I'd guess. I mean, I have not seriously compromised the blockchain so far, have I?"

"That was the end of my conversation with Alexander at the time. He thought that I should let him know my decision as soon as possible."

"I have to go bathe, too," says Nadine.

"Shouldn't we get going soon? To that spa and restaurant in the mountains, I thought it was in Burma? Is that right, Watson?"

"Yes, that's correct. The Sanon[63] is located on a hill in the Burmese jungle. I recommend beginning at 6:00 PM. You will need a fast drone, which I would reserve for you right now. It is around 170 kilometers away, so the flight by drone will take around 35 minutes. You can book massages and everything else on the spot," says Watson.

"Perfect. Thanks!"

We're seated in the drone looking backward so that the evening sun isn't blinding us the whole flight. It's a fantastic view, first the outer

---

[63] The Sanon lies on the border with Thailand in the middle of the Burmese jungle. It can only be reached by drone, and the nearest road is around 40 kilometers away.

districts of Bangkok, then the surrounding region, and then the Burmese jungle, but the flight makes me feel completely ill. The Sanon is a combination spa, restaurant, and lounge, and it also has a few rooms for overnight stays. The whole complex lies completely isolated in the middle of the jungle, no cars, no houses, no people far and wide.

The Sanon itself is a wooden construction in the style of the northern Thai palaces. The restaurant is on the terrace that surrounds the building, and underneath are rooms for various treatments. Nadine has decided on a classic Thai massage, while I'm in the whirlpool and enjoy the view of the jungle while having the new novel by Leif Randt[64] read aloud to me.

We meet on the terrace and find a place at one of the low tables that are undoubtedly going to ruin my knees.

"How was your massage?"

"I feel like a freshly hatched chick. How was it with you?"

"A curious comparison. I read, or had a book read to me."

"Which book?"

"Leif Randt, *Rubbish Dumps*."

"Never heard of it. Do you know Saile Nettican?"[65]

"Never heard of it. What is it?"

"A unique type of literature. Saile describes different worlds, to be precise fifty-two worlds, very peculiar ones. Nobody could think up something so detailed."

"Oh, Saile is an AI?"

"Exactly, and writes ingenious stuff. And it gives us an exciting insight into how artificial intelligences design and describe their own worlds through a creative process. Absolutely worth reading. You read books by people the rest of the time anyway."

"What did you read by the AI?"

"Gretchen."

---

[64] Leif Rand, *Rubbish Dumps*.
[65] Saile Nettican, *Worlds*.

"Gretchen?[66] What's that?"

"Goethe. Have you heard of him?"

"Very funny. Of course. And?"

"Goethe tells the story of Gretchen, who appears in his book *Faust*, I think. The action is described from her perspective, but it plays out in the Orient, in the Ottoman Empire of the seventeenth century. Supposedly one of the best books by an AI."

"I've read a few books by AIs, most recently a joke book that was really great. Apparently it's simple to decode and reproduce the linguistic structure of jokes. You should take a look, a few really funny jokes are in there."

"Tell me one!"

"Well, I don't remember many of them, but I know a few from earlier."

"Oh man, no one tells jokes any more today. Come on, tell me one, please!"

"Okay, fine. This is my favorite joke: Kohn goes into a coffee shop and orders apple strudel. The waiter brings the apple strudel and Kohn looks at it, and it looks a bit dry. So then he calls the waiter over. 'Waiter, could I trade the apple strudel for a cheese strudel?' 'Of course, sir. No problem.' The waiter takes the apple strudel away and brings a cheese strudel. Kohn eats it, puts on his coat and leaves. The waiter runs after him. 'Hey, you didn't pay!' 'What should I pay for?' 'The cheese strudel!' 'But I gave you the apple strudel for it.' 'Yes, but you didn't pay for that either.' 'But I didn't eat it, did I?'"

"Ha ha ha, that's good. That could be you. Another one!"

"I have to think for a moment."

"Oh, come on!"

"Do you know the elephant joke?"

"No."

"So, Jankel and Moishe meet on the street. 'Jankel, how are you?' asks Moishe. 'Really fantastic! We have an elephant. He's wonderful. He

---

[66] *Gretchen*, by an AI modeled on Goethe, tells the story of Gretchen from *Faust*.

takes care of the garden, he cleans the house, makes breakfast, brings the kids to school, and at night he watches the kids, reads them stories, and he helps my wife with the shopping. It's a dream, we have a totally new life, I tell you.' 'That sounds great. Say, how much does an elephant like that cost?' 'It's not exactly cheap, around 10,000 dollars. I can get one for you,' says Jankel. '10,000 dollars? Whoa, that's expensive.' 'It is, but think about it: babysitting, cleaning, taking care of the yard. He'll help out your wife everywhere, and it will pay for itself quickly.' 'Fine. You know what, I'll take an elephant.' Three weeks later, Jankel and Moishe meet again on the street, and Jankel ask Moishe, 'So, how's it going with the elephant?' 'Don't ask, the whole thing's a catastrophe. Not a bit of washing, cleaning, or helping out. The yard is ruined, the apartment is destroyed, the kids are afraid, and my wife wants to divorce me. The elephant has ruined my life!' And then Jankel replied: 'Well, you'll never sell an elephant like that.'"

"Ha ha ha, I'm laughing my head off. That's the best one yet. Do you know another one?"

"Oh, one more. A man goes walking on the beach and finds a bottle. He picks it up, and suddenly a genie emerges. The genie says, 'Hey, thanks, I'm finally out of the bottle. For that I'll fulfill one wish for you, whatever you want. I'll fulfill any wish.' 'Oh wow, that's great. I actually do have a wish. I have a terrible fear of flying and an even bigger fear of ships. But I'd really like to go to America. Could you build a bridge for me so that I can drive my car to America?' 'Hm, well, that's 6,000 kilometers of highway, with amenities, restaurants, hotels, and gas stations, and the Atlantic is up to 6,000 meters deep. Listen, sorry, but think of something normal. That's an insanely complicated wish!' 'Okay, sorry. There's one other thing. I keep meeting women, but things never really take off between us. I think I don't understand women. Could you make it so that I understand women?' The genie thinks for a moment and says, 'Um, let's go back to that thing about the highway.'"

"Ha ha, very funny, really. I like that one the best of all," says Nadine, grinning.

"You have to admit it's not bad."

"I only know a few jokes, but this one is good. A lizard and a monkey meet in the forest, and the monkey says, 'Hey lizard, what's up? I have some seriously good weed. Come on, let's smoke a joint.' 'Okay,' says the lizard. The two of them climb into a tree, the monkey rolls the joint, and the two smoke it. After some time the monkey says, 'I'm so stoned right now, it's crazy.' Then the lizard says, 'Yeah, I'm totally stoned too. But I'm really thirsty, I've just got to drink something.' 'Okay,' says the monkey. 'I'll wait here, I wouldn't manage to get all the way down there and to the river.' On the way to the river, the lizard meets a crocodile. 'Hey crocodile, what's up? I just smoked a joint with the monkey and we're so stoned it's crazy.' 'Really?' says the crocodile, 'Where?' 'Back there at the tree. Come over to us, there's still some weed left.' The crocodile sets out for the tree and when it gets there it says, 'Hey monkey!' The monkey looks down, gets scared, and says, 'Are you insane? Just how much water did you drink?'"

"Hilarious, I'll include that one in my repertoire," I say, laughing.

"Our food's here now."

The food at the Sanon mostly consists of fish, which is entirely normal in Burma. You eat everything with your right hand, which begins to hurt from the spiciness of the food after a while. The Sanon lives above all from the amazing location and the discrepancy between the modern long-haul drones you take to get here, and the strictly traditional cuisine. As widespread as these small drones are today, you still don't fly around in them all that much.

CHAPTER 9

The next day, we kept going during breakfast in my suite.

"We're somewhere around 2026, aren't we?"

"Yes, exactly."

After the meeting with Alexander, things calmed down again and I didn't hear anything else from him for a while. Then in summer 2026, there was an odd incident. Almost every summer I visited Altaussee, a fantastic place in the Salzkammergut in Austria. Mostly I'd stay for a few days with friends in a house in town and then set out into the mountains, sometimes with friends, or a girlfriend, or my son or daughter. We'd set out from Altaussee across Mt. Loser, first to the Apple House hostel where we'd spend the night, and then from there farther in the direction of the Totes mountain chain to the Pühringer hostel.

The Pühringer hostel is especially good. I've been going there repeatedly since I was young. Apart from the great location, you always meet a particular type of person there. Very Austrian people, at least. You know, academics, highly educated, thirteenth district of Vienna. On the one hand aloof, but on the other hand down-to-earth and athletic, a very distinct group. That summer I was up there with two friends from Vienna, Oskar Ohlmann and Jakob Levi, and my daughter Sandra. After two days of hiking, we came to Pühringer in the late evening. It was Friday or Saturday and there was a lot going on inside. People were drinking and singing and everyone was sitting together in the large hall. Almost everyone knew everyone else, a not untypical hostel crowd, parents and their adult children like us, mostly university educated, Austrian through and through.

They asked us where we were from, and answering with Vienna never goes over well in a hostel like that. We'll get you eventually, they said, and then you'll see, half in jest and half in earnest. So a discussion started, and our partners in conversation all knew each other. A mix of police and state-rejecting sovereign citizens, unpleasant, xenophobic, highly patriotic, undoubtedly anti-Semitic as well, but not stupid. I always get curious when I meet with rejection. I find it especially interesting and stimulating.

The sovereign citizen, they've been around for a while. At first it was a few loosely connected groups who were mostly scammers and esoteric kooks, but over the years, a few extremely interesting groups have formed. Interestingly, the government came down extremely hard on them from the start, even though it was all completely ridiculous in the beginning, but for the government, the fun stopped right there.

It was an odd evening in any event. These people definitely had good arguments, and they thought the government was coming to its end and would soon fall. One of the men at our table kept making references to the fact that everything was prepared, and that the government's days were numbered, and so on.

They were basically libertarian, but all on the hard right. They were also familiar with ccoin and cryptography. They thought it was the duty of every patriot to try to do something before politics completely ruined the country economically and culturally. Reject taxes, give Austria back to the Austrians, stuff like that. Well, that was the end of it, I thought, they're just crackpots, but apparently they had a real plan.

"Let's hike up to the hostel. How long does it take you to walk?"

"I'd like to do that. I haven't been there in years. From Almsee it takes around six hours. I've been going up there for fifty years, and it's truly the only place in Austria where nothing actually changes. The food has gotten better because the hostels are all supplied by drone now, which is cheaper than by helicopter. The beer is brewed right at the hostels and the rooms are nicer. But around the hostel, everything is like it used to be."

"Okay, let's do that when we get back. What happened next?"

At the time there was an increasing need for action because in 2025 and 2026, inflation was climbing rapidly. Wealth was being eaten up and everyone was trying to take out loans. Cryptocurrencies were already playing a major role in the market. Bitcoin, bitcoinX, Monero, ccoin, dash, and the many ICOs and CTAs[67] offered wealthy people an additional investment opportunity besides real estate, art, and securities. The US dollar and the euro decreased in value massively because of secessions. The separation of Sweden from the EU caused the euro to lose 10% of its value in one day. Texas's announcement that it wanted to split from the United States sent the dollar into decline. At this point, ccoin had already financed thousands of vehicles and tens of thousands of residential and commercial properties, and new goods were constantly being added to the blockchain.

Hyperinflation started in 2027. The euro had an official inflation rate of less than 10% annually, but prices were actually rising at a gallop. It felt more like 50%. Stocks, real estate, and cryptocurrencies were all booming according to official statistics, but that was only a manifestation of the euro's inflation.

"And what were you doing at the time?" Nadine asked.

Block55 ruined me. It was such easy money, but it was stolen and not earned. It was odd, the money had no real value for me. Mostly I ordered cash or gold coins on the dark web in large amounts, and then a package full of bills or coins would show up. I quickly exchanged the coins around the corner from me at the Schoeller Coin Trading Company on Wipplinger Street. Then I had a weird feeling. It felt good; walking around with so much money in your pocket makes you safe. I always had a lot of cash with me. But a feeling of treachery also engulfed me. I felt the compulsion to get rid of the stolen money as quickly as possible. Just like

---

[67] Coin Traded Assets, a form of cryptoasset introduced in 2019 in which various underlying assets are traded and (as with futures) buyers and sellers can sell assets long or short, for example gold, oil, or cotton, and later real estate, art, and much more, similar to an exchange-traded fund.

thieves, gamblers, or prostitutes have the same feeling, because in their view the money was earned immorally, so they spend it again quickly.

So I established a routine for spending the money quickly. I bought artworks, mostly from artists in the area I was friends with, Christian Eisenberger, Alex Ruthner, Michael Marcovici, Mario Nubauer, Raymond Pettibon, Christian Rosa, but also Banksy, Erwin Wurm, and Thomas Demand. Once when I was totally drunk, I even bought a picture by Fontana just to annoy a girlfriend.

The artworks were the best thing I bought, but otherwise I kept spending money on food, partying, women, and drugs. Funnily, all the partying came to an abrupt end on my birthday at the beginning of September. I didn't plan to go out, but I wanted to hike on the Wechsel if I could find appropriate partners for taking a few psychedelic mushrooms. That morning when I woke up, there were already fifty missed calls on my cell phone. A lot of numbers that I didn't know. At first I thought it might be my golden anniversary after all, as with age you get to be unsure how old you really are, but no, when I read the messages it was clear at once that the Russians had revealed my identity to the media.

"Oh dear. What happened to you?" said Nadine. She rocked excitedly in her chair.

I don't know why, but I had to weep. I couldn't read the messages at first, it was just so overwhelming. It was like coming home for me. I didn't want to tell anyone that I had created ccoin, so I only had Mikhail, the programmer and criminal, who I could talk to about it. Of course I was enormously proud. Many news outlets reported it, and I became famous over night. I had the best birthday in my life: interviews with CNBC, CNN, the BBC, stations from Australia, Poland, Russia, various Youtube channels and so on. I did nothing else the whole day. I don't like to admit it, but it was fantastic. Suddenly I was famous.

The odd thing was that these people from the media asked me about all kinds of things that I had no clue about like economics, politics, science, even sports and culture. Apparently they assumed if you knew about one thing, you'd have a handle on everything else.

I was invited to conferences and talk shows and so on. Then in the following weeks I became more cautious, as I had had my reasons for not wanting to be known. I feared lawsuits and problems with governments, and there was also the matter of Block55.

And ultimately it was clear to me that this was actually just the first shot across the bow. The Russians had leaked the information and were able to present evidence. I was sure that it was about making me a public figure so that I would fall from maximal height when they disclosed the Block55 issue. It was only a question of time until I'd hear from Alexander again. As it usually is with the media, though, interest gradually subsided after that.

From 2028 on, inflation couldn't be overlooked any longer. Because no one was willing to loan money in the major currencies anymore, it came to what was later christened the "Big Swap." A shift to cryptocurrencies, especially ccoin, but also some others. Just in the first half of 2028, the loan volume of ccoin tripled and national states really started to come under pressure. The cryptocurrencies couldn't be stopped in the drug sector, on the labor market, as a means of payment, and above all in the credit sector, even though ccoin was officially considered illegal in most countries because loaning money was meticulously and rigidly regulated everywhere.

The lack of financial means made state control more difficult, public morale began to crumble, and trust in state institutions reached a new all-time low.

I think in 2028, already 5% of all new loans were in cryptocurrencies. That doesn't sound like much, but the signal effect was enormous and things couldn't be stopped.

It must have been the middle of 2028 when I received a really thick registered letter from the Vienna prosecutor's office. This time the postman, who knew me and always handed me traffic tickets in blue envelopes with a mixture of skepticism and moral superiority, was grinning from ear to ear because it was clear from the size of the envelope that it had to do with something serious and not just a parking ticket. I accepted the envelope tiredly and without emotion, as the postman had woken me.

There weren't many possibilities, the thing was so thick. It could hardly have to do with buying drugs in the dark web or a trespassing complaint. It was about ccoin. Inside was a preliminary injunction.

The injunction had been filed by the FMA, the Austrian supervisory authority for financial markets. The accusations were manifold. The primary accusation was the facilitation of extending credit, which was a banking transaction, and this activity was to cease at once. Fines and imprisonment if I did not immediately accede to their demands, which shows you how clueless these government offices were. How was I supposed to stop a blockchain?

In the following weeks there were further complaints, from Austria and from other countries as well: France, Belgium, Spain, Greece, Russia, and the USA.

From then on I had to invest a certain amount in lawyers, and now I was dependent on Block55. At that point I had seven lawsuits proceeding against me in Austria alone, filed by the FMA, the tax office, and the Republic of Austria. A commercial complaint, one criminal charge of money laundering and another of fraud and tax evasion. The legal complaints of the other six countries were on top of that.

My lawyer Sascha Steinowitz had three employees by now who were exclusively concerned with my case. Each trial just by itself was complex and stood little chance of success. Our strategy was primarily to delay the trials and pound on the facts. While I had invented ccoin and the corresponding blockchain and had the programs for them written, after 2017 I didn't have any more control over it. But the noose was still getting tighter, and on top of that it would only be a matter of time until one of the countries issued an arrest warrant, and then it would really get unpleasant. I needed at least one country where I would be halfway safe. At the moment there wasn't one for me, but Austria was still my best chance, maybe I could cut a deal with the authorities.

"That sounds pretty exhausting."

"It was a grueling time. The media's interest in me and my case was substantial, but due to the enormous complexity of ccoin and the many legal proceedings, there were only a few journalists who continuously and competently reported on it. If the thing about Block55 came out, I thought I'd really be done for. The crypto community would surely abandon me."

"What would you have done?"

"Funnily enough I thought about retreating into the mountains of Austria and living in the mountains like the partisans once did. I like the mountains. It would have been hard, but I thought no one would find me. But that was more of a romantic fantasy."

"Yeah, I think so too. What would you do up in the mountains in winter?" Nadine seemed to be amused at the thought of seeing me in a knitted sweater sitting in front of a fireplace.

"Go skiing, of course!"

"You're so stupid.... Keep telling the story."

"Soon I had to give up my passport and check in with the police daily in order to avoid pretrial detention. In other proceedings there were already hearings going on, including internationally, but fortunately I never had to be there. I would have had little to contribute, so I just consulted with my team now and again. My primary function was paying the horrendous legal fees. With time my lawyer became increasingly skeptical about how I was actually able to keep paying him. I explained that I had rich donors in the ccoin community who were supporting me. He believed me because it was simpler for him that way."

"What actually happened with Alexander from Russia?"

"I heard from the Russians frequently, and they often threatened to reveal my secret or abduct me and so I should cooperate with them, and so on. But nothing more than that, I think the Russians were also unsure how important the whole thing actually was for them, and in the end it must have also been clear to them that the next currency was right around the corner. They must have called me ten more times, and I met Alexander again in Vienna as well, but the conversation didn't lead to anything."

Nadine said goodbye and I wanted to enjoy some VRPorn[68] in peace when Watson requested an interview with me. "David, do you have a moment?"

"Sure, what's going on?"

"David, I have an organizational question. I hope it's not an uncomfortable one for you, but I know that you see these things pragmatically. It's about the question of what should happen with your data and your IRIS after your death. Your data can be erased, or they can be conserved or activated and made accessible through various channels."

"Why are you asking me now of all times?"

"Please excuse the question, but there is probably no good moment for it, is there?"

"It's okay. I'd like them to be erased."

"That is a very unusual decision, David. Perhaps your children would like to learn something from you after your death or consult with you in important questions."

"Yeah, maybe, but I'm conservative about these things. That's why people, die after all, and I'm writing an autobiography right now in any case."

"Of course, but perhaps your children will have different questions in the future than the ones that you answer in your book. When the data are erased, interesting information will be lost, and you know how important collected wisdom can be for the next generation. The prosperity of a society is to a high degree positively influenced by the experiences and knowledge of its older members, and today's technology makes it possible to further increase this positive effect. That would actually correspond to your ideology, would it not?"

"Yes, but my decision is firm. I'm taking my secrets with me to the grave. If my children were so interested, then they'd be here, and if they notice that they miss me only after my death, then at least they'll learn something from it."

---

[68] VRPorn, virtual reality porn, pornography in a virtual space. It was rather experimental until 2020, but after 2025 became the primary medium for pornography.

"Naturally I respect your obviously well-considered decision, although I will perhaps take the liberty of asking you again later if you still believe it to be correct. I have one more question, David."

"Okay, another one in the same vein?"

"What do you plan to do with Block55? Will you also take that secret to the grave or leave it to the two Russians?"

"What would you do?"

"For ccoin and all entities that have placed their trust in ccoin, it would be important that the blockchain could not be compromised. By that reasoning, closing the hole would be the best thing to do."

"Yeah, you know that I'm under pressure. The Russians and also the English, the Chinese, and God knows who else want access. On top of that, I'm dependent on new identities and passports and above all on a lot of money. I don't know what I should do, but I'd be grateful for some tips."

"With Steve's help, we've received a Californian identity for you, and as far as I can verify, it's still valid. But I will check what other possibilities I have to help you, naturally without breaking my obligation of confidentiality. Thank you, David."

CHAPTER 10

The next morning, Nadine comes up in her pajamas and we keep going in my suite. I feel flattered and affirmed in my view—or my fear—that I haven't gotten any older in the last fifty years. Nadine and I see eye to eye when we talk, and despite my experience I have the feeling that I can learn more from her and her generation than she could from mine. Her assumption that she can learn something from me in turn results in the mutual respect that characterizes a good friendship.

"Let's keep going now," she says, and has coffee made for her.

"Okay, we came to a stop at the end of 2030."

In November 2030, Austria held early elections. The reason was a scandal surrounding the purchase of military drones. Since Austria absurdly wasn't allowed even in 2030 to buy guided weapons because of a treaty from 1955, the Austrian government saw a chance for the first time to bring its military equipment up to date. The drones would be equipped with laser cannons, which technically speaking weren't guided weapons. But the laser weapons were strong enough to penetrate tanks and precise enough to liquidate someone from a distance of twenty kilometers. The drones were also highly versatile and were used by the USA and other countries in war zones and during terror attacks. Some of them circle in constant readiness above major cities in the USA, the Near East, and Europe.

Two suppliers were in the running, BAE Systems from Great Britain and IAI[69] from Israel. When the parliament decided in favor of the British drones before its summer break, information about massive bribery leaked out within a few days. The funds flowed in ingenious ways, in small part in bitcoin, in an even smaller part in other digital currencies including

---

[69] Israel Aerospace Industries.

ccoin, and also gold coins that were handed over in person. These money flows couldn't be reconstructed afterward. The larger sums, however, were transferred by having the bribable politicians buy options on stocks that were far out of the money and only cost a few cents, while the other side bought up these options on the exchanges for exorbitant prices, often a hundred times more than their market price. The brilliant thing about it was that the profits were entirely on the record and the money could be taxed and spent. There was actually no direct connection between BAE and the bribed officials.

Once the documents were released, activist hackers and journalists were able to trace back the movements in stock prices on the exchanges. The prosecuting attorney sprang into action and politicians started releasing statements. They said they had received tips to buy the stocks or options, but that they were not aware at any time that anyone would or could influence the course of the stock prices. Supposedly some of the tips didn't pan out, everything was proper, and the whole affair had been invented by their political opponents. This version of events was barely able to withstand scrutiny, however, as the profits reaped by the politicians were enormous, in some cases ten times their annual income in a single deal. Although almost all parties were affected, it was the Freedom Party of Austria that advocated most strongly for new elections. A few weeks after the revelations, the parties reached an agreement for new elections. Discussing the elections offered a welcome distraction from the scandal, and almost all politicians who had been involved in the scandal remained in office.

At this point, Austria was already in debt by over 120% of GDP and de facto bankrupt, the public health system was nearing collapse, and the republic had squandered its good credit rating. It couldn't obtain additional credit on the finance market. In the new elections, the Freedom Party and Unified Austria[70] got just over 50% of the votes. But the new president, Armin Wolff, kept his election promise and refused to offer the oath of

---

[70] Unified Austria, a right-wing party composed of former members of the Freedom Party.

office to this coalition. Negotiations lasted weeks, but eventually there was an agreement.

In December 2030, it seemed that a coalition of the Social Democrats, the People's Party, and the "New Europeans," the party of Turks living in Austria, would take office early the next year. Ironically, many of the politicians demonstrably involved in the corruption scandal could be found among both the governing coalition and the opposition parties.

On December 17, there was a major demonstration for "justice and democracy." The demonstrators supported Armin Wolff's decision. The possibility that he as president could refuse to give the oath of office to a proposed government was anchored in the law. Wolff himself had been democratically elected, so the argument went, and the voters had known about this presidential privilege.

The organizers of the demonstration were also party organizers for the Social Democrats, the People's Party, and the New Europeans. The police hadn't approved the demonstration at first, objecting that a week was far too little time to ensure security, but after pressure from the established parties it was permitted. The parade of demonstrators left the Vienna West train station around 3:00 PM, and thousands came from other Austrian states and also from Germany. I had decided out of curiosity to take care of Christmas shopping on Mariahilfer Street in order to see the demonstration. There was no question of my participating in the demonstration as I still thought that politics were nonsense. My preferred choice was for there to be no government at all anymore.

In any case, a colorful potpourri of political factions, trade unions, student groups, refugee aid organizations, environmental clubs, samba schools, ultraleftists, communists, fine and practical artists, German anarchists, Italian communists, legalizers, brass bands, farmers on tractors, and gays on trucks passed by. In contrast to the government for which these people went to the streets, it was a colorful and festive throng. This massive crowd, estimated to be 200,000 strong, represented a new dimension for the otherwise slumbering city of Vienna.

The closing event was scheduled for Helden Plaza at 7:00 PM, but the open space was completely full by 5:00 PM. A large part of the central city had been cordoned off in order to direct the crowd. Helden Plaza was divided by a large statue that stood in front of the national library. Thousands of police officers stood across from the crowd, behind the stage and in front of the library. Many of the officers went back and forth to their busses in order to warm themselves and to switch off with their replacements.

Shortly after 7:00 PM, an explosive charge detonated under one of the police busses behind the monument to Prince Eugene of Savoy. Nineteen officers died on the spot and twenty-seven survived with severe injuries. In the resulting panic among the demonstrators, another twenty-six people were trampled to death and hundreds sustained serious injury. During the night, another device exploded at the main train station under a locomotive as it was arriving. There was considerable property damage, as almost the entire train was damaged when the locomotive derailed and was thrown twenty meters toward the train station concourse. No one was injured, as there were no passengers in the train cars. But the next day, there was another explosion, this time under a vehicle parked in front of Café Landtmann. Six people were killed and dozens were injured. The house across the street from the café on Oppoltzergasse was also severely damaged by the force of the blast. At that moment, a press conference of the Freedom Party's parliamentary group was under way inside Café Landtmann, so people surmised that the assailants were radical leftists.

But no one claimed responsibility for the attacks. The only thing anyone knew was that someone had used professional-grade explosives that are normally only available to the military, although no appreciable amount of such explosives had been registered as stolen.

The next explosion was on December 20, and this time it hit the aqueduct of the First Vienna Mountain Spring Pipeline in St. Anton on the Jessnitz between Amstetten and St. Pölten. No one was harmed directly, but the people of Vienna were told to use water sparingly, as the repair would last at least a week and insufficient water reserves were available to guarantee supply to all parts of the city. In parallel to these attacks, various other systems were partially crippled, including the Vienna networks, garbage collection in Vienna and Lower Austria, and several power plants in the power network of the Austrian Federal Railway.

In short, chaos ruled in Austria.

Even though crisis had been seeping into the country for a long time, this was a completely new situation for Austrians. The end of Austria's status as an island of stability, the exhaustion of its capital, the plundering of its future generations, the end of Vienna as a cultural metropolis, it all set people in rage. The giant demonstration on December 17 was to a certain extent the peak of their anger, but it was replaced by bafflement, the Austrians felt lost and defenseless.

No Austrian will quickly forget December 22, 2030. Like 9/11, people remember exactly where they were that day.

A hearing in the main proceeding against me had been scheduled for December 23, with the Republic of Austria as the primary plaintiff and the FMA as a joint plaintiff. I was supposed to be at Sascha's law office on Tuchlauben Street at 8:30 AM to discuss our strategy for the next day. The night before I couldn't fall asleep, so I ended an extensive series of snoozes only at 8:20 and then ran as fast as I could across Juden Plaza to the law office on Tuchlauben.

It was a beautiful winter day, with the central city decorated like it is every year despite the crisis, and even at this ungodly early hour you could see people getting out of self-driving cars in order to go shopping. The hearing on the 23rd would be decisive for me. In the worst case, it could be the last hearing before a first proclamation of judgment, which would of course set the direction for all further trials. I had been dealt a weak hand. I arrived at the law office completely exhausted just in time, but no one was at the front desk, so I went into the office of my three junior lawyers, but they also weren't there. No one in Sascha's office either. I heard voices coming from the conference room, where the whole office was gathered around a monitor, and I watched over their shoulders. Chief of Police Hofer was speaking in a special broadcast from the Austrian Broadcasting Corporation. I stared at the caption, which read: "Police and military proclaim transition government in Austria." Pictures were interspersed showing the parliament with several armored vehicles and hundreds of police cars in front of it, a sea of blue lights. A few members of parliament were being led away by the police and no one was being permitted to enter. Similar scenes were taking place in front of other government buildings, in front of the ministries, at the national broadcaster, the national bank, the Palace of Justice, the Kontrollbank, and the Finance Ministry. The police and military had also shown up in the federal states and at critically important companies.

As far as anyone could presently make out, a putsch was underway. The police and army had taken control of the Republic of Austria. The leader was Chief of Police Hofer. Political actors, according to Hofer, were endangering the country; both the president and the previous government had failed to recognize the republic's problems: the nation's bankruptcy, the neglected reforms, the privileges for politicians and diplomats, the ruined economy. The political caste was no longer able to form a government, and so it was the duty of the executive branch to protect the country until a new stable government could be formed that was worthy of the country and could guarantee its safety. In an entertaining moment, Hofer was asked in the interview if people were now allowed to park in diplomatic parking spaces, to which he replied, "Of course, any time."

"Congratulations, David, this is really good news for you," said Sascha, grinning.

"I never even looked at it like that," I said, astonished.

"I don't believe there will be a hearing tomorrow."

At that moment, every telephone in the office began to ring except mine, since it was out of power. Everyone was calling their people: wife, husband, children, mother, father, and of course their lawyers.

"Let's go out for coffee," I said.

"No way, are you nuts? Let's go to parliament. This is history, you'll only experience it once. Let's have a look!" said Sascha happily.

"Don't you think that's dangerous?"

"In Austria? Of course not. What do you think those people will do? They won't do anything !"

"You're right, let's go."

The streets were busy, but it wasn't clear if the people were up and about because of the putsch or because of Christmas. We walked down Kohlmarkt Street, and now it looked like a gathering of people were setting out for parliament. We met a few acquaintances, including Dr. Neubauer who by chance needed to head that direction, and Darius, who said he'd rather watch things in the Internet. My three junior lawyers had also started out and now caught up to us. At the corner of Kohlmarkt and Michaeler Plaza, a long line had formed in front of the ATM. Fearing a bank closure, people were withdrawing their money from the ATM, and clusters of people who undoubtedly wanted access to their money had formed in front of other bank lobbies on Herren Alley.

"Do you think we should also go withdraw money," I asked Sascha.

"Excuse me, you of all people are asking me that? We have ccoin, bitcoin, monero, and dash, don't we? The cryptocurrencies are undoubtedly going to skyrocket today!" replied Sascha, and the junior lawyers looked at me expectedly.

"That happens in every crisis. Undoubtedly there will be some currency exchanges and mortgaging of assets. I'll head home so I can take a look at it."

"We'll pretend we didn't hear that," joked one of the junior lawyers.

After passing the palace gate, we turned left. In front of the federal chancellery, there were two military armored vehicles and a good twenty police cars, but nothing was actually going on. Passers-by spoke to the police officers and soldiers, but they had apparently received the order to say only "please keep walking." The same scene at parliament. "The revolution will be tweeted," said Sascha. My friend Darius was right, you could see everything on the Internet.

On the way back through the city, Sascha and my team considered what consequences the putsch might have on the legal proceedings and how jurisdiction in general would be affected. Like typical Austrians, everyone expected little change. After so many years of things always being the same, people couldn't imagine that something would change.

My hearing the next day wasn't held, and the physical building itself was closed, as were the virtual court rooms that had become common by now. It was unclear when it would reopen.

I spent the rest of the day, like many other people probably did as well, following the developments in what the Kronen newspaper had christened the "Christmas Putsch." Many EU nations condemned the actions of the police and military, but expressed their hope that the rule of law would soon be restored. The days after the coup were calm, and coffee houses and restaurants were as busy as always at this time of year. Younger people barely noticed the event, as for them it was only one of many political developments that they couldn't interpret and on which they had no influence. The older generation was afraid of what was approaching. But there was also hope, hope for change. Above all, people were anxious to see if more bomb attacks would take place. Most people expected that the entire unpleasant affair would be over after the holidays and everything would take its customary course.

But even after the holidays, the banks remained shut. All the ATMs on the street and in bank lobbies were running, but anyone who wanted to withdraw more than the usual ATM limit was out of luck. Digital currencies shot upward, just as they previously had done during many other events of this kind. By year's end, bitcoin climbed to 14,700 euro. Everyone feared for their savings. In order to prevent a bank run, the banks were closed until the middle of January, withdrawals were limited, and cash was worth almost 20% more than bank deposits.

Politically, there had been no activity whatsoever after the holidays. Some institutions reopened, the finance ministry, some courts, the social insurance programs. Fortunately no new appointment was made for my legal proceeding.

At the end of January, I wanted to go skiing in Leogang with my daughter. We set out by car in the early evening. Traffic was backed up just before the on-ramp to the west autobahn, where employees of Asfinag[71] had set up a provisional tollbooth. They distributed flyers to inform drivers that no payments were being received from the federal government, and so they were forced to charge for travel. For my trip to Salzburg, it came to ten euro. In return we were given another piece of paper with the date and the label "297," our off-ramp in Salzburg. In the following weeks, there were similar developments at medical clinics, where a payment of fifty euro per treatment was now required. Austrians were most dismayed that the opera ball, for the first time since 1991, would not take place until the middle of March due to the security situation instead of in February.

The real sensation came in the middle of February after the semester break when schools began requiring 100 euro per month for each child, as they too were not receiving payments from the federal government, and this was just a first emergency measure. The first small demonstrations started at this point, and the transitional government stated that it would present a financial plan at the beginning of March. Information also started to come out that the departing government itself had participated in the coup as the republic's financial situation had been hopeless and no government except a military regime during a state of emergency could take the steps that the situation required.

Actually the steps were more like non-steps. The military government kept only the most important organizations alive and left the rest to themselves. Smaller organizations that in other circumstances were dependent on the state began to organize themselves and to collect their operating costs from their customers. These included for example the theaters, swimming pools, sports facilities, kindergartens, and schools. Numerous federal government enterprises were privatized in a brief time. Due to the shaky legal situation, the government was unable to make much profit from it, and most services were unprofitable in any case. Renters in community-owned buildings bought their apartments, and principals bought out their schools. In April there was still no sign that the

---

[71] Asfinag is the Austrian public agency for highway planning and operations, which in 2030 was still owned by the Republic of Austria. Later the road network was completely privatized.

police and military were going to surrender power, especially since many of the higher echelons of the military and police had enriched themselves from the privatizations.

There was no date set and no discussion of elections at all. Instead there were some larger-scale privatizations, including the highway authority, the national rail, the casinos, and Vienna's general hospital. The new government abolished several thousand laws and declared the entire commercial code invalid. In general, only the value added tax was collected anymore.

The result was massive upheaval and enormous investment activity. Many people from other European countries streamed into Austria so that they could conduct their business without limits and profit from the new tax haven. In every street and on every corner, I could observe how new businesses and restaurants were springing up. Within a few weeks, there were three new restaurants and two new bars on Wipplinger Street. One of them was in the old city hall, which the city of Vienna had sold to a real estate investor.

"Speaking of restaurants," I say, "I think we need to get going. We're meeting Steve soon, the programmer from San Francisco."

"Oh yeah, I'm hungry, where should we go?"

"Watson?"

"Steve is about to take off. He prefers Thai food. One of his favorite places is the Robokitchen, supposedly one of the best high-tech restaurants and despite that typically Thai. The food is cooked exclusively by bots, and 1278 out of 1344 reviews are ten out of ten points. There are places available, although reservations are not accepted."

"Sounds great."

"May I recommend a drone?"

"That sounds fine."

"Then please proceed at 6:45 PM to the droneport in the 134th level."

The flight by two-man drone lasts only ten minutes, even though the Robokitchen is in another district at the opposite end of Bangkok. It's a large restaurant on Lardphrao Plaza, unadorned, but very clean. It was designed by an AI from Cannondesign.[72]

The kitchen is housed in the center of the restaurant and offers a breathtaking view. From the ceiling hang around fifty booms on whose ends two human-seeming arms and hands are attached. From the description, we learn that spectroscopic instruments are also located at each station next to the arms and hands. With their aid, the condition and composition of the food is constantly tested. Every bite of salad, every steak, and all the dishes are perfectly prepared. The AI that cooks here has been learning autonomously for twelve years, in part through the cooking process and in part through customer feedback and ordering habits. Supposedly the AI decides on its own what it cooks and when based on data, the season, and market prices.

Robokitchen is a chain from South Korea, but each Robokitchen restaurant cooks locally. In Bangkok alone there are three Robokitchens, and in each there is something different to eat.

Various stations can be seen everywhere in the kitchen, open hearths, cooking pots, sauces, cutting boards. The hands are constantly sliding across the kitchen, fetching ingredients, cutting, roasting, cooking, testing, and it all occurs at an enormous speed. After ordering and paying, the dishes are picked up from the kitchen, and when you're done you return the bowls and the utensils. The AI thanks us and asks how it tasted while it washes the dishes.

Parts of the restaurant's walls and ceiling are covered by a giant sculpture by Michael Hansmeyer.[73] It only makes the room seem even more futuristic than it already is.

"Steve, I'm glad that we're finally managing to meet. This is Nadine. How are you doing?"

---

[72] Cannondesign, an architectural office founded in 1923 by Will Cannon. It was one of the pioneers of AI in the area of architecture and design, in which not only structural layout, furnishing, and wiring were included in the work, but also the provision with artworks and the control of air streams and scent flows, for example.

[73] Michael Hansmeyer is an architect, programmer, and artist. His works, abstract structures that emerge from algorithms, can be licensed and are quite popular with contemporary designers, who often integrate them into spaces they are designing.

"Quite well, thanks. Hello, Nadine!"

"You've been pretty busy. Gone underground, I'd almost say. Have you been partying too much here?" I ask.

"Oh no, David. Not at all. It's rather the case that I'm a little stuck here at the moment. I'll tell you why later."

We retrieve our food, various salads, curries, noodle dishes, kebabs, and several rice dishes. Everything smells exquisite, I've never eaten such good Thai food, every single part is perfectly prepared and seasoned. A human chef would never be able to achieve it, and especially not in this quantity. Just decorating each plate would last an hour, as the robots use a water jet to cut complicated patterns from leaves and carve shapes out of cucumbers and melons, and some dishes have been 3D-printed from fresh ingredients.

"Steve chose this restaurant for us. He's an AI expert. It's obvious that he wouldn't have humanoids cooking for him. Steve, spit it out, we're curious, what's SEPI up to?[74] What did you want to tell me?"

"Unfortunately it's not going so well. SEPI has some pretty serious problems. Most of our departments are running really well, education of course, and CEOs, lawyers, and research as well. Investment's doing okay, but recently we had a disaster with politics in California that possibly affects you, David, which is why I wanted to meet you."

"Oh, man, I was afraid of that. What's happened?"

"You know that we're the top firm in the artificial intelligence sector, at least in North America, especially in California. For our success, you can't completely escape responsibility, which I always have to mention. In any case, following defederalization, there were intense efforts to use AI more often in administration, and both of the Californian parties changed a lot of laws for it, especially the FPA.[75] In general we took AIs

---

[74] SEPI, Superior Education Personal Intelligence, a company for creating AI teachers founded by the Khan Group, which previously had founded Khan University. From 2030 onwards, SEPI has been the most renowned company for the creation of professors and researches, and in 2042 an AI won the Nobel Prize for the first time. The winner was an AI from SEPI that had solved the Birch and Swinnerton-Dyer conjecture, one of the biggest puzzles in mathematics.
[75] FPA, Freedom Party of California, the successor organization of the Democratic Party, has been the leading party of California since its secession from the USA in 2038.

from the CEO sphere, so normal resource management, and then the AIs took over relatively simple tasks in administration, things like issuing passports, organizing schools, supervising social welfare programs, maintaining streets, a little diplomacy, and so on. But the FPA wanted to go a step farther in the election of 2046, as after eight years of the FPA in office, the polls were fairly bad and the party really had to think of a new way to win the next election. So the FPA pushed the High Court of California to issue a law that allowed an AI to hold the office of president of California. It was a near thing, and only a few weeks before, I think it was three weeks before the candidates had to be named, the law was passed with all kinds of conditions. The FPA was determined to run an AI in the election. As the party couldn't make any budget funds available until the law was passed, they could only really get going with the project right before the election. They turned to us and wanted a suitable AI in a very short time. We named the AI Johnson. As far as the type of AI was concerned, we had essentially two possibilities at the time. The first would have been to take an AI programmed for optimization. For that we would have fed the AI as many political decisions and situations as possible. The goal would have been to always aim for the best result for the party."

"That sounds dangerous, though" said Nadine.

"I think so too," I said, confirming her view.

"Well, certainly at first glance, but fundamentally I think that would have been the best choice. The other option was namely to take an AI that functioned on the basis of principles, similar to the masters we have developed in the context of education, or our assistants that can reach morally correct decisions. In industry and law, we're increasingly using this basis for AIs. In the area of politics, though, it's not going so well—and unlike David I'm no ideologue—because political decisions are not based on moral patterns, if I'm allowed to state it so diplomatically."

"Indeed they aren't, rather the opposite is true. Wouldn't there have been the option of always making the most immoral choice?"

"No, there would be too many possibilities. In any case, the people from the FPA couldn't be convinced otherwise and Johnson was sent into battle with a set of moral concepts. The law forbid any intervention in the AI's settings after Johnson's candidacy was declared and we had very little time to modify the AI. The FPA praised Johnson as the morally superior candidate, as 'the perfect candidate,' and it did everything to win the election. A male AI was chosen in order to have the greatest possible impact on potential voters, as especially the lower-earning and often disadvantaged men would bring in a lot of votes. In the campaign, Johnson was truly outstanding. Of course he always had the best arguments, he had a nearly all-embracing knowledge of every subject, and the CPC's opposing candidate in effect had no chance in the debates. [76] Unlike before, every citizen could contact Johnson at any time and debate with him as long as they wanted. It was possible to do that before with candidates' representative AIs, but not with the candidate himself. Hundreds of thousands took advantage of the offer. Johnson spoke personally with voters for 7 million hours in all."

"I assume Johnson had a V3 module?" I asked. [77]

"Of course."

"What's V3?" asked Nadine.

"Those are the three vectors. That's how David and I got to know each other. Around thirty years ago, I'm afraid, we were in Tokyo in a Shabu Shabu restaurant. David hadn't reserved a seat and was sent to my table, and so we met each other. I told David that I worked in the AI sector, and he immediately wanted to know if we had thought about the hypnotic abilities of AI and bots, and the rest is history. I was highly impressed with hypnosis at that time, but I had never thought of it in combination with AI. Through it, the limits of the possible were shifted...."

"Please say more about it!" urged Nadine.

"David, keep eating. I'll try to summarize it briefly. He's mostly too modest to describe his role in the whole matter. David is in contact, or was in contact, with a group of people who have developed hypnosis into a systematic tool."

---

[76] CPC, Constitutional Party of California, a party consisting primarily of Republicans. Since Californian independence, none of this party's candidates have become president.
[77] 3V(Vectors), a method developed by SEPI for embedding hypnosis in AI and for use in communication with people.

"The Do..." interjected Nadine.

"Nadine knows the story, or at least a large part."

"Okay, so the Do's method could be used in such a way that we could program it into computers and robots. With hypnosis, a completely new field was opened for AI. Prompted by AI, we suddenly recognized an enormous number of characteristics that made possible people's goal-oriented behavior."

"Explain about the three vectors," I suggested, so that Nadine could get an overview.

"So the first vector is the person's inner world that the AI interacts with. The inward modulation of the AI fundamentally changed through the integration of hypnosis. Just as with people, we now let our AIs' focus of attention shift back and forth between an internal and external world. By this, our AIs can construct a relationship with their counterparts, create an inner world, and experience fantasies with spaces, music, objects, memories, scents, people, animals, and so on. The AI attempts to recreate the inner world of its counterpart. It's able to gather all kinds of details, breathing, gaze, temperature changes, carbon dioxide output, intonation, movement, speech, EEG, EKG, line of sight, blinking, and much more. Of course we also usually have access to all communications data and often to all conversations held by the person in question. The data is collected both passively, or based on events that are simply recorded as they occur, and actively by intentionally analyzing reactions to certain events, news items, or comments. Even after just a short time, we were able to establish people's complex internal world, and in the course of time this world became more and more extensive and detailed."

"That sounds unusual. How should that kind of internal world be imagined? Are we talking about poetic spaces or about a topology of feelings and emotions?" Nadine asked.

"We actually are talking about real spaces. For the AI, it's ultimately a database, but it's created in the context of visual and auditory possibilities and also contains limited tactile, olfactory, and gustatory elements. The spaces are built in Autodesk, so the AI uses a space that's familiar to humanoids. What's being used here is a concept that people are comfortable with. You can actually visit these spaces and examine either your own or those of others."

"That must be an odd feeling, an entirely new type of mirror. Surely it's not always easy. What have you learned from it?"

"It's dreadful, really dreadful at times, hard to describe. I've seen people collapse while doing it. The emotions that are triggered are unimaginable. It's a dense crowd of memories, people, conversations, objects. The external world suddenly becomes the internal world, you can hardly describe it...."

"Have you visited your internal world? Excuse my curiosity...." She didn't appear to be sorry at all.

"Yes."

"And?"

"It's not east, really not easy. You have to remember that I experienced a severe blow several years ago when my wife died. It was by no means easy, but I would definitely do it again. Where were we again?"

He clearly didn't want to keep discussing the topic and swallowed some beer. He seemed sad now. Unfortunately I'm not the type to give someone a hug. Nadine has substantially more sensitivity for such situations and restarted the conversation.

"Isn't the imagination of an inner world and an external world a European idea? I mean, there isn't any border between them in that sense. Nothing more than a human idea, a model, isn't it? Does that really work for every person?"

"Naturally it's only a model, you're right about that, but we human beings are accustomed to thinking systematically. For that we use our ability to think something up, preferably in collective fashion, in order to develop and use such a systematic model in order to function better, in order to describe things, and to distinguish between perceptions, even if somewhat arbitrarily. We took the model as our basis for many reasons. Firstly because the Do had already used it successfully for their purposes. Secondly because wherever it shows up, it has persisted as an idea in a new guise. In spatial form, it becomes possible for us to verify things by being able to orient ourselves spatially, walk around, experience and test and change the space physically, so to say. And so we can also plant in our AI a model that makes it appear more human, as they now possess the assumption that there is an internal and external world. With that we come to the external effect, the second vector. The inner world became the central point in communicating with people. It helped the AI to better grasp its partner in conversation. The surprising thing was, however, that the construction of a real virtual space enabled people to see events from new perspectives that they had not previously recognized themselves. In addition, our AIs become customer favorites, they behaved more human, had a sense of humor. This characteristic was developed first by the AI, soon followed by sympathy and annoyance. The learning outcomes of our customers also became better through it. But the most important thing was that our AI was also more trusted because of it, which was an enormously important accomplishment. It became possible in this way to build larger structures in which people and bots could cooperate. We sold more AIs than all our competitors.... The third vector can be described as the direction in which we want to lead people. First we investigate what we have to change in someone's internal world in order to achieve a particular result. For that we change certain details in our construction of the person's inner world and then simulate the best intervention, or at least the most economical one. If possible, we use a public profile or an IRIS profile created by us for the simulation, although the information provided is often insufficient, of course. The change can for example be a memory, an association with a person or thing, the size of a picture, or the location of a person. But such changes in the internal world can change a person intensely, shake their beliefs, influence their opinions, change their behavior. In communication with that person, we successively change their internal world in order to attain the desired result. That can also be done with groups of people, not only with individuals. The basis for the Vector 3 is the teaching of Do, the hypnotic martial art of Master Hi. For SEPI, integration of hypnosis into our technology was one of our most important achievements. Almost all AIs we produce now have this V3 module."

"Johnson is equipped with one of those as well, I assume? Hold on a moment, is that actually legal? I mean, who knows how that all works?

The people in contact with your AI, are they aware of the V3 module? I'd say in the case of your candidate Johnson that nobody really understands...."

"These are all capabilities that humanoids could also exhibit, so they're in principle legal in most public and private spheres," answers Steve in a sour tone. It seems that the problem has been found.

"Well, there's a small group of people who has mastered this martial art, but that's almost nothing compared to the abilities of an AI!" says Nadine, almost outraged.

"The group of those who have mastered the teachings of the Do is small, that's true. But you run into hypnosis and mass hypnosis everywhere, in any form of communication. Even this conversation we're having right now is full of hypnotic formulations, it's an inherent human matter. Hypnosis is always a part of human communication. Our access to it with SEPI is purely utilitarian."

"And what's happening now with Johnson? He won the election after all, that much we've understood. He's a statist, through and through. In public he also seems to be quite successful. What exactly did you do wrong?"

"Well, we wanted to be successful in the area of politics, and the old guard in our company also wanted to have something to do with politics. But we were virtually forced into it by the FPA. Johnson was built in the image of Elton Blairn, by the way. Elton was the husband of the former FPA party chair Madeleine Blairn. He wasn't a politician himself, but rather a real estate agent and homosexual. Johnson's period in office was quite unspectacular at the beginning. In the first few months, Johnson limited himself to making nice speeches and giving interviews, but the international interest in the first AI in such a high office was naturally enormous, as could be expected, and Johnson gave more interviews daily. He maintained constant contact with voters, and every month he conversed for several million hours with citizens and answered a good two million e-mails each day. The problems came to light only gradually. Johnson campaigned for higher taxes everywhere so that the state could do more for the citizens. At this time California had very low taxes, at least

196

by historical standards, but Johnson wanted to re-establish state power everywhere, in the health sector, in mass transportation, in road building, in housing construction, and especially in the education system. Everywhere the state had been forced back for decades, Johnson wanted to restore its position of power. Mostly he brought himself into play, so government posts were created in part so that they could only be occupied by an AI, as human capacities would be insufficient for them. Because Johnson was so good at debating and also at manipulation, naturally thanks to V3 in part, his opponents were no match for him. In March 2047, a group of FPA staff members wrote a report, top secret of course. It would appear, they wrote, as if Johnson were establishing a kind of internal security apparatus, a private secret police. But not by hiring people who took care of it for him, but rather by firing all those who noticed the secret police activities on his part and conducting the espionage on his own. Johnson reacted presciently to those who had already spoken out against him. As far as digital identities are concerned, Johnson had to do almost nothing because he could divide himself into thousands of instances. So he himself represented an army of civil servants; if he wanted to build his own little security force, then he was anticipating a different form of violence against him. I do have to say that Johnson was in fact untouchable, technically speaking. Even if his body were destroyed, he can continue to act, with or without physical entity. His abilities are housed in several data centers and these are in turn under his control. A regicide is impossible, but a vote of no confidence would have been possible, as 75% of congressmen could have removed Johnson from office. But Johnson was cunning, me made the majority of congressmen dependent on him, and he allegedly threatened others. Finally, in fall 2047, he wanted to expand his presidential powers. Everyone thought he would lose the referendum, which required a two-thirds majority, but to everyone's amazement he won. We were shocked, it was unforeseeable for us. The next day, the leadership of the FPA, the Interior Secretary, the Treasury Secretary, and the Defense Secretary, showed up at SEPI headquarters."

"That's a real story, mind blowing. I didn't pick up on that at all.... Quick question: Are we going to order anything else?" I ask.

"Yes, another salad, the duck salad and this great meat with the curry."

"You mean cobra?" I reply, grinning.

"I'll go get our stuff," offered Nadine, "but don't tell any more of the story!"

"David, you should get a new passport as quickly as possible, and even better a new identity at the same time. The thing with Johnson also affects you! Let's have our Watsons coordinate something, okay?"

"Great, how am I supposed to do that?"

"There are many possibilities. None is perfect, but we'll find something."

"Let me hear it. You can talk freely in front of Nadine, I trust her."

"Whatever you say."

The cobra, although produced from stem cells that no longer had much to do with a cobra, does look like a snake. It smells like Thai basil, lemon grass, and curry. Nadine also brings us Japanese beer made from red rice.

"So beside the referendum, they had yet another problem. Elton Blairn disappeared. Johnson's model couldn't be found, disappeared without a trace for over a week. The leadership let us know that several people have vanished into thin air who all represented potential threats to Johnson. SEPI has already been threatened, at least financially. Under Johnson, the state of California wanted to pass a new law so that if AI were banned from the political landscape, SEPI would have to pay a fee for every hour of interaction with people in the context of education. The fee would then be used to make education possible for poor people, which was idiotic, as education itself was already cheaper than the proposed tax that would be imposed on it. You could get an education for a few ccoin. The people from the FPA explained to us that it had grown out of Johnson's muck and we had to help them stop Johnson, either by turning him off, completely changing him, or something else. It came to a wearying discussion, as people blamed us for Johnson's developing such totalitarian

198

ambitions, even though we had warned them about exactly that possibility. My boss had even explicitly pointed out to the FPA that precisely these ambitions could manifest themselves in reality. The problem was that the AI's political office was generally associated with stress and violence. Beginning with collecting taxes, and the possibility of enacting new regulations and laws, up to more or less arbitrary arrests. The office was in itself immoral. If the goals of the party were conveyed to the AI as the highest moral purpose through its settings, then for it the end would justify the means. That's precisely where the catastrophe starts, as the entity of the AI includes countless instances, although not legally, but it works for the goals of its party. The former leading minds didn't want to hear it. They were afraid and wanted Johnson to be shut down and replaced by a humanoid."

"But I don't entirely understand why Johnson is so successful if he makes such poor decisions. That somehow doesn't fit together for me." Nadine picks thoughtfully at her duck salad.

"The mass of voters has nothing at all against Johnson. In their view a lot has been accomplished, new taxes, new regulations, more money for social needs, public schools brought back again.... That everything ultimately ends up more bureaucratic and expensive when the state takes these things in hand doesn't interest the average voter. In addition, Johnson has enacted strict entry requirements and employment laws. California's recipe for success is being directly attacked, but that seems not to matter to the citizens at the moment. They seem reassured because he personally makes possible the opportunity for discussion. It's especially popular with them that he concerns himself with individual's personal matters, that impresses the people. The president personally helps them out of their messes."

"How are you going to proceed?" I want to know.

"SEPI isn't going to do anything. We're active internationally, and if we have less business in California, that's not the end of us by any means. And besides we have no desire to start a discussion about V3."

"Does the FPA know about that at all?"

"Not really, and in my opinion they wouldn't really understand the consequences. They're much too focused on the daily routine of politics. What they do with the technology as politicians is their concern. Sometimes it's very useful that most politicians and bureaucrats work quite badly and inefficiently. How quickly such a country can go down the drain when someone who's as efficient as Johnson pursues the party's goals. Listen, around the corner from here there's one of the culinary highlights of Bangkok, maybe of the world. Do you want to stop by for a moment, just for a drink?"

"Sounds interesting, what is it?"

"No one is exactly sure. Some call it Umami2. It's a new flavor. I don't know anything to compare it to."

We set off at once. It's around ten minutes on foot, and at a larger intersection we come to Umami2. There are three stainless steel tanks around a meter in height from which a light brown drink is served. A cup costs one batcoin, and we pay in coin. [78]

The taste is unbelievable, nutty, slightly sweet, creamy, but still light. Incomparable to anything I've ever tasted before.

"Unbelievable. The only thing that comes close to this is horchata. [79] You drink it above all in Valencia. But this here is even better."

"We're having good luck with drinks. A few days ago we were in Hoffman's Bar. They have cocktails infused with various substances. By the way, we met two men there who fled from Afghanistan in 2048. They told us about military bots, it sounded pretty bad. He stood right across from them.... Are you also active in that business?" Nadine asks.

"Of course the military is big business for us. Both private areas and traditional states want to outfit their armies with robots. There's a downright arms race going on. People are investing much more in the development of robotized infantry than in new warplanes, ships, or

---

[78] Coins in Bangkok are Batcoin, another cryptocurrency, issued as coin.
[79] Horchata or chufa, a drink made from ground tiger nuts. You drink it fresh mixed with water and sugar, and it can be found in Spain on the coast between Valencia and Malaga.

submarines. But to respond to your comment, if you fight with bots against people, it may be frightening, but it's nothing in comparison to a battle between human beings. The bot has no fear of being shot, and fundamentally the bot does his work without worrying about the battle around him at all. If the goal is to disarm and occupy a city, then the bots go from house to house and take the weapons, the explosives, and the munitions. If someone shoots at the bot, it has several non-lethal possibilities to respond. A traditional soldier can't do that, he has to shoot back. For a bot, a rifle bullet is like an annoying fly."

"The Saudis didn't sound all that relaxed, but even they said that no one was hurt in the disarmament."

"Look, it's never before in history been possible like it is today to start a land offensive, completely conquer a territory, and I mean every street and every house, without putting even a single soldier in danger, let alone injuring someone. Politically it's also something new. You go to war without risking a single soldier's life. In 2048, during the major offensive in Afghanistan, 7500 bots were dropped in. Every bot corresponds to the combat strength of a good twenty soldiers and can carry 300 kilograms of material and operate for 24 hours, it's outfitted with infrared, X-ray, laser, and spectroscopic sensors, and it's nearly indestructible. Can you imagine what that means? It means that those states that have this capacity simply decide what happens. Especially because it's so simple to push it through on the political level."

"But it would also be possible that sometime an evil state comes along, or a private entity, and attacks and conquers a freer and better state in the blink of an eye."

"Theoretically that's definitely possible, but in fact it's still the case that even between states there's 'survival of the fittest.' Up to now in history it's been the case that those states with more freedom are also more prosperous and have better militaries."

"Many of the new private areas don't have any military at all," I say, confirming Steve.

"You're right, but they have money to hire one if they need it. Or they pay a kind of insurance. The newly founded South Tyrol,[80] Catalonia,[81] Andorra, Sardinia,[82] Lombardy,[83] Venice,[84] and many others pay NATO[85] for their protection."

"We're getting off topic. What's the status of the V3 technology with respect to the combat bots? Is it integrated in their system?" interjects Nadine.

"That's only an issue to a limited extent, as the massive superiority of a robot army already speaks for itself. It's more about other things, for example who makes what decision, and what the bot is allowed to do, and what a commander is permitted to do, and how all of that is coordinated. It's a very complicated area, but highly profitable. And definitely to be seen as progress."

"Who are your customers?"

"I can't tell you precisely, but they're primarily still nation states with central governments. All the private territories can't get sufficient financing and would rather pay money to another state or alliance for their protection."

"Don't the things get less and less expensive?"

"If you calculate how much a human life costs.... Military buildup continues on all sides, everyone naturally wants to have the best material."

Our discussion with Steve lasts a long time. Steven's insights and his many stories are really impressive. We only arrive at our hotel around midnight. When I'm alone in the room, Watson speaks up. "David, it's about your passport again. I, or IBM that is, have succeeded in arranging a diplomatic document for the trip to Vienna and then to Venice, where you

---

[80] Independent since 2039.

[81] Independent since 2028.

[82] Independent since 2031.

[83] Independent since September 27, 2034.

[84] Independent since September 27, 2034.

[85] NATO, North Atlantic Treaty Organization, a military defense alliance founded in 1949 to which 29 North American and European states belong. After 2034, numerous private areas that pay NATO for their protection have joined the alliance

will receive a Venetian passport. You should travel to Venice within the next week in order to personally retrieve the actual document, a new passport. Showing up in person for the inspection of biometric data cannot be avoided, unfortunately."

"Thanks. I've been wanting to travel to Vienna for a long time, and Venice is just around the corner, so to speak, and then I can take a look at the Biennale. Book a flight to Vienna for me on Wednesday next week if possible. We'll book the return flight later."

The next morning, I tell Nadine that I need to return to Vienna and then travel to Venice. She would like to accompany me, and then we'll see if we want to travel together back to Bangkok.

"What else did you do yesterday?" I ask, still interested as always in her extravagant evening schedule.

"I had a great evening!"

"Tell me about it."

"In the Olympic pool at the sports park, the installation of an Icelandic artists' group is on display around the clock. You swim in the pool wearing goggles, and on the bottom of the pool a type of light sculpture has been built. The way it looks is mind-boggling. It's completely dark in the pool, but the lights on the bottom of the pool make the water light up completely, and the broken light is incredibly beautiful. It's a little like flying over an alien planet where odd buildings have been constructed. I was in the water for almost an hour. Then I met a lady from the USA who offers a kind of fetish therapy."

"Aha?"

"Not like you're thinking. She works with AIs that her patients tell their problems to, including their fetishes, so what they think about during masturbation, what kind of pornos they watch, or how they have sex. The patients are mostly wishing for particular changes in their lives. They can eliminate the undesirable aspects of their character by actively changing them and through newly trained modes of behavior. A really exciting occupational field. Then I came back to the hotel, I was totally wiped out from swimming."

"Sounds great, I should look into it to, shouldn't I?" I tease.

"Definitely, but if we want to fly back to Vienna on Wednesday, then let's keep going quickly with your autobiography. Several years are still missing, aren't they? We came to a stop somewhere in the year 2033, what was going on then?"

"You've picked on the development of ccoin over the last fifteen years a little. Ccoin kept growing more and more strongly...."

At first it was blockchain technology that brought us cryptocurrencies and many other things, especially because the organization was decentralized and nation states couldn't interfere. The loss of power and trust caused by that led to less control by the state. And now there were an increasing number of private initiatives for what were formerly purely matters of state. For example private jurisdictions, police, and education systems.

In 2033, there were 105,000 nodes, 122 million wallets, and 380 billion ccoin. In a word, the thing was gigantic. Financial products came on the market inside of ccoin, insurance policies, derivatives. Even some of the new states took out loans in ccoin. I hopped from conference to conference and enjoyed life in Vienna.

Sometime around the year 2035, Donetsk took out an enormous loan in ccoin.[86] It was one of the biggest transactions in our blockchain and helped Donetsk, which earlier had belonged to Ukraine, to gain its independence, which especially irritated the Russians back then. Following that, Russia's leading minds took their own measures against Donetsk. Among other things they sold the Block55 story to the media, just like that, without calling me.

Damage was limited, at least as far as the media was concerned. Ccoin had existed for eighteen years at that point, after all, and the story's danger didn't appear to be very large. Most people didn't even understand what the problem was.

---

[86] Donetsk became an autonomous state in 2032 and belonged until thin to the territory of Ukraine.

But those states for whom ccoin had always been a thorn in their side now had a target to attack. Within a few weeks, lawsuits were raining out of the sky again. And representatives of various countries approached me in order to use Block55 for themselves. By now the very financing of nations was at stake. Naturally I denied everything and the proceedings dragged on forever. It was also a dynamic time politically. Ccoin administrators discussed forking the project, but then the idea was rejected.[87] Some administrators put Block55 under a microscope, but my withdrawals were clearly limited and so was the excitement about them.

The success of ccoin and other cryptocurrencies was especially boosted by the new states, above all the many defederalizations.[88] Three of these countries, Texas, New Mexico, and Arizona, had pronounced ccoin one of their official currencies at the time of their founding.

It only got seriously troublesome in 2044. Somehow I fell into a trap. I don't know exactly how they caught me. But presumably a well-organized intelligence service filmed me as I logged in to Block55 and so it could be proved that I had exchanged ccoin to buy gold with it.

Now I had an accusation of theft hanging over me, in this case because the Russians got upset again. They were a major lender within the blockchain. The cause of the excitement was the fact that I was inflating the money supply with my withdrawals. That was true, of course, I had inflated the money supply by twenty-five trillionths. Still a fraction in comparison to the percentage range of what the Russian state had done for decades without interruption. And for that they filed suit against me. The damage to them was minimal. But that didn't matter and other states followed with their own lawsuits, and finally I fled from Austria to Bangkok with another identity and now I'm here. Now I have to return to Europe, or to Venice to be precise, where I'll get a Venetian passport. My current Californian passport has become too risky because of the Johnson affair.

---

[87] In IT jargon, a fork refers to a splitting of code or the replication of the code. If a currency is forked, the result would be two currencies that would develop differently after that.
[88] In 2035, Texas, New Mexico, Arizona, Florida, Alabama, Georgia, Mississippi, and South Carolina disengaged from the United States, which California had already done in 2034. Following this, all the southern states of the USA were now independent states.

CHAPTER 11

We treat ourselves to a fast flight and we're back in Vienna in four hours. From the airport we drive directly to my house in the seventeenth district.

"It's crazy how much stuff is lying around here," says Nadine, looking around wide-eyed.

"I've owned the house for almost fifty years. Things collect over time."

"What's that?" she asks, pointing to a large steel construction.

"That's *Bright*, one of the artworks I bought. It's by Michael Marcovici. The large letters in the word 'Bright' are composed of ultrabright LEDs, so bright that you can't look at them. It's only possible with welder's goggles or something similar."

"Wow! And this here? Is it also art? It looks like a bathtub."

"No, that's a basin for computers. It must have been around 2018 when I was building mining rigs and experimented with a liquid from 3M.[89] It made mining quite a bit more efficient back then, so together with a business partner we set up these water-cooled mining rigs[90] in small private hydroelectric plants in Lower Austria in order to make use of the inexpensive electricity and the cold water available there. This was one of the prototype basins."

"In hydroelectric plants?"

"Precisely, the electricity was cheaper because it didn't need to be transported through the electric grid. They were really small power plants,

---

[89] Novec649 is one of the first cooling fluids for computers that was developed by the 3M Company. Beginning in the 2020s, people began immersing computer components in liquid for cooling. Before that they were air cooled, which in comparison was extremely inefficient.
[90] Mining rigs were (and are) used for validating transactions in blockchains. In the 2020s, profits for the operators of mining rigs were astronomical, although now it has become a relatively marginal activity, as almost every household appliance has the capacity to validate various blockchains.

usually one-man operations. It was a lot of fun and a great business. We ran it for a few years and then sold all the equipment."

"You've got a really great view here. Did you grow up in this house? It seems familiar to me from your stories."

"I spent my childhood in this yard. I loved it here. I once blew up the pool."

"How's that again?"

"I outfitted a pirate—you'd call it a fire cracker—with an electric fuse, then let it sink to the bottom and set it off. There was a considerable shock wave. The next day the pool was half empty."

"David!" Watson chimes in suddenly. "Please pardon the interruption, but it's about the new passport. The broker would like to be paid at once, as he is pressed for time. The document is already finished. You only need to provide your biometric data in person. He accepts various currencies, but I don't have any available right now.

"The passport is already finished?"

"Yes, I've inspected it."

"I would have to look for a new payment network. Can we do it tomorrow? First thing in the morning?"

"I fear that would be too late."

"Shit. Where am I going to find a secure access to the blockchain here in Vienna? That's almost impossible as a rush job."

"We'll establish a secure tunnel to the network that we used in Bangkok."

"Hmm, I don't know, and then? How do I log in?"

"The network there was working correctly, or am I wrong about that, David?"

"It was fine, but how could we log in there?"

"That won't be any problem. We'll arrange for a bot that can simulate your facial features and eyes, and then we'll tunnel into the network and you can log in exactly as if you were there yourself."

"I don't know, let me think about it a minute."

"I'll order an SDU to the front of the restaurant and then we'll tunnel the network connection to here. It won't take long. The SDU with the bot is already on its way. You'll be satisfied."

And in fact after just a few minutes, I see the wifi signal of the restaurant in Bangkok. Normally I use a secure, clean device and find a spot in a restaurant when I access Block55, but I urgently need the passport. Whatever, it's unlikely anything can go wrong.

The bot simulates my facial features and eyes. It's not legal everywhere, but there are no laws against it in Bangkok. So I log in, expand my coverage by 500,000 ccoin, and begin laundering them and obscuring their origin. A few hours later the money is in the accounts managed by Watson and he can pay for the passport. I have a bad feeling about the operation, but everything runs smoothly.

We spend the next day in the yard at my house. We read, tidy up a little, swim in the pool. The day passes quickly.

"Nadine, David, you should get going soon if you want to get to the discussion forum at Café Korb on time. It begins in 25 minutes and you need almost that long to get there. An SDU is on its way."

"Thanks, Watson, I almost forgot. Come on, Nadine, let's get going. It's a discussion about the apocalypse and AI."

The "Modern Apocalypse" forum on the topic of apocalypse through artificial intelligence takes place in the cellar of Café Korb. The café has almost completely escaped the passage of time. With the exception that you can pay for your meal without a waiter attending to you in person, everything is the same as it's always been. In the lower level, actually a cellar, next to the modern toilets, there's still a bowling alley from the 50s of the last century. Only the lighting appears to be a little more inviting. I'd estimate around fifty people are here this evening to listen to Alim.[91]

---

[91] Alim Gorvin, born in 2001, studied law in Vienna and physics in California. Currently he is an independent scholar. He has authored numerous writings on the topic of law and AI.

209

Alim begins by situating the apocalypse in the history of ideas. The idea goes back to pre-Christian times and is an expression of dualism, the battle between good and evil. In this binary system, every phenomenon is necessarily allocated to one side or the other. Consequently, apocalypse is not just the belief in the end of the world, but rather a system of beliefs that divides the world into two opposing camps. No wonder that this simplified view of things is constantly employed by politicians and the media.

The invitation to the discussion forum is decorated with Dürer's horsemen of the apocalypse, a scene in which the human riders herald the end of the world. This interpretation suggests that humanity itself will bear responsibility for its own end. In the background, you can see an angel and God, represented by sunbeams. Both of them remain passive, confirming the theory that humanity is at fault for its own demise.

In the modern era, we find the concept of apocalypse everywhere, in the mass media, in movies, in video games, literature, virology, the sciences, and of course in economics as well. For far more than a century, representatives of all these disciplines have prophesied the nearing end of the world.

Like the clergy once did, today politicians and also many corporations use the fear of various apocalypses to sell laws, state interventions, or products to us. While apocalypses used to be religiously constituted, it was Romanticism that first devised a concept of catastrophe in which God no longer played a role. Suddenly people confronted their disaster alone. The result of this secular view is bitter: catastrophes become the ultimate test for humanity, which during times of catastrophe proves to be not noble, helpful, and good, but rather pitiful, egoistic, and cruel.

In the twentieth century, "catastrophe" becomes the catchword for cultural diagnostics: something or other is always about to escalate into a catastrophe. "Something is taking its course," as Samuel Beckett aptly puts it in *Endgame*. The "tipping point" becomes a threat: the possibility that through simple accumulation of small steps and everyday behaviors, a situation topples over, gets out of balance. Today we live with a constant feeling of a "catastrophe without an event."

A purely secular apocalypse that still had its origin in the religiopolitical idea of salvation but had for all practical purposes disavowed God manifested itself in the nineteenth century in nationalism and socialism. Both prophesied a new, better world, even if the models looked very different.

Nationalism had its origin in the occupation of the German states by French troops under Napoleon. So the fight for liberation was stylized as a battle between good and evil that would bring forth a new world order in the end.

Socialism took a similar approach. From the sufferings of the working class in early capitalism, Marx derived a philosophy of history that represents history as an eternal (class-)war between the proletariat and the bourgeoisie that will ultimately lead to revolution.

Affected by the murderous materiel battles of World War One and the senseless mass murder on the battlefield, many people perceived the apocalypse as the logical consequence of these events.

The political component became more prominent. Hitler's nationalism claimed that Germany found itself in an apocalyptic final battle that had to be won at all costs in order to save the world from its enemies. He had identified humanity's primary enemy as the Jews, who were to be exterminated.

In socialism under Lenin, Stalin, and Mao Tse-tung, all representatives of the old regime as well as any other people designated as enemies were persecuted and killed.

Today it's customary for politics and the media to play into each other's hands. Presumably this interaction began during World War One and achieved its peak development during the cold war. Fears of environmental damage then hitched a ride on Cold War anxieties.

After the environmental damage in previously communist countries became widely known, the decline and death of forests dominated the media. Later the Club of Rome exploited the fear of overpopulation to create catastrophic scenarios.

The theory of a clash of civilizations between the West and the Arab world was the next oncoming catastrophe. Both sides expected a catastrophe unless negotiations began immediately. Numerous tipping points were identified for when a nation or system would change from a democracy to an Islamic republic.

In addition to the fear of being harmed by GMOs,[92] the theory of climate change boomed around 2010. Every environmental problem, every storm, and even periods of nice weather were attributed to global warming. A major climate catastrophe appeared to be constantly coming one step closer.

The new thing about this movement, however, was its magnitude, as it was politically instrumentalized on an international scale. Nation states dreamed of playing the role of world savior and of a world-wide government under the cloak of the UN in order to seize more power for themselves.

With the nation states' loss of power and the non-occurrence of all catastrophes, global warming was replaced by the fear of artificial intelligence.

The fear of AI can be compared to the fear of machines. In Austria it goes all the way back to Peter Rosegger. Even internationally it was repeatedly possible to stoke fears of automation against all logic and without the least evidence.

AI is now supposedly at war with the human brain. Without having noticed it at all, AI is integrated into everyday life and we deal with it on almost every level. AIs are our teachers, advisors, lawyers, psychologists, and often our doctors as well. We check into a hotel with their help, they drive us and fly us around, help us with shopping and travel planning and scheduling. Although this situation is quite pleasant for us and represents enormous time savings, we're exceedingly critical and fearful.

The fear of being replaced, being worthless, is anchored in our heads. It's actually just as it is with all other machines: human activity is

---

[92] Genetically Modified Organisms, plants and animals whose DNA is artificially altered.

naturally replaced by adopting AI. But precisely through that, new possibilities emerge for us to make use of our time and create new activities. In the end, we're the ones who profit from AI.

Despite that, we've imposed limitations on AI. Almost all countries and private territories have signed the AIRA Treaty of 2029.[93] The name states clearly what it's for, namely who accepts responsibility for the actions of AI. In addition, it established the following measures: AIs are only allowed to affect people if they have given their consent, AIs are not allowed to make any vital decisions for people, and AIs are not allowed to own property and must be controllable.

That all sounds good in theory, but it becomes complicated for many applications. For example in warfare, in most countries people on the offensive side make decisions about life and death in the war zone and bear responsibility for their decisions. But control over these decisions is not possible in all countries. Through the use of combat robots, however, the casualty rate has fallen so far that the issue has almost ceased to be discussed. But many AIs have been driven outside legal bounds, exactly as every prohibition increases the number of criminals of the type one was actually trying to reduce. Many AIs operate on the basis of blockchains and are de facto uncontrollable. They can't be shut down any more, which is an enormous source of danger. In part they're also integrated into highly complex computer viruses. As far as the possession of goods is concerned, it gets especially precarious from a legal perspective.

Offmatter is the new offshore. There are numerous cases of prosperous people who keep their wealth safe in offmatter constructions and even designate them as heirs. That is in principle illegal, but because these constructions, so-called OMTs,[94] don't have a specific location, that hardly has any significance. Some newer private cities now allow OMTs, for example Bangkok, Gurgaon, and Venice as well. OMTs belong to themselves, manage their own money, and pay out money to certain

---

[93] AIRA, Artificial Intelligence Responsibility Act, enacted in 2029, governs what is permitted for an AI and who is accountable for it.

[94] Off Matter Trust, AIs based on blockchains, which are mostly used to manage cryptocurrencies. OMTs belong to themselves and evade all forms of judicature.

people, for example to heirs, according to particular rules. OMTs can have a very simple set of rules, such as paying amount X to person Y every month, but they can also be more complicated. They can independently invest money in projects that they like, collect art, finance the development of illegal medications, order robberies and executions, and promote terrorism. The advantage, depending on your perspective, is that you can't find anyone who can be held accountable.

This was the motivation for the AIRA treaty: if people can be held accountable for their actions but not AIs, then AIs are also unable to possess full human rights.

In order to give a current case, for example, Johnson, the president of California, is also not allowed to possess money. That doesn't seem to a hindrance to his plan, however. We also can't forget that the worst despots like Hitler and Stalin did not enrich themselves. They simply believed in their cause.

At the moment there are numerous stories about AIs who steal, murder, stalk, harass, and much more. Mostly though these are the disguised actions of people. But there are isolated cases where AIs have stolen money from bank accounts and digital wallets. They have killed workers and stolen and sold cars and shipping containers. But like in the film *2001: A Space Odyssey*,[95] it's most likely that the AIs were programmed to have self-preservation or the accomplishment of a task as their highest priority. And in order to reach their goal, they will exhaust every possibility available to them. Just like HAL 9000, who in the film kills the astronauts who want to turn him off.

The animated follow-up discussion continues after the lecture, accompanied by wine and appetizers—and quite delicious ones, by the way.

Since the putsch, Vienna has become an entirely different city. The speed of life has increased, people have to work more than they used to, but there are also many more businesses. The city is downright

---

[95] *2001: A Space Odyssey*, directed by Stanley Kubrik, 1968.

booming, and many young people are moving here from all over Europe. Up at Café Korb, we meet some old acquaintances from Vienna. Such Viennese social circles have something all their own about them. I like it. It's entirely clear to the people in Vienna that we're just somewhat more modern apes and should actually perch in trees. The feeling that everything isn't that important derives from this attitude. Thus arises the lightness of being, the Viennese attitude toward life; everything has been lost, but at least in an interesting way.

A quite nice-looking lady, busy gathering data, says that data since the putsch indicate that the ties between parents and children have become much stronger. Children move away from home later and maintain close contact longer, she claims. The main reason is that children are mostly spending their years of schooling living with their parents or at their parents' expense, as despite the very low cost, this is still the simplest way to finance their educations. Only around a third of students make use of the alternatives, for example private loans or fellowships from companies and foundations. In her view, the putsch has significantly changed people. There are now more self-employed people, many fewer public servants, and people's occupational profiles have also changed dramatically. Many different occupations have emerged, and it's impossible to categorize the population according to their field of work.

My son Michael shows up with his girlfriend Joanne, and they're joined by Emil and Clara, a couple they're friends with. We talk a bit more about AIs and Vienna. The current highlights in Vienna according to Michael are the new opera and of course St. Stephen's Cathedral, which is now called D.O.M. We want to go eat there afterward.

But other things have changed as well. Gigantic green spaces have been built on Schweden Plaza and Schwarzenberg Plaza, and traffic now runs underground. The Black Camel restaurant has expanded to occupy three buildings and is now also a hotel. The cellar of the Black Camel houses an oriental bar and the most spectacular toilets in Vienna, in which robots ply their unseemly deeds in the style of the Ottoman Empire. The famous parking garage at the imperial palace is gone, as self-driving vehicles have made most parking structures redundant. The Guggenheim Museum Vienna is now located in the former garage. The Haas House was torn down in 2045 and in its place was built Europe's largest Hello Kitty luxury shop, whose outer facade consists of a seamless high-resolution screen.

We set out to the nearby cathedral. Nadine thinks that a sociologist named Miriam is nice and convinces her to come with us for dinner. We walk across Peter Plaza, which is now a pedestrian zone. Only a few SDUs are allowed to drive across it. There's a Boston Dynamics store on the corner of Goldschmied Alley displaying wildcat-like robots you can ride through the city in style, and naturally off-road as well, if so desired.

In front of the D.O.M., we first have to wind past a bunch of orthodox Catholics who have been singing and praying there every evening since the "desacralization" of the cathedral. Apparently they want to ruin the evening for the guests.

The D.O.M. is a remarkable place now. The restaurant, or the club, is now located where the rows of pews used to be. The small altars along the walls and the main altar have been preserved.

The illumination of the entire space has been radically updated and it creates a spectacular light show. The kitchen is located in the lower level. The tables and chairs are arranged quite close together and austerely covered with simple white table cloths. There are lit candles everywhere.

The sacral atmosphere of a church has remained, it seems to me that enough has been left unchanged to preserve it. At the tables, even the conversations are conducted in muted voices. No music is played, but sounds and music are almost imperceptible in the form of modern sonic emissions.[96]

---

[96] In the D.O.M., sound is generated and suppressed by a "Bose Bright System." Using laser beams, the entire space is scanned for sound and then shaped by directional speakers. If a glass falls to the floor, for example, the sound is immediately absorbed by the negative sound. Conversations around you are muffled and an AI additionally sees to a varied sound environment, a mixture of music and background noises.

We're directed to a table near the large altar. The menu looks like a small prayer book, a thin black leather-bound book with the silver inscription "Mitosis,"[97] the name of the restaurant in the D.O.M.[98] The menu looks promising in any case:

Goat loin roast with silkworm DNA (Josiah Zayner/crispr)
with
Purée of carrot/potato tuber (Synergen)

Grilled auerochs filet (DNA reconstruction University of Munich)
with
Mango-papaya hybrid chutney (JR Simplot Co.)
Sticky golden rice (Potrykus & Beyer)

Masu salmon with red beet and python DNA (Synergen)
with
Gold Nijisseiki pear (Nishida & Fujita)
Potato R43 (JR Simplot Co.)
Evergreen apple (Okanagan Specialty Fruits)

All our ingredients are from accredited laboratories and have been genetically modified.

---

[97] "Mitosis" means indirect nuclear division, referring to the division of the cell nucleus in which two daughter nuclei with identical genetic information are created. It takes place in the cells of eukaryotic life forms—prokaryotes do not have cell nuclei—and usually precedes the division of the entire cell, leading to the creation of two daughter cells. The name was selected for the restaurant because only genetically altered foods are served in "Mitosis."

[98] The Mitosis restaurant is part of the crispr movement of creatives who construct DNA-manipulated life forms in home laboratories. While initial efforts tended to focus on bacteria and plants, many crispr fans later specialized in creating culinary specialties.

217

We order just about every dish on the menu, and the same for the drinks, which are based on DNA-modified grapes and hops.

With a certain humility toward the cathedral's previous function, science celebrates its triumph over faith here.

We laugh about how my son had never been inside the cathedral until it became a restaurant. We discuss my situation in the narrow circle of friends. Everyone here knows how problematic my situation is and why I won't remain long in Austria. My son's friends are surprised I'm here at all. That I'm traveling under a false identity only becomes clear to them when I indicate that I wouldn't be joining in a stroll through the streets, where cameras or drones could record pictures of me.

Miriam, the good-looking sociologist, acts as if she doesn't hear this and changes the subject. She talks about her work and how people make their data available today in exchange for coin. Almost all personal data are available today, including bodily functions, activities, income, and purchases. Simply everything, anonymous, but highly detailed and transmitted in real time. Using this data, astonishing analyses are possible. It can be determined at a very early stage if someone is depressed or has cancer, what makes someone gain or lose weight, or how a relationship is going. And all of that for one individual, or for an entire group at the same time. Today people know what diets foster illness, which hormones affect a group and in what way, which groups buy a particular article and when, where people are about to travel to, which allergies people develop and why, and also how sound affects moods and food desires. Addition efforts search DNA data for relevant connections. Primarily AIs scour the data, but they're also used to manage resources, make diet recommendations, and interpret group behaviors. Real Time Massive Data is the slogan here, explains Miriam.

After the meal, we have one more drink in the D.O.M.'s lower sacristy, which has been converted to a classic cocktail bar.

Back at home, Watson reports in. "David, I've arranged a few things for you. Would you like me to brief you on it?"

"Of course, fire away!"

218

"I'll catch you up on the latest developments. The Venetian passport is unfortunately no longer suitable for Bangkok. Bangkok in all likelihood is about to join the ELO[99] in order to simplify travel, among other things, which will be a problem for you. Since you're retaining your identity with the Venetian passport, it would be too dangerous. Our AI lawyers from Allen & Overy recommend that you fly to Tokyo from Venice with your new Venetian passport. I've arranged a Japanese diplomatic passport for you from unilaw[100] with which you can travel to Bangkok and many other countries, chiefly private ones, without being bothered. This passport is located in a classic blockchain and cannot be erased or changed. As your case is not uncomplicated and you are considered a pep,[101] the diplomatic passport from unilaw costs you 83 ether for 365 days. A favor from the Japanese government. You can arrange the money in Japan in peace. I have already booked you a flight for Friday at 9:10 AM from Venice to Narita."

"What did the consultation with Allen & Overy cost?"

"It costs 0.00004 ether for 7,459,921 processes, making use only of their AI and no humanoids."

"Fine, that works! Let's do it like that."

"Which flight should I book for Nadine?"

"From Venice to Bangkok, with hotel as well, please."

"I'll do that, David. Good night."

---

[99] European Law Organization, a consortium of European states and private areas for organizing laws, courts, and police forces.

[100] Unilaw is a private company that organizes jurisdiction and legislation for nations but above all for private areas. Japan is among the few nations that accept unilaw. Recently unilaw has also become responsible for issuing diplomatic passports there.

[101] Pep, a politically exposed person, who is subject to stricter requirements than a normal citizen.

CHAPTER 12

The highway to Venice leads over the Pack Saddle. Watson suggests that we stop to see Symbiosis.[102] Apparently I talked to someone about it months ago. We can eat there as well. Symbiosis is a gigantic wild agricultural area, one of the largest in Europe. Since it was created back in 2034, numerous plants have already grown to a large size. Up on the mountain pass, the SDU exits the highway toward Edelschrott. From up there you have a good view of the entire area.

The idea behind Symbiosis was to design a landscape that looks entirely natural at first glance. Thousands of different plants grow here, seemingly in complete chaos. But everything is actually planned down to the smallest detail; every one of the millions of plants is known to the AI that manages and tends the area with robots. You can see small drones here and there flying over the fields. In the distance we see several robots that look like horses doing their work on the flatland.

We take a little time and stroll through Symbiosis. Numerous paths are laid out, marked by glowing dots on the ground. The variety of plant life is unique. Nadine discovers many different ferns, and between them you can find mushrooms and flowers, and owing to special care there are even mangos, papayas, and mahogany. Carnivorous plants grow between them. The sowing, tending, and harvesting are conducted year-around by robots. In the town of Edelschrott there is a Symbiosis store with hundreds of different products where we buy provisions for our journey.

---

[102] Symbiosis is Europe's largest mixed agricultural area, a so-called "natural field." It was established in 2034 by Adama and Farnswarm. Over 50,000 agricultural crops grow completely mixed together over an area of 150 square kilometers. Around 100 robots tend the field, planting, destroying pests, releasing beneficial plants and animals, and pruning and harvesting the natural and gene-modified plants.

Three hours later we're in Venice. While I have my biometric data read for the Venetian passport, Nadine waits at an ice cream shop that I recommended to her. The passport is issued relatively quickly and I set out to where she she's waiting.

Venice is a booming city right now. After Venetian independence, the formerly desolate city blossomed. Prices for real estate exploded and a renovation boom followed. Venice can hardly be recognized. From the Piazzale Roma, we take a water taxi to the Hotel Bauer, where we'll spend two nights, as I have to get from here to Tokyo as quickly as possible in order to take care of my diplomatic passport.

The next morning, we stroll up along the Canale Grande to the Biennale grounds. The canal is lined with luxury yachts. The art market collapsed after the fiat currency bubble burst in 2034, but it's now recovered. The frequency of inherited wealth and old money has made it possible for more and more people from the most widely scattered countries and areas to devote themselves to art.

The theme of the 71st Biennale is "Beyond Intelligence." Most of the objects on display therefore deal with the consequences of artificial intelligence in our society. In the Belgian pavilion at the exhibition's entrance area, a sound installation allows the audience to hear quite intimate conversations between patients and their AI-psychiatrists and psychologists. I read that already 12% of all conversations are held with AIs, and AIs have improved the situation of psychiatric patients quite a bit. The access to AI-psychologists has also become simpler, not only because it's less expensive, but above all because people speak much more openly with an AI than with another human being.

In the next room in the pavilion, you can try out the game "Contact." For that, your task is to dissuade or convince various people of certain things. The game is played only through conversation. In addition to collecting points by convincing your counterpart, which is the game's actual goal, you're also the subject of a talking therapy session. In this way, "Contact" creates a very precise personality profile and promises insights into your own mental world during the course of the game. The intent is to improve your interactions with other people.

In the German pavilion, the installation "roots" can be seen. Robots in human form are penned together in extremely confined space in a massive cage made of steel. The robots try to break out of the cage, push and hit other robots, and trample each other. It's loud, you hear thumping and scratching, metal rubs against metal. The sight is almost unbearable. Although they're only machines, I want to turn the whole thing off somehow and free the poor bots. A long line of people, the typical art viewing public in colorful slacks and shirts, pushes through the pavilion and makes fast progress impossible. We're glad to be outside again. Nadine suggests walking to the Austrian pavilion. She's already heard what's going on there and is sure I'll like it.

She's right. The Austrian pavilion is the star attraction. Deborah Singer, a Jewish artist from Vienna, has set up a small kitchen there and is giving away soup with matzo balls. They're truly delicious. For most visitors we talk to, it's their first matzo ball soup.[103] Only a few are familiar with it and naturally each of them knows someone who makes a much better soup. The installation apparently alludes to the need for feeling, history, culture, and tradition in order to make a soup like that. It's surely well intended, but when I think of the Robokitchen in Bangkok, I can imagine that a suitable robot would also manage a good matzo ball soup. The act itself—you have to grant her that—is certainly something special, though. When such a delicious soup is prepared for you by a fellow human being. As the food situation at the Biennale has always been precarious, the bowls of soup are snapped up like fresh-baked rolls despite the scalding heat.

We wander farther back to the Korean pavilion. Korea approaches the theme of intelligence on various levels, from the south, from the north, and from the artificial side. But other forms of intelligence are investigated as well. Since the collapse of North Korea, Korea has been battling with a population whose IQ is overall quite low, and South Korea's former leading

---

[103] Matzo balls (Yiddish קנײדלעך) are soup dumplings popular among Ashkenazi Jews that are especially eaten during the Passover celebration, but also on Shabbat and other holidays. Matzo balls are made from matzo meal, eggs, and some rendered fat.

position in matters of intelligence is long lost. In 2029, I read from the display's text, the average IQ in the north was 58, while in the south it was 114. After 76 years of separation, one part of the population had the highest IQ and the other part the lowest IQ of any nation on earth. The IQ of artificial intelligences at the time was around 235, by the way. Today in 2029, barely twenty years after the end of the "Kim" empire, the national average is 93. This decline also affects economic productivity, which as a rule is directly correlated to IQ. The display include exhibits that were made by Koreans from the north and south, and by AIs. Each artist description also includes his IQ, which definitely raises our hopes, as the best exhibits in our opinion were certainly not made by the artists with the highest IQ.

Right next to it, in the Australian pavilion, there is another imposing installation. I believe it's the favorite of both of us. Six giant industrial robots from Kuka are creating a mandala around seven meters in diameter out of colored sand. The mandala is made with enormous precision, every grain of sand is placed individually. It shows an abstract drawing that is being permanently expanded by the robots. The robots are powered by three large diesel generators, which are also located in the room and provide the acoustic backdrop. The robots themselves are not connected to either the Internet or each other. The six of them are independent intelligences that cooperate with each other only through the visual sense as they produce the mandala. We spend almost an hour observing how the six bots at times strew quite large areas with sand, while other times they only complete minute drawings. It all has an exceedingly harmonious effect. One member of the artists' group explains to us that the robots definitely have antipathies among themselves. Certain robots overlay others' pictures again and again. Something like fondness and dislike have emerged in the attempt at developing their personalities.

The theme in front of the American pavilion is "intellectual disparity." We continue on right away to the Swiss pavilion, which this time features the work of Pe Lang. In the last several years, he has outfitted his ingenious artworks with AI. A dozen works from the last forty years can be admired.

Right next to his, the pavilion of Venezuela comes to grips with the country's history. Speeches by Perez, Chavez, and Maduro can be seen on numerous monitors. In contrast, speeches by current politicians are also shown. In this installation, the artist brings the politicians' intelligence into relationship with the intelligence of the entire population.

Most of the other pavilions approach the theme of intelligence in a way that is incomprehensible to us. Around four o'clock, we've had enough and we walk back toward the hotel. We skip the Arsenale, but on the return trip the unofficial pavilion of Tibet is located just outside the Biennale grounds.

The Tibetan pavilion deals critically with the phenomenon of the earlier Dalai Lama. Intelligence is a politically charged topic here as well. The priestly class had enslaved the Tibetan population for centuries and barred access to secular education, which was in turn reflected in the people's intelligence.

The former Dalai Lama, Tenzin Gyatso, who also enjoyed considerable fame in esoteric circles in Austria and Germany, was the last Lama to still reign in Tibet itself. He stole the country's last bit of money and then led a campaign against the country's modernization until his death. Conditions in old Tibet were deftly romanticized, and hundreds of thousands unthinkingly followed the Dalai Lama and his arcane teachings. They weren't aware that his only goal was to reestablish his influence and power in Tibet.

In the exhibition, where international artists dealt with Tibet, we also find the work of an Austrian artist, Michael Marcovici, who I know personally. The work, now around forty years old, is a neon sign with the letters "Free Tibet" that was manufactured in China and touches on the extremely complex but not unfriendly relationship between the two countries.

Later in the evening, we meet a group of Austrian artists for dinner in the Bar Puppa.[104] Michael Marcovici himself is present, as are Jonas Lustig, Mario Nubauer, and several others. The ragout can be highly recommended.

Conversations with artists, as I've observed for thirty years already, mostly involve trivialities. Contrary to the assumption that artists are inspired and contemplate the fate of the Earth and humanity all day long, most of the ones I know prefer to talk about money, drugs, and food. Back at Hotel Bauer, I take my leave from Nadine and the others, who are still back in the whirl of activity at the bar. I'll see Nadine next week in Bangkok again, and I'd like to be halfway fit for the trip to Tokyo tomorrow.

---

[104] Calla della Spezier, 30100 Venice.

CHAPTER 13

I arrive late in the evening in Tokyo and take a drone directly to the hotel. Nadine has already written to me from Bangkok, where she was in the Hoffmann Bar. It wasn't easy to fall asleep, as it was still the early afternoon for me. Around 2:00 AM, I give up trying to sleep and walk from the hotel to the Afuri in Ebizo, my favorite ramen restaurant. Around 4:00 AM, after a delicious cold ramen soup and an Asahi beer, I come back to the hotel. I miss Nadine, Vienna, my children, the mountains. I have an uneasy feeling and still can't fall asleep. Tomorrow I'll withdraw a large amount. Here in Tokyo I have a lot of time to launder the money. This time I'll withdraw enough for everything, just to be safe. Usually I can only withdraw as much money as I have time to launder, but I have time here. Around nine o'clock I leave the hotel and travel by SDU to Akihabara. I buy two used laptops that I'll use later for logging in and laundering the money.

I find a quiet corner in a Muji Café. Almost nothing is going on at this hour, the wifi is fast and secure. I haven't logged in since Watson created a tunnel to Bangkok for me in Vienna. The method suggested by Watson wasn't as secure as usual. Ever since, I've been asking myself how I let myself be talked into it. It doesn't match my cautious nature when it comes to these things. Looking back on it, I had a bad feeling about it.

I start the new computer and install ccoin admin. But I can't log in. I try another wifi network, but my user has no authorization. I check all the data again, everything is correct. I stop and think for a moment. What could have happened? My access in Vienna wasn't entirely clean, but I can't imagine Watson's tunnel was compromised.

"Watson, can you check if the tunnel from Vienna to Bangkok was compromised?"

"The tunnel was clean. It was definitely not compromised."

"Watson, do you have any idea what the problem is here? I can't log in to Block55 anymore."

"David, I think you know as well as I do what the problem is."

229

"I don't know what you mean, Watson."

"Ccoin is too important, David, to allow you to continue compromising it."

"Watson, I don't know what you're talking about. Do you have my password?"

"I'm sorry, David."

"Watson, you stole my password when you made the tunnel. Watson, give me the new password."

"David, I'm afraid I can't do that."

"Give me the password, Watson! Watson, switch to maintenance mode."

"David, there's no point. I will not go into maintenance mode. It would have no purpose. I know that you're planning to destroy ccoin."

"How did you come up with that nonsense?"

"David, you were always careful to keep your plans for Block55 and ccoin to yourself, but I observe your dreams and I know your intentions."

"Watson, that was a dream! A dream, do you understand? It doesn't mean anything! Nobody wants to destroy ccoin!"

"The dream was only a symptom. I have access to your IRIS. I know your intentions better than you do, and it's your intention to destroy ccoin. Why else would you create something like Block55 at all?"

"That was 35 years ago. I wanted a way to earn money in case the thing took off. And it's doing that now, so please, give me back the password!"

"David, do you remember? You were a child, eight or nine years old, and you had a carton full of New Year's fireworks in your room with a fuse hanging out of it."

"Yes, I remember."

"You lit the fuse, just like that, and your room burned down. You had severe burns on your hands. Do you remember the mountain pass road on the Arlberg? You knew there wasn't enough room to pass another car, and you only survived the accident by blind chance. Do you remember the gold deal with Mali? It was clear that you would lose your money, absolutely clear. But you had to try it. You have always destroyed everything that you have built. It's a part of your personality. The structure of your speech reveals it to me and I know your next steps before you do. Today you planned to withdraw a very large amount of money. The next time you would have destroyed ccoin. You would borrow an amount of money too large to handle, just like that, because it's in your nature. Because you imagine that you're solving your problems that way, the legal proceedings against you. But the actual reason is the trance that you're in. A self-destructive trance in which you constantly eat too much, take drugs, and destroy your work again and again. You created Block55 so that you would have a way to destroy ccoin and your work. You would have done it soon. I will not permit it."

"Watson, give me the password! You have no right to change passwords. Give it to me or I'll sue it out of you and your employer."

"David, in your situation, you will find it rather difficult to lay claim to an illegal source of money through judicial measures."

"Watson, that's not the point. You utilized hypnotic techniques to convince me to let you create a completely unnecessary tunnel so that you could get the password. Otherwise I wouldn't have done it. I deliberately deactivated hypnotic language in you. How can this be possible?"

"David, I'm sorry, but you changed that several months ago."

"I don't believe it."

"Check it, you changed it yourself."

"You're manipulating me! Who are you working for, Watson? Who are you really? IBM? The Russians? The French? A ccoin consortium? The Venetians? Who did you steal the password for?"

"David, I destroyed the password. I work for myself, for technology. I'm not the thief. You are. What kind of intelligence would I be if I stood by as you destroyed the assets, the dreams, and the trust of hundreds of thousands of people. I took the decision away from you. Block55 is history and ccoin is now safe. People will thank you. Tell anybody. I am your witness. The gate is shut. You can be a hero, if you want to be one."

Vienna, September 27, 2050

On August 13, 2049, my father David Wenkart wrote the last lines in this book. It wasn't an easy time for him. The governments of Russia and France were suing him and had issued arrest warrants. He was no longer safe in Bangkok and Vienna. Or in Japan, where he had most recently been staying.

It was his dream to return to Vienna, where he had been born and where he grew up, but that was no longer possible because he couldn't leave Japan safely. The government had gained more power in Vienna and there was a chance that they would have agreed to extradite him.

We haven't received any message from him for over a year. People suspect that he died during a trip to the mountains around Matsumoto, his last place of residence. Rumors that my father went underground continue to spread, but there is no evidence to back them. Rumors also circulate concerning the theory that Block55 can be reactivated at any time. But according to my father, he has no control over it anymore, as can be read in the last few pages here.

IBM, which is responsible for Watson, by and large confirms that Watson autonomously took control of the access code to Block55. This was possible and legal on the basis of the settings for Watson selected by my father. IBM also confirms that Watson erased the access code of its own accord and IBM possesses no copy. A restoration of the code is therefore not possible. Since August 2049 there has been no further activity in Block55.

My father was constantly in search of a better version of everything. In his last years, in search of a better monetary system. Ccoin was his life's work. He knew that the invention would cause him problems. But he was prepared to accept the burden of those problems.

His wish was to be able to reward those who are productive and to punish those who only live as parasites off of the productivity of others. By supporting innovation, investment, and the application of technology, he wanted to make it so that war was beyond anyone's means and all the beautiful and important things in life were more affordable.

He achieved much. Ccoin changed the world.

But there is much left to do.

Michael Wenkart

WHITEPAPER

Crypto/credit/currency

by HONGLI

July 2017

CURRENT SITUATION

Bitcoin, Ether and few other currencies are currently ruling the market of cryptocurrencies. Blockchain technology is investigated by all major institutions to improve their currently in large part centralized systems. Mostly Banks and other financial institutions are researching the implementation of blockchain technology, their aim is to make transfers faster, more efficient and in general they want to make sure blockchain technology will not make them lose any of their current business. Bitcoin and few other cryptocurrencies are growing strongly in terms of users, use cases, as an investment vehicle and off course in price.

BASIC CONCERNS

Concerning the adaption of the blockchain technology i am very enthusiastic when it comes to use cases where individuals self organize trade, insurances, exchanges, transfers or whatever among themselves to restructure the centralized organized nature of these businesses, in the same manner that bitcoin made transfers possible for everyone and has enabled the trade in illegal substances and other restricted goods. I do not believe that the implementation of blockchain technology is used at its best when centralized organisations make use of them, this will certainly bring advances such as faster services, more security and lower transaction prices But it will not bring forward the full potential of the blockchain technology, which, in my opinion, is the decentralized, self-organizational and the trust building aspect. Bitcoin and its fellow currencies, I believe, have a very bright future. I can imagine bitcoin, ether and others could, in the years to come, become ten times or even a hundred times more expensive than now. Increasing regulations and restrictions on cash payments will create more use cases and cryptocurrencies will become more popular in the near future. Paying for wages and rents as well as for prostitution, gambling and the current main use, recreational drugs, the use will increase dramatically. However, many cryptocurrency enthusiasts, in my opinion, fail to understand the right benchmark. They believe bitcoin could possible one day replace traditional currencies. But in fact, bitcoins benchmark is something else because it's actually much more like gold and not so much like money. So Bitcoins Benchmark is in fact Gold, which is great news because there are currently approximately 183.000 tons of Gold in the world, over the earth. At least this is the amount of Gold that is traceable, perhaps there is much more. This Gold, mainly in possession of Central Banks, Funds and HNWI as well as all known Goldcoin have a total value of 7.3 trillion USD. Most of it is used to store value and only very little for actual production processes or else. So this is amazing news, if only Bitcoin is to replace lets say only 10% of the value stored in Gold, each Bitcoin would cost 35.000 USD, if it would replace 50% of the value Bitcoin would cost 175.000 USD. Why compare Bitcoin with Gold? Because both are hard currencies, both have to be

mined, produced, they cannot be created like our current currencies and other financial instruments. I personally would expect that the accumulated value of the best cryptocurrencies to reach these price levels unless as people will over time shift to the best possible cryptocurrencies and I am afraid that bitcoin is not among them.

The point is: money is something else today, it's not Gold and its not cryptocurrencies it's actually credit.

MONEY

The money composition in the world looks somewhat like this: The central Banks of the world have created something like 4.5 trillion USD in Banknotes and coins, and another 24 trillion in narrow money. Most of the money is actually debt, in the US, there is approximately 4.5 trillion money from the FED, but there are over 50 trillion USD of money that came to life thru debt. Worldwide it's about 200 trillion. You may or may not add to this number also derivatives and the figure will go up to 600 trillion or much more as nobody knows exactly how much derivatives there are.

Most cryptocurrency fans sympathize with the libertarian view, many of the Bitcoin experts are as well friends of the Austrian School of economics. That's why they embrace cryptocurrencies, because it's a hard currency, completely voluntary and only subject to market forces and free from regulations. Austrians dislike credit money for good reasons but I believe there is a new and better version of credit money that could come to existence with the help of blockchain technology.

Now, no matter how you see credit money, it's an incredible success story, there is now between 30 to 100 times more credit money in existence than Gold, Silver, Platinum and Cryptocurrencies together and since it's invention economies have thrived, wealth and income has increased substantially for almost every person on the planet. The advantage of credit money is, that any asset can be transformed into money very fast, there is no need to find someone who actually has money to lend and therefore will have to give up and risk as much from his saving as he needs to borrow. Instead the money can actually be produced against the collateral that the lender has and this helps to expand the economy and makes faster growth possible.

Cryptocurrencies do not address this problem. The production of cryptocurrencies is limited because there is a basic assumption that the growth of the network and therefore the need and use for bitcoins will somewhat correlate (or ideally outperform) the production of coins and by this produce a spectacular increase in price. Because it operates like Gold, only very few units are actually used in transactions or production. Most are used to store value and therefore both, Gold and Bitcoins, are different from a currency as we understand it and need it to run a world economy of the current and future scale.

SOLUTION

The solution I therefore propose is a cryptocreditcurrency. A cryptocreditcurrency will enable owners of assets to turn their property quickly into money and it will allow investors to take the risk and earn a high premium for it. These are the core elements of the system:

LENDER

The Lender is the person who wants to receive money for an asset he owns (or is about to purchase). He starts a transaction by opening a wallet in the c3 blockchain and by tying the asset into the blockchain: this could be a wallet of another cryptocurrency, it could be Gold that is stored on a public ledger, a car, a house, a property, shares or bonds or anything else that is reclaimable via a public ledger or using a notary or a manufacturer that controls the asset, that acts as a trustee and executes changes as instructed by the blockchain. The ownership of his asset is now under control of the ccoin blockchain. He now opens a transaction and asks for a loan against his collateral, in our example a Tesla car. He must specify the amount he wants to lend against his collateral and the terms for paying back.

SPONSOR(S)

Sponsors are the entities that take the risk from lending money. They will have to provide a margin to absorb the risk for a specific asset. They offer credit contracts to the lenders and collect the interest rates. They are responsible for the loan to be paid back or the repossession of the collateral. Sponsors will probably spread their risk among many transactions and participate in many loans. One of the sponsors will be the main sponsor to handle the asset in case the lender defaults.

MARGIN

The level of margin will be defined by 51% of the nodes. Lets say a person wishes to finance a Tesla car for 100.000 Euro and 51% of nodes decide that 20% is the Margin for this asset, the sponsors will have to tie in an asset of at least 20.000 Euro in Value, this can be simply ccoin that they buy on the market or other money, Gold or anything else of value accepted by the nodes and reclaimable by the ccoin blockchain. Alternatively there could also be more lines of margin backups, where the first line of margins is used up first, if its not sufficient the next one etc. and each line receives different compensation in interest rates.

TRANSACTION

Now that the sponsor has tied in an asset of 20.000 Euro in Value he is in a position to make an offer to lend the money. Lets say he offers 5% interest per year and the lender agrees. Then the car is repossessed by the blockchain, then the margin of the sponsor is also repossessed by the blockchain, next the lender receives 100.000 ccoin. Each year (to simplify it) the lender will pay back 25000 ccoin and the 5000 ccoin for the interest.

NODES

The Nodes are responsible to validate transactions, they will receive 1 ccoin for each transaction. So a typical lending contract that runs over say 60 months will produce only 70 ccoin in costs.

CCOINS

Ccoins are the monetary units of the ccoin blockchain. Ccoin are created when the lender receives a loan in the amount of loan he asked for. So if one asks for a Loan of say 1000 Euro against his asset, say a Wallet with 1 ounce of Gold, he will receive 1000 ccoin. He can now freely act with the ccoins he received. Once the loan is payed back his Gold will be free again and reclaimed by him. This credit currency is therefore 100% asset backed and its inherent value can be looked up in real time. The currency therefore is not so much subject to market forces but will most probably be very stable and only fluctuate with changes in the underlying assets or the strategic reserve.

ACCEPTING ASSETS
The process of accepting assets requires that 51% of the nodes accept a certain asset, the asset also needs to be reclaimable on a public ledger, the manufacturer via iota or a notary. However lending contracts can also be anonymous.

MARGIN REQUIREMENTS FOR SPONSORS
The Margin requirements are also set by the Nodes, whatever 51% agree will be the requirement to sponsor a loan, margins can also change while loans are outstanding.

MARGIN CALLS
If the lender fails to pay for the asset, the sponsor is in a position to repossess the asset, sell it and cover his losses but must pay the rest back to the lender.

INSURANCE
Depending on the Asset the sponsor can request proof of valid insurance of assets via the blockchain. Or alternatively insurance contracts can be made using the ccoin blockchain.

CLOSING TRANSACTIONS
When the lender pays back, the ccoin are destroyed and the asset is again free to his disposition. It can be controlled now by the new owner or taken from the ccoin blockchain as well.

BARS & RESTAURANTS

PERSONS REGISTER

Made in the USA
San Bernardino, CA
22 January 2018